Change of Heart

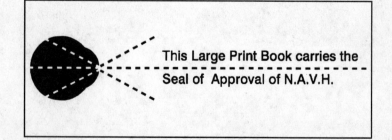

This Large Print Book carries the
Seal of Approval of N.A.V.H.

CHANGE OF HEART

JUDE DEVERAUX

THORNDIKE PRESS
A part of Gale, Cengage Learning

Farmington Hills, Mich • San Francisco • New York • Waterville, Maine
Meriden, Conn • Mason, Ohio • Chicago

GALE
CENGAGE Learning

Thorndike Press® Large Print Core.
The text of this Large Print edition is unabridged.
Other aspects of the book may vary from the original edition.
Set in 16 pt. Plantin.

LIBRARY OF CONGRESS CATALOGING-IN-PUBLICATION DATA

Deveraux, Jude.
    Change of heart / Jude Deveraux. — Large print edition.
        pages ; cm. — (Thorndike Press large print core)
        ISBN 978-1-4104-7396-7 (hardcover) — ISBN 1-4104-7396-1 (hardcover)
    1. Large type books. I. Title.
PS3554.E9273C47 2014
813'.54—dc23   2014035590

Published in 2014 by arrangement with Pocket Books, a division of Simon & Schuster, Inc.

Printed in the United States of America
1 2 3 4 5 6 7 18 17 16 15 14

ACKNOWLEDGMENTS

I'd like to thank my readers who respond to my many questions on Facebook. Thank you for your encouragement and for listening to the ups and downs of being a writer. For everyone else, please join me on Facebook and hear the truth about writing.

PART ONE

1

The man behind the desk looked at the boy across from him with a mixture of envy and admiration. Only twelve years old, yet the kid had a brain that people would kill to have. I mustn't appear too eager, he thought. Must keep calm. We want him at Princeton — preferably chained to a computer and not allowed out for meals.

Ostensibly, he had been sent to Denver to interview several scholarship candidates, but the truth was, this boy was the only one the admissions office was truly interested in, and the meeting had been set to the boy's convenience. The department dean had arranged with an old friend to borrow office space that was in a part of town close to the boy's very middle-class house so he could get there by bike.

"Ahem," the man said, clearing his throat

and frowning at the papers. He deepened his voice. Better not let the kid know that he was only twenty-five and that if he messed up this assignment, he could be in serious trouble with his advisers.

"You are quite young," he said, trying to sound as old as possible, "and there will be difficulties, but I think we can handle your special circumstances. Princeton likes to help the young people of America. And —"

"What kind of equipment do you have? What will I have to work with? There are other schools making me offers."

As the man looked at the boy, he thought someone should have strangled him in his crib. Ungrateful little — "I'm sure that you'll find what we have adequate, and if we do not have everything you need, we can make it available."

The boy was tall for his age but thin, as though he were growing too fast for his weight to catch up with him. For all that he had one of the great brains of the century, he looked like something out of *Tom Sawyer:* dark hair that no comb could tame, freckles across skin that would never tan, dark blue eyes behind glasses big enough to be used as a windshield on a Mack truck.

Elijah J. Harcourt, the file said. IQ over 200. Had made much progress on coming up with a computer that could *think*. Artificial intelligence. You could tell the computer what you wanted to do and the machine could figure out how to do it. As far as anyone could tell, the boy was putting *his* prodigious brain inside a computer. The future uses of such an instrument were beyond comprehension.

Yet here the smug little brat sat, not grateful for what was being offered to him but demanding more. The man knew he was risking his own career, but he couldn't stand the hesitancy of the boy. Standing, he shoved the papers back into his briefcase. "Maybe you should think over our offer," he said with barely controlled anger. "We don't make offers like this very often. Shall we say that you're to make your decision by Christmas?"

As far as the man could tell, the boy showed no emotion. Cold little bugger, the man thought. Heart as frigid as a computer chip. Maybe he wasn't real at all but one of his own creations. Somehow, putting the boy down made him feel better about his own IQ, which was a "mere" 122.

Quickly, he shook the boy's hand, and as he did so he realized that in another year the boy would be taller than he was. "I'll be in touch," he said and left the room.

Eli worked hard to control his inner shaking. Although he seemed so cool on the exterior, inside he was doing cartwheels. Princeton! he thought. Contact with *real* scientists! Talk with people who wanted to know more about life than the latest football scores!

Slowly, he walked out the door, giving the man time to get away. Eli knew that the man hadn't liked him, but he was used to that. A long time ago Eli had learned to be very, very cautious with people. Since he was three he had known he was "different" from other kids. At five his mother had taken him to school to be tested, to see whether he fit into the redbirds or the bluebirds reading group. Busy with other students and parents, the teacher had told Eli to get a book from the shelf and read it to her. She had meant one of the many pretty picture books. Her intention had been to find out which children had been read to by their parents and which had grown up glued to a TV.

Like all children, Eli had wanted to impress his teacher, so he'd climbed on a chair and pulled down a college textbook titled *Learning Disabilities* that the teacher kept on a top shelf, then quietly went to stand beside her and began softly to read from page one. Since Eli was a naturally solitary child and his mother didn't push him to do what he didn't want to do, he had spent most of his life in near seclusion. He'd had no idea that reading from a college textbook when he was a mere five years old was unusual. All he'd wanted to do was to pass the reading test and get into the top reading group.

"That's fine, Eli," his mother said after he'd read half a page. "I think Miss Wilson is going to put you with the redbirds. Aren't you, Miss Wilson?"

Even though he was only five, Eli had recognized the wide-eyed look of horror on the teacher's face. Her expression had said, *What* do I do with this freak?

Since his entry into school, Eli had learned about being "different." He'd learned about jealousy and being excluded and not fitting in with the other children. Only with his mother was he "normal." His mother didn't think he was unusual or strange; he was just *hers.*

Now, years later, when Eli left his meeting with the man from Princeton, he was still shaking, and when he saw Chelsea he gave her one of his rare smiles. When Eli was in the third grade, he'd met Chelsea Hamilton, who was not as smart as he was, of course, but near enough that he could talk to her. In her way Chelsea was as much a freak as Eli was, for Chelsea was rich — very, very rich — and even by six she'd found that people wanted to know her for what they could get from her rather than her personality. The children had been two oddities in the boring little classroom, and they'd become eternal friends.

"Well?" Chelsea demanded, bending her head to look into Eli's face. She was six months older than he, and she'd always been taller. But now Eli was beginning to catch up to her.

"What are you doing in this building?" Eli asked. "You aren't supposed to be here." Smugly, he was making her wait for his news.

"You're slipping, brain-o. My father owns this place." She tossed her long, golden, glossy hair. "And he's friends with the dean at Princeton. I've known about the meeting for two weeks." At twelve, Chelsea was already on the way to being a beauty. Her problems in life were going to be the stuff of dreams: too tall, too thin, too smart, too rich. Their houses were only ten minutes apart, but in value, they were miles apart. Eli's house would fit into Chelsea's marble foyer.

When Eli didn't respond, she looked

straight ahead. "Dad called last night and I cried so much at missing him that he's buying us a new CD-ROM. Maybe I'll let you see it."

Eli smiled again. Chelsea hadn't realized that she'd said "us," meaning the two of them. She was great at the emotional blackmail of her parents, who spent most of their lives traveling around the world, leaving the family business to Chelsea's older siblings. A few tears of anguish and her parents gave her anything money could buy.

"Princeton wants me," Eli said as they emerged into the almost constant sunshine of Denver, its clean streets stretching before them. The autumn air was crisp and clear.

"I *knew* it!" she said, throwing her head back in exultation. "When? For what?"

"I'm to go in the spring semester, just to get my feet wet, then a summer session. If my work is good enough, I can enter full-time next fall." For a moment he turned to look at her, and for just that second he let his guard down and Chelsea saw how very much he wanted this. Eli passionately hated the idea of high school, of having to sit through days of classes with a bunch of semiliterate louts who took great pride in their continuing ignorance. This program would give Eli the opportunity to skip all

15

those grades and get on with something useful.

"That gives us the whole rest of the year to work," she said. "I'll get Dad to buy us —"

"I can't go," Eli said.

It took a moment for those words to register with Chelsea. "You can't go to Princeton?" she whispered. "Why not?" Chelsea had never considered, if she wanted something — whether to buy it or do it — that she wouldn't be able to.

When Eli looked at her, his face was full of anguish. "Who's going to take care of Mom?" he asked softly.

Chelsea opened her mouth to say that Eli had to think of himself first, but she closed it again. Eli's mom, Miranda, *did* need taking care of. She had the softest heart in the world, and if anyone had a problem, Miranda always had room to listen and love. Chelsea never liked to think that she needed anything as soppy as a mother, but there had been many times over the years when she'd flung herself against the soft bosom of Eli's ever-welcoming mother.

However, it was because of Miranda's sweetness that she needed looking after. His mother was like a lamb living in a world of hungry wolves. If it weren't for Eli's con-

16

stant vigilance . . . Well, Chelsea didn't like to think what would have happened to his mother. Just look at the horrid man she'd married. Eli's father was a gambler, a con artist, promiscuous, and a liar of epic proportions.

"When do you have to give them your answer?" Chelsea asked softly.

"My birthday," Eli answered. It was one of his little vanities that he always referred to Christmas as his birthday. Eli's mom said that he was her Christmas gift from God, so she was never going to cheat Eli because she'd been lucky enough to have him on Christmas Day. So every Christmas, Eli had a pile of gifts under a tree and another pile on a table with a big, gaudy birthday cake, a cake that had no hint of anything to do with Christmas.

In silence, the two of them locked their bikes, then walked down Denver's downtown streets, forgoing the trolley that ran through the middle of town. Chelsea knew that Eli needed to think, and he did that best by walking or riding his bike. She knew without asking that Eli would never abandon his mother. If it came to a choice between Princeton and taking care of his mother, Eli would choose the person he loved best. For all that Eli managed to appear cool and calculating, Chelsea knew that when it came to the two people he loved the most — her and his mother — inside, Eli was marshmallow cream.

"You know," Chelsea said brightly, "maybe you're overreacting. Maybe your mother can get along without you." *Without us,* she almost said. "Who took care of her before you were born?"

Eli gave her a sideways look. "No one, and look what happened to her."

"Your father happened," Chelsea said heavily. She hesitated as she thought about the matter. "They've been divorced for two years now. Maybe your mother will remarry and her new husband will take care of her."

"Who will she marry? The last man she went out with ended up 'forgetting' his wallet, so Mom paid for dinner and a tank full of gas. A week later I found out he was married."

Unfortunately, Miranda's generosity didn't just extend to children but to every living creature. Eli said that if it were left up to his mother, there would be no need for a city animal shelter because all the unwanted animals in Denver would live with them. For a moment, Chelsea had an image of sweet Miranda surrounded by wounded animals and uneducated men asking her for

18

money. For Chelsea, "uneducated men" was the worst image she could conjure.

"Maybe if you tell her about the offer, she'll come up with a solution," Chelsea said helpfully.

Eli's face became fierce. "My mother would sacrifice her *life* for me. If she knew about this offer, she'd personally escort me to Princeton. My mother cares only about me and never about herself. My mother —"

Chelsea rolled her eyes skyward. In every other aspect of life Eli had the most purely scientific brain she'd ever encountered, but when it came to his mother, there was no reasoning with him. Chelsea also thought Miranda was a lovely woman, but she wasn't exactly ready for sainthood. For one thing, she was thoroughly undisciplined. She ate too much, read too many books that did not improve one's mind, and wasted too much time on frivolous things, like making Eli and Chelsea Halloween costumes. Of course, neither of them ever told her that they thought Halloween was a juvenile holiday. Instead of tramping the streets asking for candy, they would go to Chelsea's house and work on their computers while dripping artificial blood. They sent the butler out to purchase candy that they'd later show to Eli's mom so she'd think they were "normal" kids.

Only once had Chelsea dared tell Eli that she thought it was a bit absurd for them to sit at their computers wearing uncomfortable and grotesque costumes while calculating logarithms. Eli had said, "My mother made these for us to wear," and that had been the *final* decree. The matter was never mentioned again.

As Eli rode his bike onto the cracked, weedy concrete drive of his mother's house, he caught a glimpse of the taillights of his father's car as it scurried out of sight.

"Deadbeat!" Eli said under his breath, knowing that his father must have been watching for him so he could run away as soon as he saw his son.

Every time Eli thought of the word *father* his stomach clenched. Leslie Harcourt had never been a father to him, nor a husband to his wife, Miranda. The man had spent his life trying to make his family believe he was "important." Too important to talk to his family; too important to go anywhere with his wife and child; too important to give them any time or attention.

According to Leslie Harcourt, other people were the ones who really counted in life. "My friends *need* me," Eli had heard his father say over and over. His mother would say, "But Leslie, *I* need you too. Eli needs school clothes and there are no groceries in the house and my car has been broken for three weeks. We *need* food and we *need* clothes."

Eli would watch as his father got that look on his face, as though he were being enormously patient with someone who couldn't understand the simplest concepts. "My friend has broken up with his girlfriend and he has to have someone to talk to and I'm the only one. Miranda, he's in pain. Don't you understand? Pain! I *must* go to him."

Eli had heard his father say this same sort of thing a thousand times. Sometimes his mother would show a little spunk and say, "Maybe if your friends cried on the shoulders of their girlfriends, they wouldn't *be* breaking up."

But Leslie Harcourt never listened to anyone except himself — and he was a master at figuring out how to manipulate other people so he could get as much out of them as possible. Leslie knew that his wife, Miranda, was softhearted; it was the reason he'd married her. She forgave anyone anything, and all Leslie had to do was say "I love you" every month or so and Miranda forgave him whatever.

21

And in return for those few words, Miranda gave Leslie security. She gave him a home that he contributed little or no money to and next to no time; he had no responsibilities either to her or to his son. Most important, she provided him with an excuse to give to all his women as to why he couldn't marry them. He invariably "forgot" to mention that all these "friends" who "needed" him were women — and mostly young, with lots of hair and long legs.

When he was very young, Eli had not known what a "father" was, except that it was a word he heard other children use, as in "My father and I worked on the car this weekend." Eli rarely saw his father, and he never did anything with him.

But Eli and Chelsea had put an end to Leslie and all his Helpless Hannahs two years ago. It was Chelsea who first saw Eli's father with the tall, thin blonde as they were slipping into an afternoon matinee at the local mall. And Chelsea, using the invisibility of being a child, sat in front of them, twirling chewing gum (which she hated) and trying to look as young as possible, as she listened avidly to every word Eli's father said.

"I would like to marry you, Heather, you know that. I love you more than life itself, but I'm a married man with a child. If it weren't for that, I'd be running with you to the altar. You're a woman any man would be proud to call his wife. But you don't know what Miranda is like. She's utterly helpless without me. She can hardly turn off the faucets without me there to do it for her. And then there's my son. Eli needs me so much. He cries himself to sleep if I'm not there to kiss him good-night, so you can see why we have to meet during the day."

"Then he started kissing her neck," Chelsea reported.

When Eli heard this account, he had to blink a few times to clear his mind. The sheer enormity of this lie of his father's was stunning. As long as he could remember, his father had *never* kissed him good-night. In fact, Eli wasn't sure his father even knew where his bedroom was located in the little house that needed so much repair.

When Eli recovered himself, he looked at Chelsea. "What are we going to do?"

The smile Chelsea gave him was conspiratorial. "Robin and Marian," she whispered, and he nodded. Years earlier, they'd started calling themselves Robin Hoods. The legend said that Robin Hood righted wrongs and did good deeds and helped the underdog.

It was Miranda who'd first called them

Robin and Marian, after some soppy movie she loved to watch repeatedly. Laughingly, she'd called them Robin and Marian Les Jeunes, French for "youths," and they'd kept the name in secret.

Only the two of them knew what they did: They collected letterhead stationery from corporations, law firms, doctors' offices, wherever, then used a very expensive publishing computer system to duplicate the type fonts, then sent people letters as though from the offices. They sent letters on law-office stationery to the fathers of children at school who didn't pay child support. They sent letters of thanks from the heads of big corporations to unappreciated employees. They once got back an old woman's four hundred dollars from a telephone scammer.

Only once did they nearly get into trouble. A boy at school had teeth that were rotting, but his father was too cheap to take him to the dentist. Chelsea and Eli found out that the father was a gambler, so they wrote to him, offering free tickets to a "secret" (because it was illegal) national dental lottery. He would receive a ticket with every fifty dollars he spent on his children's teeth. So all three of his children had several hundred dollars' worth of work done, and

Chelsea and Eli dutifully sent him beautiful red-and-gold, hand-painted lottery tickets. The problem came when they had to write the man a letter saying his tickets did not have the winning numbers. The man went to the dentist, waving the letters and the tickets, and demanded his money back. The poor dentist had had to endure months of the man's winking at him in conspiracy while he'd worked on the children's teeth, and now he was being told he was going to be sued because of some lottery he'd never heard of.

In order to calm the man down, Chelsea and Eli had to reveal themselves to the son who they'd helped in secret and get him to steal the letters from his father's night table. Chelsea then sent the man one of her father's gold watches (he had twelve of them) to get him to shut up.

Later, after they'd weighed the good they had done of fixing the children's teeth against the near exposure, they decided to continue being Robin and Marian Les Jeunes.

"So what are we going to do with your father?" Chelsea asked, and she could see that Eli had no idea.

"I'd like to get rid of him," Eli said. "He makes my mother cry. But —"

"But what?"

"But she says she still loves him."

At that, Chelsea and Eli looked at each other without comprehension. They knew they loved each other, but then they also *liked* each other. How could anyone love a man like Leslie Harcourt? There wasn't anything at all likable about him.

"I would like to give my mother what she wants," Eli said.

"Tom Selleck?" Chelsea asked, without any intent at humor. Miranda had once said that what she truly wanted in life was Tom Selleck — because he was a family man, she'd added, and no other reason.

"No," Eli said. "I'd like to give her a *real* husband, one who she'd like."

For a moment they looked at each other in puzzlement. Eli had recently been trying to make a computer think, and they both knew that doing that would be easier than trying to make Leslie Harcourt stay home and putter in the garage.

"This is a question for the Love Expert," Chelsea said, making Eli nod. Love Expert was what they called Eli's mom because she read romantic novels by the thousands. After reading each one, she gave Eli a brief synopsis of the plot, then he fed it into his computer data banks and made charts and graphs. He could quote all sorts of statistics, such as that 18 percent of all romances are medieval, then he could break that number down into fifty-year sections. He could also quote about plots, how many had fires and shipwrecks, how many had heroes who'd been hurt by one woman (who always turned out to be a bad person) and so hated all other women. According to Eli the sheer repetition of the books fascinated him, but his mother said that love was wonderful no matter how many times she read about it.

So Eli and Chelsea consulted Miranda, telling her that Chelsea's older sister's husband was having an affair with a girl who wanted to marry him. He didn't want to marry her, but neither could he seem to break up with her.

"Ah," Miranda said, "I just read a book like that."

Here Eli gave Chelsea an I-knew-she'd-know look.

"The mistress tried to make the husband divorce his wife, so she told him she was going to bear his child. But the ploy back-fired and the man went back to his wife, who by that time had been rescued by a tall, dark, and gorgeous man, so the husband was left without either woman." For a moment Miranda looked dreamily into the distance. "Anyway, that's what happened in the book, but I'm afraid real life isn't like a romance novel. More's the pity. I'm sorry, Chelsea, that I can't be of more help, but I don't seem to know exactly what to do with men in real life."

Chelsea and Eli didn't say any more, but after a few days of research, they sent a note to Eli's father on the letterhead of a prominent physician, stating that Miss Heather Allbright was pregnant with his child, and his office had been directed to send the bills to Leslie Harcourt. Sending the bills had been Chelsea's idea, because she believed that all bills on earth should be directed to fathers.

But things did not work out as Chelsea and Eli had planned. When Leslie Harcourt confronted his mistress with the lie that she was expecting his child, the young woman didn't so much as blink an eye, but broke down and told him it was true. From what Eli and Chelsea could find out — and Eli's mother did everything she could to keep Eli from knowing anything — Heather threatened to sue Leslie for everything he had if he didn't divorce Miranda and marry her.

Miranda, understanding as always, said they should all think of the unborn baby and that she and Eli would be fine, so of course she'd give Leslie the speediest divorce possible. Leslie said it would especially hasten matters if he had to pay only half the court costs and only minimal child support until Eli was eighteen. Generously, he said he'd let Miranda have the house if he could have anything inside it that could possibly be of value, and of course she would assume the mortgage payments.

When the dust settled, Chelsea and Eli were in shock at what they had caused, too afraid to tell anyone the truth — but if Heather *was* going to have a baby, then they *had* told the truth. One week after Eli's father married Heather, she said she'd miscarried and there was no baby.

Eli had been afraid his mother would fall apart at this news, but instead she had laughed. "Imagine that," she'd said. "But Miss Clever Heather *did* get her baby, whether she knows it yet or not."

Eli never could get his mother to explain that remark, but he was very glad she wasn't hurt by the divorce.

So now Eli had just seen the taillight of his father's car pull away, and he knew without a doubt that the man had been there trying to weasel out of child-support payments. Leslie Harcourt made about seventy-five thousand a year as a car salesman — he could sell anything to anyone — while Miranda barely pulled down twenty thousand as a practical nurse. "As good as I make people feel, they don't pay much for that. Eli, sweetheart, my only realistic dream for the future is to become a private nurse for some very rich, very sweet old man who wants little more than to eat popcorn and watch videos all day."

Eli had pointed out to her that all the heroines in her romance novels were running corporations while still in their twenties, or else they were waitressing and going to law school at night. That made Miranda laugh. "If all women were like that, who'd be buying the romance novels?"

Eli thought that was a very good consideration. His mother often had the ability to see right to the heart of a matter.

"What did he want?" Eli asked the moment he opened the door to the house he shared with his mother.

For a moment Miranda grimaced, annoyed that her son had caught his father there. Escaping Eli's ever-watchful eye was like trying to escape a pack of watchdogs. "Nothing much," she said evasively.

At those words a chill ran down Eli's back. "How much did you give him?"

Miranda rolled her eyes skyward.

"You know I'll find out as soon as I reconcile the bank statement. How much did you give him?"

"Young man, you are getting above yourself. The money I earn —"

Eli did some quick calculations in his head. He always knew to the penny how much money his mother had in her checking account — there was no savings account — and how much was in her purse, even to the change. "Two hundred dollars," he said. "You gave him a check for two hundred dollars." That was the maximum she could afford and still pay the mortgage and groceries.

When Miranda remained tight-lipped in silence, he knew he'd hit the amount exactly on the head. Later, he'd tell Chelsea and allow her to congratulate him on his insight.

Eli uttered a curse word under his breath.

"Eli!" Miranda said sternly. "I will not allow you to call your father such names." Her face softened. "Sweetheart, you're too young to be so cynical. You must believe in people. I worry that you've been traumatized by your father leaving you without male guidance. And I know you're hiding your true feelings: I know you miss him very much."

Eli, looking very much like an old man,

said, "You must be watching TV talk shows again. I do not miss him; I never saw him when you were married to him. My father is a self-centered, selfish bastard."

Miranda's mouth tightened into a line that was a mirror of her son's. "Whether that is true or not is irrelevant. He *is* your father."

Eli's expression didn't change. "I'm sure it is too much to hope that you were unfaithful to him and that my real father is actually the king of a small but rich European country."

As always, Miranda's face lost its stern look and she laughed. She was as unable to remain angry with Eli as she was to resist the whining and pleading of her ex-husband. She knew Eli would hate for her to say this, but he was very much like his father. Both of them always went after whatever they wanted and allowed nothing to stop them.

No, Eli wouldn't appreciate such an observation in the least.

Eli was so annoyed with his mother for once again allowing Leslie Harcourt to con her out of paying the child support that he couldn't say another word, but turned away and went to his room. At this moment his father owed six months in back child support. Instead of paying it, he'd come to

Miranda and shed a few tears, telling her how broke he was, knowing he could get Miranda to give him money. Eli knew that his father liked to test his ability to sell at every opportunity. Seeing if he could con Miranda was an exercise in salesmanship.

The truth — a truth Miranda didn't know — was that Leslie had recently purchased a sixty-thousand-dollar Mercedes, and the payments on that car were indeed stretching him financially. (Eli and Chelsea had been able to tap into a few credit-report data banks and find out all sorts of "confidential" information about people.)

Eli spent thirty minutes in his room, stewing over the perfidy of his father, but when he saw that his mother was outside tending her roses, he went back to the living room and called the man who was his father.

Eli didn't waste time with greetings. "If you don't pay three months' support within twenty-four hours and another three months' within thirty days, I'll put sugar in the gas tank of your new car." He then hung up the phone.

Twenty-two hours later, Leslie appeared at the door of Miranda's house with the money. As Eli stood behind his mother, he had to listen to his father give a long, syrupy speech about the goodness of people, about how some people were willing to believe in others, while others had no loyalty in their souls.

Eli stood it for a few minutes, then he looked around his mother and glared at his father until the man quickly left, after loudly telling Miranda that he'd have the other three months' support within thirty days. Eli restrained himself from calling out that within thirty days he'd owe not three months' support but four.

When Leslie was gone, Miranda turned to her son and smiled. "See, Eli, honey, you must believe in people. I told you your father would come through, and he did. Now, where shall we go for dinner?"

Ten minutes later, Eli was on the phone to Chelsea. "I *cannot* go to Princeton," he said softly. "I cannot leave my mother unprotected."

Chelsea didn't hesitate. "Get here fast! We'll meet in Sherwood Forest."

"What are we going to do?" Chelsea whispered. They were sitting side by side on a swing glider in the garden on her parents' twenty-acre estate. It was prime real estate, close to the heart of Denver. Her father had bought four houses and torn down three of them to give himself the acreage. Not that he was ever there to enjoy the land, but he got a lot of joy out of telling people he had twenty acres in the city of Denver.

"I don't know," Eli said. "I can't leave her. I know that. If I weren't there to protect her, she'd give everything she owned to my father."

After the story Eli had just told her, Chelsea had no doubt of this. And this wasn't the first time Leslie Harcourt had pulled a scam on his sweet ex-wife. "I wish . . ." She trailed off, then stood up and looked down at Eli. His head was bent low as he contemplated what he was giving up by not taking this offer from Princeton. She knew he hated the idea of high school almost as much as he loved the idea of getting on with his computer research.

"I wish we could find a husband for her."

Eli gave a snort. "We've tried, remember? She only likes men like my father, the ones she says 'need' her. They need her tendency to forgive them for everything they do."

"I know, but wouldn't it be nice if we could make one of those books she loves so much come true? She would meet a tall, dark billionaire, and he'd —"

"A *billionaire*?"

"Yes," Chelsea said sagely. "My father says that, what with inflation as it is, a millionaire

— even a multimillionaire — isn't worth very much."

Sometimes Eli was vividly reminded of how he and Chelsea differed on money. To him and his mother two hundred dollars was a great deal, but the woman who cut Chelsea's hair charged three hundred dollars a visit.

Chelsea smiled. "You don't happen to know any single billionaires, do you?"

She was teasing, but Eli didn't smile. "Actually, I do. He . . . he's my best friend. Male friend, that is."

At that Chelsea's eyes opened wide. One of the things she loved best about Eli was that he always had the ability to surprise her. No matter how much she thought she knew about him, it wasn't all there was to know. "Where did you meet a billionaire and how did he get to be your friend?"

Eli just looked at her and said nothing, and when he had that expression on his face, she knew she was not going to get another word out of him. Eli had an unbreakable ability to keep secrets.

But it was two days later that Eli called a meeting for the two of them in Sherwood Forest, their name for her father's garden. Chelsea had never seen such a light in his eyes before. It was almost as though he had a fever.

"What's wrong?" she whispered, knowing it had to be something awful.

When he handed her a newspaper clipping, his hand was shaking. Having no idea what to expect, she read it, then knew less than she did before she'd started. It was a small clipping from a magazine about a man named Franklin Taggert, one of the major heads of Montgomery-Taggert Enterprises. He'd been involved in a small accident and his right arm had been broken in two places. Because he had chosen to seclude himself in a cabin hidden in the Rocky Mountains until his arm healed, several meetings and contract finalizations had been postponed.

When Chelsea finished reading, she looked up at Eli in puzzlement. "So?"

"He's my friend," Eli said in a voice filled with such awe that Chelsea felt a wave of jealousy shoot through her.

"Your *billionaire*?" she asked disdainfully.

Eli didn't seem to notice her reaction as he began to pace in front of her. "It was your idea," he said. "Sometimes, Chelsea, I forget that you are as much a female as my mother."

Chelsea was not sure whether or not she liked that statement.

"You said I should find her a husband, that I should find her a rich man to take care of her. But how can I trust the care of my mother to just any man? He must be a man of insight as well as money."

Chelsea's eyebrows had risen to high up in her hairline. This was a whole new Eli she was seeing.

"The logical problem has been how to introduce my mother to a wealthy man. She is a nurse, and twenty-one percent of all romance novels at one point or another have a wounded hero and a heroine who nurses him back to health, with true love always following. So it follows that her being a nurse would give her an introduction to rich, wounded men. But since she works at a public hospital and rich men tend to hire private nurses, she has not met them."

"So now you plan to get your mother the job of nursing this man? But Eli," she said gently, "how do you get this man to hire your mother? And how do you know he's a good man, not just a wealthy one? And if they do meet, how do you know they'll fall in love? I think falling in love has to do with physical vibrations." She'd read this last somewhere, and it seemed to explain what her dopey sisters were always talking about.

Eli raised one eyebrow. "How could any

man *not* fall in love with my mother? My problem has been keeping men away from her, not the other way around."

Chelsea knew better than to comment on that. Making Eli see his mother as a normal human being was impossible. He seemed to think she had a golden glow around her. "Then how . . ." She hesitated, then smiled. "Robin and Marian Les Jeunes?"

"Yes. I think Mr. Taggert is at the cabin alone. We have to find out where it is, send my mother a letter hiring her, give her directions, then get her up there. They will fall in love and he'll take care of her. He is a proper man."

Chelsea blinked at him for a moment. "A 'proper man'?" She could see that Eli wasn't going to tell her another word, but she knew how to handle him. "If you don't tell me how you know this man, I won't help you. I won't do a thing. You'll be all alone."

Eli knew that she was bluffing. Chelsea had too much curiosity not to go along with any of his projects, but he did want to tell her how he'd met Frank Taggert. "You remember two years ago when my class went on a field trip to see Montgomery-Taggert Enterprises?"

She didn't remember, but she nodded anyway.

"I wasn't going to go, but at the last moment I decided it might be interesting, so I went."

"For the stationery," Chelsea said.

He smiled at her, glad of her understanding. "Yes, of course. We didn't have any from the Montgomery-Taggert industries, and I wanted to be prepared in case we needed it."

He told her how when he was standing there, bored, with a condescending secretary asking the children if they would like to play with the paper clips, Eli looked across the room to see a man sitting on the edge of a desk talking on the telephone. He had on a denim shirt, jeans, and cowboy boots. Maybe he was dressed like the janitor, but to Eli the man radiated power, like a fire generating heat waves.

Quietly moving about the room, Eli got behind him so the man couldn't see him, then listened to his telephone conversation. It took Eli a moment to realize that the man was making a multimillion-dollar deal. When he talked of "five and twenty," he was talking of five *million* and twenty *million*. Dollars.

When the man hung up, Eli started to move away.

"Hear what you wanted to, kid?"

Eli froze in his tracks, his breath held. He couldn't believe the man knew he was there. Most people paid no attention to kids. How had this man seen him?

"Are you too cowardly to face me?"

Eli stood straighter, then walked to stand in front of the man.

"Tell me what you heard."

Since adults seemed to like to think that children could hear only what the adults wanted them to, Eli usually found it expedient to lie. But he didn't lie to this man. He told him everything: numbers, names, places. He repeated whatever he could remember of the phone conversation he'd just heard.

As the man looked at Eli, his face had no discernible expression. "I saw you skulking about the office. What were you looking for?"

Eli took a deep breath. He and Chelsea had never told an adult about their collection of letterheads, much less what they did with them. But he told this man the truth.

The man's eyes bore into Eli's. "You know that what you're doing is illegal, don't you?"

Eli looked hard back at him. "Yes, sir, I do. But we only write letters to people who are hurting others or ignoring their responsibilities. We've written a number of letters to fathers who don't pay the child support they owe."

The man lifted one eyebrow, studied Eli for a moment, then turned to a passing secretary. "Get this young man's name and send him a complete packet of stationery from all Montgomery-Taggert Enterprises. Get them from Maine and Colorado and Washington State." He looked back at Eli. "And call the foreign offices too. London, Cairo, all of them."

"Yes, sir, Mr. Taggert," the secretary said, looking in wonder at Eli. All the employees were terrified of Frank Taggert, yet this child had done something to merit his special consideration.

When Eli got over his momentary shock, he managed to say, "Thank you."

Frank put out his hand to the boy. "My name is Franklin Taggert. Come see me when you graduate from a university and I'll give you a job."

Shaking his hand, Eli managed to say hoarsely, "What should I study?"

"With your mind, you're going to study everything," Frank said as he got off the desk and turned away, then disappeared through a doorway.

Eli stared after him, but in that moment, with those few words, he felt that his future had been decided. He knew where he was going and how he was going to get there. And for the first time in his life, Eli had a hero.

"And then what?" Chelsea asked.

"He sent the copies of the letterheads — you've seen them — I wrote to thank him and he wrote back. And we became friends."

Part of Chelsea wanted to scream that he had betrayed her by not telling her of this. *Two years!* He had kept this from her for two whole years. But she'd learned that it was no good berating Eli. He kept secrets if he wanted to and seemed to think nothing of it.

"So you want your mother to marry this man? Why did you just come up with this idea now?" She meant her words to be rather spiteful, to get him back for hiding something so interesting from her, but she knew the answer as soon as she asked. Until now Eli had wanted his beloved mother to himself. Her eyes widened. If Eli was willing to turn his mother over to the care of this man, he must . . .

"Do you really and truly like him?"

"He is like a father to me," Eli said softly.

"Have you told him about me?"

The way Eli said "Of course" mollified

her temper somewhat. "Okay, so how do we get them together? Where is this cabin of his?" She didn't have to ask how they would get his mother up there. All they had to do was write her a letter on Montgomery-Taggert stationery and offer her a nursing job.

"I don't know," Eli answered, "but I'm sure we can figure it out."

Three weeks later, Chelsea was ready to give up. "Eli," she said in exasperation, "you have to give up. We can't find him."

Eli set his mouth tighter, his head propped in his hands in despair. They'd spent three weeks sending faxes and writing letters to people, hinting that they needed to know where Frank Taggert was. Either people didn't know or they weren't telling.

"I don't know what else we can do," Chelsea said. "It's getting closer to Christmas and it's getting colder in the mountains. He'll leave soon, and she won't get to meet him."

The first week she'd asked him why he didn't just introduce his mother to Mr. Taggert, and Eli had looked at her as though she were crazy. "They will be polite to each other because of me, but what can they have in common unless they meet on equal ground? Have you learned nothing from my mother's books? The rich duke meets the governess in a place where they are *forced* to be together."

But they had tried everything and still couldn't get his mother together with Mr. Taggert. "There is one thing we haven't tried yet," Chelsea said.

Eli didn't take his head out of his hands. "There is nothing. I've thought of everything."

"We haven't tried the truth."

Turning, Eli looked at her. "What truth?"

"My parents were nearly dying for my sister to get married. My mother said my sister was losing her chances because she was getting old. She was nearly thirty. So if this Mr. Taggert is forty, maybe his family is dying to get him married too."

Eli gave her a completely puzzled look.

"Let's make an appointment with one of his brothers and tell him we have a wife for Mr. Taggert and see if he will help us."

When Eli didn't respond, Chelsea frowned. "It's worth a try, isn't it? Come on, stop moping and tell me the name of one of his brothers here in Denver."

"Michael," Eli said. "Michael Taggert."

"Okay, let's make an appointment with him and tell him what's going on."

After a moment's hesitation, Eli turned to

his keyboard. "Yes, let's try."

Michael Taggert looked up from his desk to see his secretary, Kathy, at the door wearing a mischievous grin.

"Remember the letter you received from Mr. Elijah J. Harcourt requesting a meeting today?"

Frowning, Mike gave a curt nod. In thirty minutes, he was to meet his wife for lunch, and from the look on Kathy's face there might be some complications that would hold him up. "Yes?"

"He brought his secretary with him," Kathy said, breaking into a wide smile.

Mike couldn't see why a man and his secretary would cause such merriment, but then Kathy stepped aside and Mike saw two kids, both about twelve years old, enter the room behind her. The boy was tall, thin, with huge glasses and eyes so intense he reminded Mike of a hawk. The girl, even taller, had the easy confidence of what promised to be beauty and, unless he missed his guess, money.

I don't have time for this, Mike thought, and wondered who'd put these kids up to this visit. Silently, he motioned for them to take a seat.

"You're busy and so are we, so I'll get

right to the point," Eli said.

Mike had to repress a smile. The boy's manner was surprisingly adult, and he reminded him of someone but Mike couldn't think who.

"I want my mother to marry your brother."

"Ah, I see," Mike said, leaning back in his chair. "And which one of my brothers would that be?"

"The oldest one, Frank."

Mike nearly fell out of his chair. "Frank?" he gasped. His eldest brother was a terror, as precise as a measuring device, and about as warm as Maine in February. "Frank? You want your *mother* to marry Frank?" He leaned forward. "Tell me, kid, you got it in for your mother or what?"

At that Eli came out of his seat, his face red. "Mr. Taggert is a *very nice* man, and you can't say anything against him *or* my mother!"

The girl put her hand on Eli's arm and he instantly sat down, but he turned his head away and wouldn't look at Mike.

"Perhaps I might explain," the girl said, and she introduced herself.

Mike was impressed with the girl as she succinctly told their story, of Eli's offer to go to Princeton but his refusal to leave his mother alone. As she spoke, Mike kept looking at Eli, trying to piece everything together. So the kid wanted a billionaire to take care of his mother. Ambitious brat, wasn't he?

But Mike began to have a change of heart when Eli turned to Chelsea and said, "Don't tell him that. He doesn't *like* his brother."

"Tell me what?" Mike encouraged. "And I love my brother. It's just that he's sometimes hard to take. Are you sure you have the right Frank Taggert?"

At that Eli removed a worn, raggedy envelope from the folder he was carrying. Mike recognized it as Frank's private stationery, something he reserved for the family only. It was a way the family had of distinguishing private from business mail. His family frequently joked that Frank never used family stationery for anyone who did not bear the same last name as he did. There was even a rumor that on the rare times he'd sent a note to whichever date was waiting for him at the moment, he'd used business letterhead.

Yet Frank had written this boy a letter on his private stationery.

"May I see that?" Mike asked, extending his hand.

Eli started to return the letter to his folder.

"Go on," Chelsea urged. "This is important." Reluctantly, Eli handed the letter to Mike.

Slowly, Mike took the single sheet of paper from the envelope and read it. It was handwritten, not typed. To Mike's knowledge, Frank had not handwritten anything since he'd left his university.

My dear Eli,

I was so glad to receive your last letter. Your new theories on artificial intelligence sound magnificent. Yes, I'll have someone check what's already been done.

One of my brother's wives had a baby, a little girl, with cheeks as red as roses. I set up a trust fund for her but told no one.

I'm glad you liked your birthday present, and I'll wear the cuff links you sent me next time I see the president.

How are Chelsea and your mother? Let me know if your dad ever again refuses to pay child support. I know a few legal people and I also know a few thugs. Any man who isn't grateful to have a son like you deserves to be taught a lesson.

My love and friendship to you,
Frank

Mike had to read the letter three times, and even though he was sure it was from his brother, he couldn't believe it. When one of his siblings produced yet another child, Frank's only comment was "Don't any of you ever stop?" Yet here he was saying his brother's new baby had cheeks like roses — which she did.

Mike carefully refolded the letter and inserted it back into the envelope. Eli nearly snatched it from his hands.

"Eli wants his mother to meet Mr. Frank Taggert in a place where they will be equal," Chelsea said. "She's a nurse, and we know Mr. Taggert's been injured, so we thought she could go to this cabin in the mountains where he's staying. But we can't find where it is so we can send her there."

Mike was having difficulty believing what she was saying. He looked at his watch. "I'm to meet my wife for lunch in ten minutes. Would you two like to join us?"

Forty-five minutes later, with the help of his wife, Samantha, Mike finally understood the whole story. And more importantly, he'd figured out who Eli reminded him of. Eli was like Frank: cool exterior, intense eyes, brilliant brain, obsessive personality.

As Mike listened, he was somewhat hurt and annoyed that his elder brother had chosen a stranger's child to love. But at least Frank's love for Eli proved he *could* love.

"I think it's all wonderfully romantic," Samantha said.

"I think the poor woman's going to meet Frank and be horrified," Mike muttered, but when Samantha kicked him under the table, he shut up.

"So how do we arrange this?" Samantha asked. "And what size dress does your mother wear?"

"Twelve petite," Chelsea said. "She's short and f—" She didn't have to turn to feel Eli's glare. He wasn't saying much, and she knew that it was because he was hostile toward Mike. "She's, ah, round," Chelsea finished.

"I understand," Samantha said, getting a little notebook from her handbag.

"What difference does her dress size make?" Mike asked.

Chelsea and Samantha looked at him as though he were stupid. "She can't very well arrive at the cabin wearing jeans and a sweatshirt, now can she? Chelsea, shall we go buy some cashmere?"

"Cashmere?!" Eli and Mike said in unison,

and it made a bond between them: men versus women.

Samantha ignored her husband's outburst. "Mike, you can write a letter to Mrs. Harcourt saying —"

"Stowe," Eli said. "My father's new wife wanted my mother to resume her maiden name, so she did."

At that Samantha gave Mike a hard look, and he knew that all sense of proportion was lost. From now on, anything Eli and Chelsea wanted, they'd get.

2

Gratefully, Miranda got off the horse and went into the cabin. In the last few days, things had happened so quickly that she'd had no time to think about them. Yesterday afternoon a man had come to the hospital and asked if she'd please accept a private, live-in nursing job for his client. It was to start the next morning and would last for two weeks. At first she started to say no, that she couldn't ask the hospital to let her off. But it seemed that her absence had already been cleared with the chief of staff — a man Miranda had never seen, much less met.

She then told the man she couldn't go because she had a son to take care of and she couldn't leave him. As though the whole thing were timed, Miranda was called to the phone to be asked — begged, actually — by Eli to be allowed to go with Chelsea's family on an extremely educational yacht trip.

Maybe she should have protested that he'd miss too much school, but she knew that Eli could make up any work within a blink of an eye, and he so wanted to go that she couldn't say no.

When she put down the phone, the man was still standing there, waiting for her answer about accepting the job.

"Two weeks only," she said, "then I have to be back."

Only after she agreed was she told that her new patient was staying in a remote cabin high in the Rockies and the only way to get there was by helicopter or horse — but there was no place for the 'copter to land. Since the idea of being lowered on a rope from a helicopter didn't appeal to her, she said she'd take the horse.

Early the next morning, she hugged and kissed Eli as though she were going to be away from him for a year or more, then got into a car that drove her thirty miles into the mountains. An old man named Sandy was waiting to take her up to the cabin. He had two saddled horses and three mules loaded with goods.

They rode all day and Miranda knew she'd be sore from the horse, but the air was heavenly, thin and crisp as they went higher and higher. It was early autumn, but she could almost smell the snow that would eventually blanket the mountains.

When they reached the cabin, a beautiful structure of logs and stone, she thought they must be in the most isolated place on earth. There were no wires to the cabin, no roads, no sign that it had touch with the outside world.

"Remote, isn't it?"

Sandy looked up from the mule he was unloading. "Frank made sure the place has all the comforts of home. Underground electricity and its own sewage system."

"What's he like?" she asked. Because of the narrow trail, they hadn't been able to talk much on the long ride up. All she knew of her patient was that he'd broken his right arm, was in a cast, and that it was difficult for him to perform everyday tasks.

Sandy took a while to answer. "Frank's not like anybody else. He's his own man. Set in his ways, sort of."

"I'm used to old and weird," she said with a smile. "Does he live here all the time?"

Sandy chuckled. "There's twelve feet of snow up here in the winter. Frank lives wherever he wants to. He just came here to . . . well, maybe to lick his wounds. Frank doesn't talk much. Why don't you go inside and sit down? I'll get this lot unloaded. If I know Frank, he's out fishing and won't be back for hours."

With a smile of gratitude, Miranda did as he bid. Without so much as a glance at the interior of the cabin, she went inside, sat down, and immediately fell asleep. When she awoke with a start, it was about an hour later, and she saw that Sandy and the animals were gone. Only a huge pile of boxes and sacks on the floor showed that he had been there.

At first she was a bit disconcerted to find herself alone there, but she shrugged and began to look about her.

The cabin looked as though it had been designed by a computer, or at least a human who had no feelings. It was perfectly functional, an open-plan L-shape, one end with a huge stone fireplace, a couch, and two chairs. It could have been charming, but the three perfectly matched pieces were covered with heavy, serviceable, dark gray fabric that looked as though it had been chosen solely for durability. There were no rugs on the floor, no pictures on the walls, and only one table had a plain gray ceramic lamp on it. The kitchen was in the corner of the L, and it had also been designed for service: cabinets built for use alone, not decorative in any way. At the end of the kitchen were two beds, precisely covered in hard-wearing brown canvas. Through a door was a bathroom with a shower, white ceramic toilet, and washbasin. Everything was utterly basic. All clean and tidy. And with no sign of human habitation.

Miranda panicked for a moment when she thought that perhaps her patient had packed up and left, that maybe she was here alone, with no way down the mountain except for a two-day walk. But then she noticed a set of doors beside one of the beds, one on each side, perfectly symmetrical. Behind one, arranged in military precision, were some pieces of men's clothing: heavy canvas trousers, boots without a bit of mud on them.

"My, my, we are neat, aren't we?" she murmured, smiling, then frowned at the twin bed so near his. No more than three feet separated the beds. She did hope this old man wasn't the type to make childish passes at her. She'd had enough of those in school. "Just give me a little kiss, honey," toothless men had said to her as their aged hands reached for her body.

Laughing at the silliness of her fantasy, Miranda went to the kitchen and looked inside. Six pots and pans. Perfectly arranged, spotlessly clean. The drawers contained a matched set of stainless steel cooking utensils that looked as though they'd never been used. "Not much of a cook, are you, Mr. Taggert?" she murmured as she kept exploring. Other cabinets and drawers were filled with full jars of spices and herbs, their seals unbroken.

"What in the world does this man eat?" she wondered aloud. When she came to the last cabinet, she found the answer. Hidden inside was a microwave, and behind the tall door in the corner was a freezer. It had about a dozen TV dinners in it, and after a moment's consternation, Miranda laughed. It looked as though she'd been hired to cook for the missing Mr. Taggert as much as anything else.

"Poor man. He must be starving," she said, and she cheered up at the thought. The beds so close together had worried her, but the empty freezer was reassuring. "So, Miranda, my girl, you weren't brought here for a sex orgy but to cook for some lonely old man with a broken arm. Poor dear, I wonder where he is now."

She didn't waste time speculating but set to work hauling in supplies. She had no idea what Sandy had brought on those two mules but she soon found out. Packed in dry ice, in insulated containers, was nearly a whole side of prime beef and a couple dozen chickens. There were bags of flour, packets of yeast, some canned goods, and bags of fresh fruit and vegetables. With every item she unpacked, she felt more sure of what her true purpose here was, and thinking of someone who needed her made her begin to forget how easily Eli had said he didn't need her for the next two weeks. He'd told her in detail how very much he wanted to travel with Chelsea and her parents to the south of France, then on to Greece aboard some Italian prince's yacht.

"All in just two weeks?"

"It's a really fast boat," Eli said, then disappeared into his room.

With a sigh, Miranda put a frozen chicken in the microwave to thaw. She would *not* let herself think how Eli needed her less every day. "My baby is growing up," she said to herself as she removed the chicken and began to prepare a stuffing of bread cubes, sage, and onion.

"Don't start feeling sorry for yourself," she said. "You're not dead yet. You could meet a man, fall madly in love, and have three more kids." Even as she said it, she laughed. She wasn't a heroine in a romance novel. She wasn't drop-dead gorgeous with a figure that made men's hands itch with lust. She was a perfectly ordinary woman. She was pretty in a dimpled sort of way — an old-fashioned prettiness, not the gaunt-cheeked style that was all the rage now. And she was — well, face it, about thirty pounds overweight. Sometimes she consoled herself that if she'd lived in the seventeenth or eighteenth century, men would have used her as a model for a painting of Venus, the goddess of love. But that didn't help today when the most popular models weighed little more than ninety pounds.

As Miranda settled down to prepare a meal for her absent patient, she tried to forget the loneliness of her life, to forget that her precious son would soon be leaving her to go to school and she would be left with no one.

Two hours later she had a lovely fire going in the big stone fireplace, a stuffed chicken roasting in the never-before-used oven, and some vegetables simmering. She'd filled a bowl full of wildflowers from the side of the cabin and put a dry pinecone on a window-sill. Her unpacked duffel bags were by the bed the man didn't appear to use. She'd draped her sweater across the back of a chair and put an interesting rock on one end of the stone mantel. The place was beginning to look like home.

When the cabin door was flung open and a man burst in, Miranda almost dropped the teakettle. He was *not* old. There was some gray at the temples of his thick black hair and lines running down the sides of his tight-lipped mouth, but his virility was intact. He was a *very* good-looking man.

"Who are you and what are you doing here?" he demanded.

She swallowed. Something about him was intimidating. She could see that he was a man who was used to giving orders and being obeyed. "I'm your nurse," she said brightly, nodding toward his arm, which was in a cast nearly to his shoulder. It must have been a bad break for such a cast, and he must have great difficulty doing even the smallest tasks.

Smiling, she walked around the counter, refusing to be intimidated by his face. "Miranda Stowe," she said, laughing nervously. "But you already know that, don't you? Sandy said you had the medical reports with you, so maybe if I saw them, I'd know more about your condition." When he didn't say a word, she frowned a bit. "Come and sit down, supper's almost ready and — here, let me help you off with those boots."

He was still staring at her, speechless, so she gently tugged on his uninjured arm and got him to sit in a chair by the dining table. Kneeling before him, she started to unlace his boots while thinking that sharing a cabin was going to be a lonely experience if he never spoke.

When he started to laugh, she looked up at him, smiling, wanting to share whatever was amusing him.

"This is the best one yet," he said.

"What is?" she asked, thinking he was remembering a joke.

"You are." Still smiling, he cocked one eyebrow at her. "I must say you don't *look* the part of — what was it you called your-self? A nurse?"

Miranda lost her smile. "I *am* a nurse."

"Sure you are, honey. And I'm a newborn babe."

Miranda quit unlacing his boots and stood up, looking down at him. "Exactly what do you think I am?" she asked quietly.

"With those" — he nodded toward her ample bosom — "you could be only one thing."

Miranda was a softhearted woman. Wounded butterflies made her weep, but this tall, good-looking man, nodding toward her breasts in that way, was more than she could take. She was strong from years of making beds and turning patients, so when he reached out as though to touch her, she put her hand on his shoulder and pushed. It was harder than she meant to. As he went flying backward in the chair, he reached for the table to keep from falling. But his right arm, encased in plaster, unbalanced him so he went sprawling to the floor.

Miranda knew she should see if he was all right, but she didn't. She turned on her heel and started for the cabin door.

"Why you —" he said, then grabbed her ankle before she could take another step.

"Let go of me!" She kicked out at him, but he pulled harder, until she landed on top of him and hit his injured arm. She knew the impact must have hurt him, but he didn't so much as show his pain by a flicker of an eye.

With one roll, he pinned her body to the floor. "Who are you and how much do you want?"

Genuinely puzzled, she looked up at him. He was about forty years old, give or take a few years, and his body felt as though it was in perfect condition. "For this job I receive about four hundred dollars a week." She narrowed her eyes at him. "For *nursing.*"

"Nursing," he said in a derogatory way. "Is *that* what you call it?"

She pushed against him angrily but

couldn't budge him.

"So how did you find me? Simpson? No, he doesn't know anything. Who sent you? The Japanese?"

Miranda stopped struggling. "The Japanese?" Was the man's injury *only* in his arm?

"Yeah, they weren't too happy when I won on that last deal. But microchips are a dead item. I'm going for —"

"Mr. Taggert!" she interrupted, as he seemed to have forgotten he was lying full length on top of her. "I have *no* idea what you're talking about. Would you please let me up?"

When he looked down at her, the color of his dark eyes seemed to change. "You're not like the women I usually have, but I guess you'll do." He gave her a lascivious, one-sided smirk. "The softness of you might make for a nice change from bony models and starlets."

At that remark, made as though he were in a butcher's shop poking chickens for tenderness, she brought her knee up sharply between his legs. He rolled off her in pain. "Now, Mr. Taggert," she said as she stood up and bent over him, "just what is this all about?"

He was holding himself with one hand, and as he rolled to one side, his injured shoulder hit the table leg. Miranda's heart *almost* went out to him.

"I'm a . . ."

"A what?" she demanded.

"A billionaire."

"You're a — ?" She didn't know whether to laugh or kick him in the ribs. She couldn't conceive of the amount of money he was talking about. "You're rich, so you think I came up here to . . . to get your money?"

He was beginning to recover as he pulled himself up to sit heavily on a chair. "Why else would you be here?"

"Because you asked for a nurse," she shot at him. "You *hired* me."

"I've heard *that* story before."

She stood looking down at him, glaring, more angry than she'd ever before been. "Mr. Taggert, you may have a great deal of money, but when it comes to being a human being, you are penniless."

She didn't think about what she was doing, that she was in the Rocky Mountains and had no idea how to get back to civilization. She just grabbed her sweater from the back of the couch and walked out of the cabin.

Still raging in anger, she followed a bit of a trail, but she didn't look where she was going.

Not even Leslie had ever made her as angry as this man just had. Leslie lied to her and manipulated her at every chance, but he'd never accused her of being indecent.

She went uphill and down, unaware of the growing dark. One minute it seemed to be sunny and warm, and the next moment it was pitch-dark and freezing. Putting on her sweater didn't help at all.

"Are you ready to return?"

When the man spoke, she nearly jumped out of her skin. Whirling about, she could barely see him standing hidden amid the trees.

"I don't think I will return to the cabin," she said. "I'm going back to Denver."

"Yes, of course. But Denver is that way." He pointed in the direction opposite to the way she was walking.

She wanted to keep some of her pride. "I wanted to . . . to get my suitcase." She looked from one side to the other for a moment, then charged straight ahead.

"Ahem," he said, then pointed over his right shoulder.

"All right, Mr. Taggert," she said, "you've won. I haven't a clue where I am or where I'm going."

He took two steps around her and parted

some bushes with his hand, and there, about a hundred yards in front of her, was the cabin. Light glowed softly and warmly from the windows. She could almost feel the warmth of the fire.

But she turned away, toward the path leading to Denver, and started walking.

"And where do you think you're going?"

"Home," she said, just as she stumbled over a tree root in the trail. But she caught herself and didn't fall. With her back straight, she kept walking.

He was beside her in moments. "You'll freeze to death out here. If a bear doesn't get you first, that is."

She kept walking.

"I am ordering you to —"

Halting, she glared up at him. "You have no right to order me to do anything. No right at all. Now, would you please leave me alone? I want to go *home*." To her horror, her voice sounded full of tears. She'd never been able to sustain anger for very long. No matter what Leslie did to her, she couldn't stay angry for more than a short time.

Straightening her shoulders, she again started walking.

"Could I hire you as my cook-housekeeper?" he said from behind her.

"You couldn't pay me enough to work for

you," she answered.

"Really?" he asked, and he was right behind her. "If you're poor —"

"I am *not* poor. I just have very little money. You, Mr. Taggert, are *very* poor. You think everyone has a price tag."

"They do, and so do you. So do I, for that matter."

"If you think that, you must be a very lonely man."

"I've never had enough time alone to consider what loneliness is. Now, what can I offer you to make you cook for me?"

"Is *that* what you want? My pot roast?" At this thought there came a little spring to her step. Maybe she *did* have something to offer. And maybe she wouldn't have to spend the night running down a mountain being chased by a bear.

"Five hundred dollars a week," he said.

"Ha!"

"A thousand?"

"Ha. Ha. Ha," she said with great sarcasm.

"What then? What do you want most in the world?"

"The finest education the world has to offer for my son."

"Cambridge," he said automatically.

"Anywhere, just so it's the best."

"You want me to give your son four years

68

at Cambridge University for one week's cooking? You're talking thousands."

"Not four years. Freshman to PhD."

At that Frank laughed. "You, lady, are crazy," he said, turning away from her.

She stopped walking and turned to look at his back. "I saw wild strawberries up here. I make French crepes so light you can read through them. And I brought fresh cream to be whipped and drenched in strawberries, then rolled in a crepe. I make a rabbit stew that takes all day long to cook. It's flavored with wild sage. I saw some ducks on a pond near here, and you would not believe what I can do with a duck and tea leaves."

Frank had stopped walking.

"But then you're not interested, are you, Mr. Billionaire? I bet you could toast hundred-dollar bills on a stick over the fire and they would no doubt taste yummy."

He turned back to her. "Potatoes?"

"Tiny ones buried under the fire coals all day so they're soft and mushy, then drizzled with butter and parsley."

He took a step toward her. When he spoke, his voice was low. "I saw bags of flour."

"I make biscuits flavored with honey for breakfast and bread touched with dill for dinner."

He took another step toward her. "PhD?"

"Yes," she said firmly, thinking of Eli in that venerable school and how much he'd love it. "PhD."

"All right," he said, as though it were the most difficult thing he'd ever agreed to.

"I want it in writing."

"Yes, of course. Now, shall we return to the cabin?"

"Certainly." With her head held high, she started to walk past him, but he pulled aside a curtain of bushes. "Might I suggest that this way would be quicker?"

Once again, not a hundred yards away, was the cabin.

As she walked past him, her nose in the air, he said, "Thank heaven your cooking is better than your sense of direction."

"Thank heaven *you* have money enough to *buy* what you want."

She didn't see the way he frowned as she continued walking. If the truth were told, Frank Taggert wasn't used to being around women who didn't fawn over him. Between his good looks and his money, he found he was quite irresistible to women.

But then he usually didn't have anything to do with women like this one. Most of the women he escorted were the long-legged, perfect sort, the kind who wanted sparkling baubles and nothing else from him. He'd found that if he grew bored with one of them, if he gave her enough jewelry, she soon dried her tears.

But this one had had a chance at a great deal of money and she'd asked for something for someone other than herself.

As he watched her walk back to the cabin, he wondered about her husband. What was he like to allow his wife to go alone into the mountains to take care of another man?

Once he was inside the cabin, he sat down hungrily at the table and waited while she served the meal she'd cooked. She made herself a plate and took it into the living area, put it on the heavy pine coffee table, sat on the floor, and began to eat as she watched the fire.

Annoyed, and with great difficulty because he was one-handed, he picked up his plate and flatware and moved it to the coffee table. He'd no more than sat down when she lifted her plate and took it to the table.

"Why did you do that?" he asked, greatly annoyed.

"The hired help doesn't eat with Mr. Billionaire."

"Would you stop calling me that? My name is Frank."

"I know that, Mr. Taggert. But what is *my* name?"

For the life of him, he couldn't remember. But then, considering the circumstances under which she'd told him her name, his lack of memory was understandable. "I don't remember," he said.

"Mrs. Stowe," she answered, "and I was hired as your *nurse.*"

She was behind him, seated at the dining table, and when he twisted around, causing pain to shoot through his shoulder, he saw that she had placed herself with her back to him. Frowning in annoyance, he moved to the table across from her.

"Would you mind telling me who hired you?" he asked. The chicken was indeed delicious, and he thought a week away from canned food was going to be worth sending some kid to school — well, almost, anyway. Maybe he could write off the expense as charity. This could be advantageous tax-wise if he —

"Your brother."

Frank nearly choked. "My *brother* hired you? Which one?"

She still refused to look at him, but he could see her shoulders stiffen. They weren't fashionably square shoulders, but rather round and soft.

"It seems to me, Mr. Taggert," she said, "that a rather unpleasant joke has been played on you. I would hate to think that you had more than one brother who would have such animosity toward you as to instigate such a joke."

Frank well knew that each of his brothers would delight in playing any possible trick on him, but he didn't tell her that.

After her remark about his brothers he didn't speak again but tried to give his attention to the food. She wasn't going to put his French chef out of business, but there was a comforting, homey flavor to the food, and the portions were man-sized. In his house in Denver, his apartment in New York, and his flat in London, each of his chefs served calorie-controlled meals to ensure Frank's trim physique.

She finished eating, then silently cleared her place and his, while Frank, feeling deliciously full, moved to the couch and watched the fire. He'd never been a man who smoked, but when she served him a tiny cup of excellent coffee, he almost wished he had a cigar. "And a plump woman to share my bed," as his father used to say.

Relaxed, drowsy, he watched the woman as she moved about the room, straightening things. But then she stood on a chair and drove a nail into the ceiling beam that ran between the two beds. "What are you doing?"

"Making separate rooms," she answered. "Or as close as I can come to it."

"I assure you, Mrs. Stowe, that that is not necessary. I have no intention of imposing myself on you."

"You've made yourself clear as to your thoughts of my . . . of my feminine appeal, shall we say?" She drove another nail, then tied a heavy cotton rope from one nail to another.

Aghast, Frank watched her drape spare blankets over the rope, effectively creating a solid boundary between the two beds. He stood up. "You don't have to do this."

"I'm not doing it for you. I'm doing it for me. You see, Mr. Billionaire, I don't like you. I don't like you at all, and I'm not sure anyone else in the world does either. Now, if you'll excuse me, I'm going to take a bath."

Minutes later, Miranda stepped into a tub of water so hot it made her toes hurt, but she needed the warmth, needed the heat to thaw her heart. Being near Frank Taggert was like standing near an iceberg. She wondered if he had ever had any human warmth in him, whether he'd ever loved anyone. She'd like to think he was like one of her romantic heroes: wounded by some callous woman, and now his cold exterior protected a soft, loving heart.

She almost laughed aloud at the absurdity of the idea. All evening he'd been watching her speculatively; she could feel his eyes even through her back. He seemed to be trying to decide where she belonged in the world. Rather like an accountant would try to figure out where an expense should be placed.

"At least Leslie had passion," she whispered, lying back in the tub. "He lied with passion, committed adultery with passion, made money with passion." But when she looked into this Frank Taggert's eyes, she saw nothing. *He* would never lie to a woman about where he'd spent the night because he'd never care whether or not she was hurt by his infidelity.

All in all, she thought it was better not to think about Mr. Billionaire. With longing, she wondered what Eli and Chelsea were doing tonight. Would Eli eat properly if she wasn't there? Would he ever turn off his computer and go to bed if she didn't make him? Would he get seasick? Would — ?

She had to stop thinking about her son or she'd cry from missing him. It suddenly dawned on her that whoever had played a joke on Frank Taggert had inadvertently also played one on her. Obviously, someone thought that sending a plain, ordinary woman such as she was to spend a week with a handsome, sophisticated, rich man like Mr. Taggert was the most hilarious of jokes.

Getting out of the tub, she dried off, then opened her night case to get her flannel gown and old bathrobe. At the sight of the garments inside, she felt a momentary panic. These were not her clothes. When she saw the Dior label on the beautiful pink nightgown, she almost swooned. Pulling it out, she saw that it was a peignoir set, made of the finest Egyptian cotton, the bodice covered with tiny pink silk roses. The matching robe was diaphanous and nearly transparent. It didn't take a brain like Eli's to see that this was not something a woman who was merely a housekeeper would wear.

Wrapping a towel about herself to cover the beautiful gown and robe, she rushed out of the room, past the bed on which Frank Taggert sat, scurried behind the blanket partition, and began to rummage in her not-yet-unpacked suitcase for her own clothes.

"Is there a problem?" he asked from behind his side of the blanket.

"No, of course not. What could be the problem?" She went through her bags frantically, but nothing was familiar. If a 1930s-era movie star were going to spend a week in the Rockies, these were the clothes she would have worn. But Miranda had never worn clothes made of silk or linen, or a wool so soft you could use it as a powder puff.

She knew herself to normally be a soft-tempered person. After all, she'd had to put up with Leslie's shenanigans for years. But this was too much!

Throwing aside the blanket room divider, three cashmere sweaters in her hand, she pushed them toward Frank Taggert. "I want to know exactly what is going on. Why am I here? Whose clothes are these?"

Sitting on the side of the bed, Frank was trying to unlace his boots with one hand. "Tell me, Mrs. Stowe, are you married?"

"Divorced."

"Yes, I think I am beginning to understand. I come from a large family that is constantly reproducing itself. I believe they have decided I should do the same."

"You — ?" In shock, Miranda sat down on the edge of her bed. "They have . . . You mean, they want us to . . ."

"Yes. At least that's my guess."

"Your . . . guess?" She swallowed. "My guess is that your family sent me here because the idea of a woman like me with a man like you is a great joke."

He didn't pretend to misunderstand her. While she'd been speaking, he'd continued to work at untying his bootlaces. So far he'd not managed to even loosen the knot.

Not even thinking about what she was doing and certainly not what she was wearing, Miranda knelt before him and untied his laces, then pulled off his boots. "I don't mean to pry," she said as she removed his socks. Then, just as she did for Eli and used to do for Leslie, she gave each foot a quick massage. "But why would they choose someone like *me*? With your looks and money, you could have anyone."

"My family would like you. You look like a poster illustration for fertility."

She had her hands on his shirt collar as she began to unbutton it. "A what?"

"A symbol of fertility. A paean to motherhood. I'm willing to bet that this son of yours is your whole life."

"Is there something wrong with that?" she asked defensively.

"Nothing whatever if that's what you

choose to do."

She was helping him out of his shirt. "What better life is there for a woman than to dedicate herself to her children?"

"You have more than one child?"

"No," she said sadly, then saw that his eyes seemed to say: *I knew it.* "So your brother sent me up here in the hope that I would . . . would what, Mr. Taggert?"

"From the look of your gown, I'd say Mike did this, since his wife, Samantha, is the personification of a romantic heroine."

"A romantic heroine?"

"Yes. All she wants out of life is to take care of Mike and their ever-growing brood of children."

"*You* have not been reading what I have. Today, the heroines of romance novels want a career and control of their own lives and —"

"A husband and babies."

"Perhaps. Stand up," she ordered and began unfastening his trousers. She'd undressed many patients, and she was doing so now without thinking too much about the action.

"How many heroes have you read about who said, 'I want to go to bed with you, but I don't want to get married and I never want children'?" he asked.

"I guess normality *is* a requirement in a hero."

"And to not want marriage and children is abnormal?"

She smiled coldly at him. "I've never met anyone like you, but I assume you are not married, never want to be, never will be, and will have no children. But then, if you did, you would only visit them by court order."

She had him stripped to his undershorts and T-shirt and he was certainly in fine physical form, but she felt no more for him than she would have for a statue.

"What makes you think I have no wife? I could have married many times." He sounded more curious than anything else.

"I'm sure you could have, but the only way a woman would marry you is for your money."

"I beg your pardon?"

Maybe it was rotten of Miranda, but she felt a little thrill at having upset his calm. "You are *not* what a woman dreams of."

"And what does a woman dream of, Mrs. Stowe?"

The thought of that relaxed Miranda as she pulled back the blankets on his bed. "She dreams of a man who is all hers, a man whose whole world revolves around their family. He might go out and solve world problems and be seen by everyone as magnificently strong, but when he's at home, he puts his head on her lap and tells her he couldn't have accomplished anything without her. And, most important, she knows he's telling the truth. He *needs* her."

"I see. A man who appears to be strong but is actually weak."

She sighed. "You don't see at all. Tell me, do you analyze everything? Take everything apart? Do you put it all into an account book?" She gave him a hard look. "What are you making your billions *for*?"

As she held back the covers, he stepped into bed. "I have many nieces and nephews, and I can assure you that my will is in order. If I should die tomorrow —"

"If you should die tomorrow, who will miss you?" she asked. "I mean, miss *you*?"

Suddenly she was very tired. Turning away from him, she pushed the blanket partition aside and went to her own bed. She had never felt so lonely in her life. Perhaps it was Eli's going away to college, or maybe it was this man's talk of her looking as though she should have many children. When Eli left home, she would be alone, and she didn't think some man was going to come riding up to her front door on a black stallion and —

She didn't think anymore but fell asleep.

When Frank heard the soft sounds of her sleeping, he got out of bed and went to the fire. Without seeming to think about what she was doing, she'd banked the fire before they went to bed.

In fact, Mrs. Stowe seemed to have done every good thing without conscious thought. It seemed to be natural to her. When he'd first entered the cabin, for a moment it was as though he'd been transported back to his childhood. The delicious smell of food, bits of clothing draped on the furniture, wild-flowers in a vase, had brought it all back to him. He'd almost expected his many brothers and sisters to come running to him. And then his mother would call to him to please help her with . . . anything and everything.

His mother, overburdened with so many children and wanting to show that she could do everything herself, often said Frank was her "rock." He was her helpmate, a child who never complained, never threw tantrums, who always shared. His father said Frank had been "born old."

What none of them realized was how much Frank hid inside himself. He'd had to develop great inner strength to keep quiet and repress urges to run away and hide. Sometimes he wanted to scream, "I don't *want* to take care of three toddlers. I *want* to be all by myself and read a book or look at the stars." Gradually, being alone, being quiet, and having no little kids around him had become the ultimate goal of his life.

Frank threw a couple more logs on the fire, then sat down on the couch. He had achieved his goal so well that . . . Well, he'd almost become a joke to his family. His childhood had been inundated with sticky siblings leaping on him, trying to stick wet crackers in his ears. By the time he was twelve he could change a diaper with one hand while feeding strained carrots to another child.

But his adulthood was the opposite. Over the years his siblings had married and begun producing children of their own, and Frank had nearly run from them. He'd found that he had a talent for making money — and his ability to hide his true feelings had helped greatly. He had used what he earned to give himself an extremely orderly life. Peace. Calm. Quiet. It had all been such a glorious relief to him.

Until Eli, he thought. It was as though meeting the boy had unlocked something inside Frank. Eli wasn't like Frank's gregarious, laughing, rambunctious family. Eli was like Frank. They understood each other, thought alike, wanted the same things in life.

Frank found himself telling the boy things he'd never shared with anyone else. And Frank had begun to change. When he'd been shown his latest niece, her dad had laughed and said, "I know you're not interested, so you don't have to hold her."

But to Frank's surprise, he *had* wanted to hold the baby. The feeling had so shocked him that he'd left his brother's house right away.

As he drove home, he wondered if Eli was the cause of these new feelings or if it was the other way around. Had Frank begun to change so that he noticed a kid skulking around his office?

Frank glanced over at Miranda, lying on the bed. He was ashamed of himself for what he'd assumed about her. His family had often said that his incessant business dealings had made him lose touch with the real world. While it was true that his life consisted of doing his best to win deals, he did have a social life. In fact, right now he had a girlfriend, Gwyn. They went to one charity gala after another. He owned an entire wardrobe of tuxedos, all of which got frequent wear.

It was his sister-in-law Samantha who'd said, "But that's not real. Seeing each other at your best has nothing to do with actual life. You need to love a person at three a.m. when the baby has spit up on you and you haven't had any sleep and you're angry and crying and he puts his arms around you and says, 'Go to bed. I'll do this.' Charity balls are the dessert, not the meal."

At the time, Frank had dismissed what she'd said, but since he'd met Eli two years ago, he'd thought about it. A few months ago he'd been up all night working on a contract with some Russian businessmen. There'd been vodka and a lot of cigarettes. He was to meet Gwyn later that day so he'd planned to take a nap and clean up, but he didn't. Instead, when she arrived at his apartment, he'd been unshaven, sweaty, and stinking.

She had graciously and charmingly told him she'd return when he was presentable.

Frank got up to use the poker to move the logs around. This woman, this Mrs. Stowe, wouldn't do that. She would probably have straightened up the apartment while Frank took a shower. Or maybe he would have rubbed his whiskers on her neck, made her laugh, and they would have taken a shower together.

He liked that idea. In fact, he liked everything about her. He had treated her abominably. Horribly. But she'd returned his actions with kindness. Well, maybe she'd been a bit sassy in calling him Mr. Billionaire — the memory made him smile — but she'd fed him, undressed him, taken care of him.

When he'd told Gwyn that he'd broken his arm, she'd said, "Oh dear, how awful for you. You'll miss the museum gala. But I'll send you photos so you won't feel left out." Photos were Gwyn's idea of kindness.

What would Miranda have done in that situation? Made chicken soup?

One of the reasons Frank was so very successful was because he could make decisions quickly. In seconds, he could see down the road to where his decision would lead him, then say yes or no.

As he looked at Miranda's sleeping form, he could see where a liaison, a merger so to speak, with her would lead. There was a possible end to the deep loneliness of his life. Perhaps with someone like Miranda in his life he could at last give up hiding what was inside him.

He'd been angry at the thought of his siblings playing a joke on him, but maybe they hadn't. Maybe they'd realized what

Frank needed and had helped him find her.

But, he thought, how to present what he had in mind to her? Should he lie and say he'd fallen in love with her? She wouldn't believe that. Tell her he was overcome with lust? She'd go running out the door again. Perhaps he should suggest dating? What a waste of time! He'd made up his mind so why dally?

That she had a son she wanted to take care of was to his advantage. What if he presented it all as a business deal? He could point out that they had things the other wanted, so let's do it. Yes, he thought, that was the way.

Miranda didn't know how long she'd been asleep before a man's voice woke her.

"Mrs. Stowe."

Startled, she looked up at Frank Taggert, wearing just his underwear, his arm in its heavy cast, standing there looking at her, his dark eyes serious. Only the fading firelight lit the room.

I'll bet this is how he looks when he makes one of his million-dollar deals, she thought, and she wondered what he could possibly want of her that he needed to wake her in the middle of the night.

"Yes?"

"I have a proposition to put to you. A merger of sorts."

Pushing herself upright, she leaned against the head of the bed, unaware that the gown showed every curve of her upper body. But Frank didn't seem to notice, as his eyes were intense.

"Ordinarily," he began, "the things you said to me would have no effect on me. My relatives have said everything you have and more. However, it seems that when a man reaches forty and —"

"A billion," she interrupted.

"Yes, well, there does come a time when a man begins to consider his own mortality."

"Midas," she said, referring to the story of the man who turned everything, including his beloved child, into gold.

"Just so." He hesitated, glancing down at her bosom for the briefest second. "Contrary to what people think, I *am* human."

At that Miranda pulled the covers up to her neck. She was *not* a one-night-stand type of person. In fact, she wouldn't even read romances in which the heroine had a multitude of lovers. "Mr. Taggert —" she began.

But he put up his hand to stop her. "You do not have to concern yourself about me. I do not force myself on women."

She knew he was telling the truth and let the covers go. Besides, she didn't see herself as a woman who drove men to uncontrollable acts of lust. "What is it you're trying to say to me?"

"I am trying to ask if you'd consider marrying me."

It took her a full minute to recover herself enough to speak. "Marriage?" she asked, her eyes wide. "To me?"

"Yes." He was serious. "I can see that you're shocked. Most of the women I meet are tall, statuesque blondes who train horses and wear couture. I don't usually come across short, plump —"

"I understand," she said quickly. "So why aren't you married to one of these horsey women who spends her life trying on clothes?"

Her cattiness was acknowledged with a tiny bit of a smile. "I'm afraid that it's as you say — they care only for my money."

"Mr. Taggert," she said, looking at him hard, "I'm not interested in your money *or* you."

He gave a little smile. "Surely there are things you want that money can buy. I would imagine you live in a house with a mortgage, and I doubt that your car is less than three years old. Does your ex-husband pay you any support? You're the type who would never take a person to court for nonpayment of debt. How long has it been since you've had any new clothes? There must be many things besides an education that you want for your son."

That he'd described her life perfectly made her angry. "Being poor is not a social disease. And since slavery was outlawed some years ago, I don't have to sell myself to get a new car."

"How about a white Mercedes with red leather interior?"

She almost smiled at that. "Really, Mr. Taggert, this is ridiculous. What's the *real* reason you're asking me to marry you? If you still are, that is."

"Yes. Once I make up my mind, I never change it."

"I can believe that about you."

Again he gave her a bit of a smile, making her wonder if any of the tall blondes in his life had ever contradicted him. "My life is too perfect," he said, "and it's beginning to bore me. Everything is perfectly in order as my servants are the best. There's never so much as a hairbrush out of place in any of my houses. For some time now I've thought it might be pleasant to have a wife, someone familiar to me. I like familiarity, which is why the contents of each of my houses are exactly the same."

Blinking, she thought about this for a moment. "Same towels, same —"

"Same clothes in exactly the same arrangement, so that no matter where I am I know what is where."

"Oh my. That *is* boring."

"But very efficient."

"Where would *I* fit into this efficiency?"

"As I said before, I have considered a wife, and the women I generally meet would be as perfect as my life already is."

"Why not marry several of them?" she asked helpfully. "One for each house. For variety you could change hair color, since I'm sure it wouldn't be natural anyway."

This time he did smile. Not an all-out teeth-showing smile, but a smile nonetheless. "If wives were not so much trouble, I would have done so years ago."

She couldn't suppress a bit of a laugh. "I think I'm beginning to understand. You want me because I'll add chaos to your life."

"And children."

"Children?" she asked, blinking.

"Yes. My family is prolific. Twins, actually. I find I want children." He looked away. "Since I was quite young, I have been very aware of my responsibilities. As the oldest of many siblings, I knew I would be the one to run the family business."

"The crown prince, so to speak."

"Yes, exactly. Fulfilling my obligations has always been uppermost in my mind. But about two years ago I met a boy."

When he said nothing more, Miranda encouraged him. "A boy?"

"Yes, he was at my brother's offices, skulking around from desk to desk, pretending to play but actually listening and looking at everything. I spoke to him, and it was like looking into my own eyes."

"And he made you want to have children of your own, did he? Sort of a wish to clone yourself, is that right?"

"More or less. But the boy changed me. He made me see things in my own life. We have corresponded since that time. We have become . . ." He smiled. "We have become friends."

She was glad that he had at least one friend in the world, but he couldn't marry a woman and hope she would give him a son just like the boy he'd met. "Mr. Taggert, there is no way *I* could produce the kind of son you want. My son is a sweet, loving child. He is the personification of kindness and generosity. He would die if he knew I told anyone this, but I still tuck him in every night and read aloud to him before he goes to sleep." She wasn't going to mention that she usually read advanced physics textbooks, because that would have ruined the fairy-tale aspect of the story.

Turning his head to one side, Frank said, "I would like my children to be a bit softer than I am."

It was beginning to dawn on Miranda that this man was serious. He was coldly, and with great detachment, asking her to marry him. And produce children. For a moment, looking at him, she couldn't quite picture him in the throes of passion. Would he perhaps delegate the task to his vice president in charge of production? *Charles, my wife needs servicing.*

"You are amused," he said.

"It was just something I was thinking about." She looked at him with compassion. "Mr. Taggert, I understand your dilemma and I would like to help. If it were only me, I might consider marrying you, but others would be involved. My son would be exposed to you, and if you and I did have — well, if we did have children, I'd want them to have a real father. I can't imagine you reading fairy stories to a two-year-old."

For a moment he didn't move; he just sat on the edge of the bed. "Then you are saying no to me?"

"Yes. I mean no. I mean, yes, I'm saying no. I can't marry you."

For a few seconds he stared at her, then he stood up and silently went to his own bed.

As Miranda sat there in the dark silence, she wondered if she'd dreamed the whole thing. She'd just turned down marriage to a very wealthy man. Was she terminally stupid? Had she lost all sense? Eli could have the best the world had to offer. And she could —

She sighed. She would be *married* to a man who wanted her so she could add chaos to his life. How amusing. Plump little Miranda walking about in circles in her attempt to leave the cabin. Daffy Miranda being stupid enough to fall for an elaborate joke played on a cold, heartless billionaire.

It was a long while before she fell asleep.

The next morning Miranda was silently making strawberry pancakes while Frank sat before the fire staring at the pages of a book on tax reform. He hadn't turned a page in fifteen minutes, so she knew he was thinking rather than reading.

No doubt I'm the first thing he's tried to buy and failed, she thought. Will he take the loss in good spirits or will he try to win me over? Read a how-to book on courting? Maybe he'll send candy to Eli. A man like Frank Taggert would never take the time to find out that Eli would rather have new computer equipment than all the candy in the world.

But as she cooked, she watched him — and she began to feel sorry for him. The feeling of isolation he projected surrounded him like an impenetrable glass bubble.

It was while she was making a sugar syrup for the strawberries and thinking how she'd like to see a little fat around the middle of Mr. Trim Taggert that she began to soften. Eli was always telling her that her problem was that no matter how bad a person was, she forgave him.

But in this case, it was understandable. The little glimpse she'd had into his life last night had shown her a very lonely man.

"How long is it before we can leave here?" she asked.

"In three days my assistant will come in a helicopter to see if I'm all right."

"He's too cowardly to come on a horse with Sandy?"

He didn't smile. "Julian is pure city."

She put a stack of pancakes on the table and he sat down, but he kept his eyes downward, not meeting hers.

She couldn't bear to see anyone so unhappy. "Look," she said, "if we're going to be stuck together for three days, we can at least be friendly. Let's pretend that last night didn't happen. All right?"

He didn't look up. "Do you mean where you undressed me or where I made a fool of myself?"

For a moment she blinked at him. "Did you just make a joke?"

He looked up at her. "I believe I did, yes."

"Should I look outside to see if the sky is falling?"

He didn't smile, but there was a tiny twinkle in his eyes. "I think it's safe." He began to cut his pancakes, but the cast made it difficult to do. He looked up at her as though asking for help.

"Only if you apologize for thinking I was a lady of the evening."

"Can't do that," he said seriously. "You're quite pretty and your frame is . . ." He hesitated as he searched for a word. "Luscious."

"Oh my," Miranda said. "I should probably protest that remark but I won't." Getting up, she cut his stack of pancakes into bites.

"These are good. What's for lunch?"

"Whatever you catch. Sandy said you like to fish."

"I do. What about you? Ever been fishing?"

"No. Never. But I would like to go outside."

They smiled at each other across the table, and Miranda thought that with his big plaid shirt on, he didn't look like the owner of some Fortune 500 company. "Help me clean up the kitchen," she said, "then we can go."

He didn't hesitate as he carried his plate to the sink. She washed and he tried to dry, but with just one hand, it wasn't easy.

"Here, let me help," she said, then moved next to him to take the plate. She halted when she felt his breath on her hair, but she didn't look up at him.

Seconds later, he stepped away and went to a cabinet near the front door. It was full of fishing gear.

It took a while to pack it all, including an old iron skillet that was blackened with years of use. "Whose is this?"

"Mine," he said.

"Then who gave it to you?"

"What makes you ask that?"

Miranda turned to the cabin. "This place is yours and it is perfect. If you owned a skillet, it would be stainless steel and spotless. Did Sandy give you this?"

Frank tried to repress a smile. "He did, actually. Do you moonlight as a detective?"

"No, I leave that for my son and his friend Chelsea. But some of it does rub off on me."

Frank was glad his back was to her so she couldn't see his face because he was sure it had just drained of color. Chelsea?! Eli's friend? Was it possible that she was Eli's mother? If so, it was possible that he had just seen the reason behind everything. All this was Eli's doing, not his brother's.

Frank tried to regain his calm. "Is this the son I'm to send to school?"

"Oh, heavens!" Miranda said. "I forgot about that. I'm sorry I said that. I was just so angry I couldn't think clearly. You asked what I most wanted in life and that came out. But it's absurd to even think you'd pay for my son's schooling."

"My company gives scholarships. Is your son smart enough to qualify for one?"

Miranda picked up a nylon pack full of gear and put it on her back. "Eli is smart enough for anything. He's being offered a full scholarship, but . . ."

"But what?" Frank opened the door and they went outside to the trail.

"I can't bore you with my life story. What

about *you*? Your life must be very interesting."

"It is. Since my last board meeting, I've been worried about something. The Hong Kong market is volatile right now and I'm concerned about my stock in one of my minor companies. I can't decide whether to go public or not. What's your opinion?" He turned to look at her.

"I, uh . . . Uh . . ."

Frank started walking again. "Right. There's nothing in my mind that would interest anyone not in a business suit. So what were you saying about your son's future? Eli. Was that his name? And the girl was Sheila?"

"Chelsea. They are the most incongruous pair you've ever met. She looks like a girl who'd only care about her nail polish, while Eli . . . Well, to me, he's beautiful, but he didn't inherit my ability to put on weight."

"I should turn him over to my relatives. Two of my brothers, Kane and Mike, power lift."

"What's that?"

"It builds muscle."

"Is that where you got yours?"

Frank was in front so his grin was hidden. "Me? They think I'm fat and flabby."

"You're not!" Miranda said. "And it

wasn't very kind of them to say that."

Frank was smiling broader than he had in years. It was sinking in that this was Eli's mother and it looked like she was as sweet natured as he'd said she was. It wasn't easy, but Frank was beginning to get over his deep embarrassment from last night. Joy was replacing his discomfort. Eli had done this. Like Frank, the boy had seen what he wanted and went after it. Frank could only marvel at all the boy must have done to arrange this meeting between his mother and his friend. And Frank couldn't have been more proud!

Behind him, Miranda was talking about how Eli and Chelsea did things they weren't supposed to. "Sometimes I'm afraid to find out what those two are doing."

Again, Frank hid his smile. Twice his company had been contacted by men wanting to know about a letter they'd received. The men weren't paying child support. Each time, Frank had turned the problem over to his lawyers, who'd contacted the police.

"You've not mentioned your son's father," Frank said. They'd turned down a side path. When Miranda stumbled, he took her hand and helped her down the steep hill.

At the bottom was the wide, cold stream,

a flat, graveled area beside it. There were big overhanging rocks nearby.

"This is beautiful. Eli would like this."

"Would he?" Frank asked, glad to hear it.

"I've talked too much about me. Tell me more about your family. Are they all like you?"

He put his pack on the ground. "You mean cold, unfeeling, and dedicated to money?"

Miranda winced. "We certainly did get off on the wrong foot, didn't we? I've never before said anything like that to anyone."

"And I've never made a proposal of marriage, so we're even. At least yours wasn't ridiculous."

"I thought it was sweet," she said.

He didn't comment on that. "Are you one of those women who baits her own hook or one who squeals at the thought?"

"Neither. I'm the one who cleans the fish and cooks it. Mind if I look around for some wild herbs I can use?" She nodded toward the surrounding forest.

"Just don't go too far. There really are bears here and you do tend to get lost."

"I'll be back in a few minutes."

Miranda wandered around the area, never going too far as she looked for wild herbs. But it wasn't easy to keep her mind on anything. The Colorado mountains were so beautiful she kept stopping to look around her. It had been years since she'd had any time off.

Unfortunately, the lack of huge amounts of work was giving her time to think. She remembered Mr. Taggert's assessment of her life with a mortgage and an ex who thinks money is a game. She sounded a bit pathetic. What would it be like to be fabulously wealthy?

The thought made her smile. If she had any sense, she would go running back to Mr. Taggert and tell him yes. But the thought of trading her little house and laughter with her son for houses where all the towels were in exactly the same place gave her cold chills.

She found wild onions and thyme but not much else. But then, she wasn't looking very hard. Her mind was too full of her thoughts.

When the first drops of rain hit her, she looked up in surprise. At this high altitude, she knew that the rain would be icy. She looked about for shelter but saw none. She should go back, but the truth was that she wasn't quite sure which way the cabin was or where the stream ran.

The rain was beginning to come down harder. Just a few drops so far, but it was increasing. A clash of thunder rolled across the mountains.

She got under a clump of trees but they were pines and aspens, neither of which gave much shelter. The temperature dropped by degrees and she shivered. How did she get back?

There was a quick flash of lightning and Miranda wasn't the least surprised to see Mr. Taggert standing between two tall pines. At the moment he looked as tall and as big as the trees.

He didn't say anything, just held his big flannel shirt open. With her head bent against the rain, she ran to him and ducked inside his shirt. She put one arm around his waist and the other held on to his shirt. Together they quickly walked through the trees to the campsite.

Frank led her to an overhanging rock where it was dry underneath. "Can you build a fire?" he asked over the rain, which was coming down harder.

When she nodded, he ran back out and gathered their belongings. By the time he got back, the rain had turned into a storm and Frank was drenched.

Miranda had found a stack of dry branches piled in the back of what was almost a cave. And toward the front was a circle of rocks enclosing some burned wood.

Frank put the two packs and loose gear on the stone floor.

"You come here often, don't you?" she asked. She'd found plastic-encased matches with the wood, as well as dried leaves needed for tinder.

"When I can. Do you mind?"

He was asking her permission to remove his wet shirt.

Miranda got up and helped him, peeling the wet cloth over his cast.

"Damned thing!" Frank muttered. "I hate being helpless."

"I would too." She tossed his wet flannel shirt onto the stone, then started on his long-sleeved undershirt. It was plastered to his skin. "I think I should have left a bread-crumb trail."

"Didn't the birds eat those and the kids ended up in serious trouble?"

"So you *have* read something other than a business report. Bend down." He was too tall for her to reach to pull the shirt over his head. When she had it off, she put it on the rocks, then turned to see him, nude from the waist up.

For a moment she stared at him, at his muscular chest, with its light coating of hair. The rain outside, the darkness of the cave-like rock formation, the warm light of the fire, all made them seem very isolated. And it had been a long, long time since Miranda had felt a man's body against hers. She missed the hardness of a man's flesh, the warmth of him, the way he could make a woman feel protected and safe — and the way he could ignite a raging desire in her body.

As she went to her pack, she made herself turn away. She'd put in one of the cotton shirts she'd found in her suitcase. "Sit," she told him.

She couldn't bring herself to look into his eyes. If there was even a hint of invitation in them, she didn't think she could resist. Between the atmosphere and the longing, she knew she'd slide into his arms and they'd make love on the stone floor.

She walked behind him and began to rub his wet back with her dry shirt, rubbing hard to generate warmth in his skin. He kept his head down, letting her do what she wanted to him.

After a few minutes, he put his hand up and she handed him the shirt so he could dry his chest. He was facing the entrance to the rock formation and the fire was before them.

Miranda couldn't help herself as she ran

her hands over his shoulders. The shape, the hardness of them made her own body grow warm. There seemed to be no fat on him, just acres of warm, honey-colored skin that curved and dipped over lean muscle.

He sat very still, not moving, and she knew that if she made even the slightest gesture, he'd turn to her. Could he kiss? she wondered. Or did he think kissing wasn't needed? Not "efficient"?

She stepped back from him. "Did you bring another shirt?"

"In my pack." There was an almost sad tone to his voice, as though he knew the moment had been lost.

She got the shirt out, helped him pull it on over his cast, then tended to his wet clothes. She wrung them out and made a makeshift rack by the fire to get them dry.

"How about you?" he asked. "Dry?"

"Sure. Thanks to you. I guess you assumed I was lost."

"No," he said. "I missed your company. I've never had anyone up here before. My brothers come, but . . ." He trailed off. "I caught a few fish."

"So you did," she said. "While I clean and cook, why don't you tell me about your big family. Do they think like you?"

Frank leaned back against the rock wall.

"Not at all. Some of my brothers are fairly good businessmen, but they don't take it seriously."

As he talked, Miranda gutted and scaled the fish. She'd brought flour and butter and even capers with her, and she handed Frank the little potatoes to peel and slice.

It took a bit of encouragement from her to get him to talk about himself, but he did. What she heard was of a life with an underlying loneliness to it. His siblings had all been gregarious, laughing kids who tumbled over each other like puppies. But Frank had been quiet.

"I was changing diapers when I was eight," he said. "We had help, but —" He shrugged.

"The kids wanted you."

"Yeah," he said. "I'm not sure how it happened, but they all seemed to think of me as a second father."

Miranda hid her smile. She could understand that. If he was then like he was now, yes, toddlers would see him as an adult. "Eli was like that," she said. "Sometimes I think he knew what his father was like from the beginning. Leslie used to get angry because when he tried to hold Eli, the child would start kicking and fussing. He never really cried, just tried to get away."

Frank put the potatoes in the bowl Miranda held out. "Intuition. You probably won't believe this, but a strong and reliable intuition is a big basis for my success."

"That's the same as Eli! Many times he's said to me, 'Mom, don't do that.' He never has a reason, but it always turns out that he's right."

"It's good that you listen to him. How do he and his father get along now?"

"Not well at all." As she cooked, Miranda talked about the joy of her life with her son, Eli. Twice, she said she should stop as she was boring him, but he encouraged her to go on. Now and then he'd ask a question about Eli's schooling, how he got along with other kids, even if Eli was eating enough. Frank leaned back against the stone wall and listened as though what she was telling him was fascinating.

"You now know more about my son than his father does," she said as she handed him a metal plate full of fish and potatoes, then watched as he began to eat.

"This is very good," he said. "None of my chefs could do better. Why don't you sit here? You can get a better view."

He indicated a place beside him. Miranda hesitated, but then sat down near him. It was very pleasant under the rock, with the rain pounding outside.

"I could help you with the legalities of getting your ex-husband to pay," he said softly.

Miranda started to say that she needed help, but didn't. "That's a very kind offer but I'll manage. Tell me more about your family. What was it like growing up in a large family?"

"Hectic," he said. Long ago he'd made it a rule not to talk about his childhood, but with this woman things were different. "Shall I tell you about the time my brothers Mike and Kane decided to tame all the broncs we brought down off the winter range?" He paused a moment. "They were five."

Miranda laughed. "Yes, please do. Unless it has a sad ending. I can't bear stories with unhappy endings.

"If you mean did they live to grow up and marry and have kids, yes, it's happy. But back then, when Mom got hold of them, it wasn't happy at all."

"Then tell me," she said as she put another fish on Frank's plate. "I want to hear all the happy stories you have."

Frank had never thought of himself as a storyteller, but when Miranda started laughing, he enjoyed the sound so much that he kept embellishing his story. When he told how he, a child himself, had run under the horses' bellies to get to his little brother Mike, Miranda put her hand to her throat. She gasped in such a satisfying way that Frank told another story about his brother Mac and a rattlesnake.

Miranda was a great audience, laughing, showing fear, congratulating him. By the time they finished the meal, they were smiling at each other.

"Oh, look, it's stopped raining," she said as she cleaned their utensils.

"About half an hour ago."

Miranda smiled. "I guess we should go. We should —" When she looked at him, there was regret on her face. They'd had such a pleasant time that she didn't want it to end.

Neither did Frank. "We have two and a half days with nothing whatever to do," he said as he stood up. "Any suggestions?"

"I have no idea." Her head came up. "Do you have a secret place where you've taken no other human being? A place not even your family knows about? I'd like to see *that.*"

He thought for a moment, then said, "Actually, I do. In the 1880s a prospector was sure there was gold in these mountains and he lived alone up here. He went down twice a year for supplies. I found his cabin. It's a day's trek up there, but we could stay a night then return. I promise I'll behave myself."

"Darn!" Miranda said before she thought. "Sorry. I didn't mean — I shouldn't have —"

Bending forward, Frank smoothed a strand of hair behind her ear. "Let's go home and plan our trip."

For a fraction of a second, the backs of his fingers touched her cheek, but then he moved away.

The little touch so unnerved Miranda that she searched for something to break the silence. "Wish I'd brought my camera," she said. "Eli would love to see photos of an old cabin."

"I have one here. We can take it with us."

"Great. And what do I get if we find the prospector's gold?"

"I'll have to consult my board before I can answer that," he said solemnly.

She wouldn't have known he was teasing except for the sparkle in his eyes. "How about if I buy a fifty percent share? A raspberry tart with ground hazelnuts in the crust enough?"

"Make it almonds and I'll give you eighty percent."

"Done!" she said and held out her hand to shake his.

He took it, held her hand for a moment, then smiled warmly at her. "Best deal I ever made," he said and picked up both packs. As they walked back to the cabin, they made plans for their coming excursion.

3

Frank couldn't sleep. All his life he'd had a clear vision of where he was going with his life, but right now he couldn't seem to see what was ahead for him.

There was a faint buzzing sound and he knew what it was: Julian was calling. Reaching across to move the blanket Miranda had put up, he saw that she was asleep. She was snuggled deep under the covers so just a bit of her face peeped out.

He silently got out of bed and went to a blank log wall to the right of the fireplace, pushed a knot, and a door opened. In contrast to the rugged, almost primitive cabin, the room Frank entered was ultramodern, its walls painted a hard gloss white. Along three sides were tables, each covered with machines: computer, fax, television with the stock market playing on it, telephones, and other devices of communication.

He picked up a blue phone, the one Julian used. "What is it?"

"And good evening to you too," Julian said. "There are some problems with Tynan Mills that you need to decide about. And Tokyo needs to talk to you. I know you weren't planning to return for another day but I think I should send the chopper tomorrow. Besides, Gwyn has been here asking for you. I better warn you that she had a bridal magazine in her briefcase. She —"

"Don't come here until Thursday."

"But that's three days away!"

"Right," Frank said. "And pay Gwyn off with the usual gifts."

For a moment, Julian was stunned into silence. "Are you sure you want to do that? I thought maybe this one was serious. I know Gwyn certainly thinks so."

Frank didn't comment on that. "I want you to check on someone for me. He's a kid. Elijah J. Harcourt. Make sure he's all right. And find out about his friend Chelsea Hamilton. And pay off the mortgage of Eli's mother. No! Wait, that might cause some problems with the dad. Find out what that bastard is up to."

"Anything else?" Julian asked.

"Yeah, call one of my brothers and tell

114

him to take care of Tynan Mills."

Julian drew in his breath. "You're going to delegate? You're going to trust your financial-genius brothers to handle a family business?"

"Julian?" Frank said. "Cut the sarcasm. Just do the job and don't give me any more problems. And don't call here again. You might wake —" He broke off. "Thursday. Late afternoon." He hung up and went back to bed.

"You okay?" Frank asked as he stopped on the trail that led up the side of the mountain. He had on a fifty-pound pack full of the things they'd chosen last evening — and he'd enjoyed planning with Miranda.

Gratefully, she sat down on a rock and drank from her water bottle. Her pack was less than half the weight of Frank's but it was still heavy.

"It's the altitude," he said.

"You're being kind. It's also my lack of aerobic exercise. I should spend more time in a gym."

"In your line of work, have you ever saved anyone's life?"

"A few times," she said, smiling.

"I have a full gym off my office and I work out at least an hour a day, but I have *never* saved a human life. Which of us do you think has accomplished more?"

For a moment she blinked at him, then smiled. "What a very kind thing to say. And you know what? You've made me feel better." She stood up. "But just in case of a relapse, is it much further?"

"A mile at most." His face was serious. "If you falter I could get behind you and push." He gave such a lecherous lift to his brows that she laughed.

"I think I'll manage. Lead on, oh fearless leader."

"Sounds good. I think I'll put that title on my office door."

They reached the old cabin in the late afternoon. It was a three-sided shed, with the flat side of a giant boulder as the back wall. Inside was a crude fireplace and to one side was a little fenced area. "For his donkey friend," Frank said. There was a little cabinet with a chipped porcelain bowl and an old, crude bed frame in the far corner.

Miranda saw that repairs had been made to the roof and one wall. "You keep it from falling down?"

"I do," he said. "I carried all the wood up here and I reset the stone for the fireplace. One year I got caught in an early snowstorm and spent a week up here. I was glad my dad taught me about hunting or I might have starved."

"Spoken like a man who has never dieted. Trust me on this, but a week without food will only make you *feel* like you're going to starve."

Again, Frank looked serious. "As a man who spent half a day walking behind you, I can swear that you don't need to lose an ounce."

Miranda laughed but she also blushed.

"Come on," he said, "I'll show you why the old guy built his cabin here."

They put down their packs and she followed him outside into the soft light. She could feel autumn in the air. He led her down a well-worn trail, around the big boulder, then up again. At one point, he put his hands on her waist and swung her over a place where the trail had washed out. For a moment they stared at each other, but then Frank turned away and they kept going up.

At last they came to a very pretty little freshwater pool. Water trickled down the mountain into the pool, then flowed out at the far side. Since the water was always moving, the pond never became stagnant.

Frank pointed at the far end. "I found the

remnants of some hollowed-out logs. I think he made a viaduct."

"So he had running water all year," Miranda said. "How ingenious."

"It froze in winter, but by then he had piles of snow outside his door." When Frank sat down and began to try to untie a boot-lace, Miranda took over. She removed his boots and socks, then her own. They sat side by side, pants rolled up, their feet soaking in the cool, clean water.

"This is wonderful," she said. "Thank you for bringing me here."

Turning, Frank looked at her. Right now he was feeling the best he had in years. But Julian's mention of Gwyn had thrown him somewhat, and had made him think of her seriously. She belonged to his real world, the one of money and board meetings. Even what social life he had with her dealt with money, as every function they attended was a charity fund-raiser.

Gwyn fit into that world perfectly. She was charming to everyone. She had an ability to coax people into opening their wallets in support of whatever cause she was working with. Orphaned children, homeless people, literacy groups were all better off because of Gwyn.

But there was no way she'd travel up a

mountain to dangle her bare feet in an icy mountain pond. Frank had once joked that he thought her feet were like a Barbie doll's, permanently bent upward for high heels. Gwyn hadn't laughed.

"You're looking at me very hard," Miranda said.

"I was thinking how you fit here."

"You can see me in a pair of overalls? Maybe with a pickax?" She was teasing, but when he didn't answer and turned away to look at the pond, Miranda frowned. Obviously, something had upset him. "Did the prospector find any gold?"

"Not that anyone knew about, but there were rumors. He's a chapter in a few books and they said that people believed he found gold and buried it in a cave near his cabin."

"Have you looked?"

"A little," he said, "but no luck. My nieces and nephews are getting old enough that I thought I might bring them up here and let them scrounge the area. Nobody can find things like a kid can."

"You seem to know so much about children. You don't have any of your own?"

"Not that I know of," he said as he stood up. "How about if I build a fire and we cook some of that food you brought?"

"Sure," Miranda said. As she pulled on

her boots, she thought, Something has changed. He had gone from laughing to serious in seconds.

They sat outside with their dinner, the stars bright above them. The air was quite cool, but they had on layers of clothes.

"Are you all right?" Miranda asked, her voice full of concern.

"Sure. I come up here to think and . . ."

"And I'm hindering you?" She started to get up.

"No, please, I didn't mean that." He turned to her. "I asked you about your ex-husband, but you didn't answer. What's he like?"

She took a moment before replying, "Leslie likes to win. It's everything to him. He doesn't care about the cost or future consequences. He just has to win right now. You know how I got custody of our son?"

"I can't imagine."

She took a breath. "It still terrifies me to remember what I did, and I pray that Eli will never find out. At the divorce, I told his father I didn't want the child. I said that his extraordinary intelligence made him a freak and I didn't want to have to spend my life with the kid."

Frank looked at her in astonishment. "I agree that no child should hear that."

Miranda had to swallow back tears in memory. "Eli thinks that I'm blind to Leslie's selfishness, but I know my ex very well. When he comes over and does his little whining act about how no one's ever given him anything, I hand him money. I don't give very much, but he knows I'm poor so even a little is a lot."

"I see," Frank said. "And that lets him feel that he's won."

"Right," she said. "And if he feels that he's winning, I don't have to fear that he'll do something bigger."

"Like fight you for custody of Eli," Frank said softly.

"Exactly."

"In your circumstances, I think that's a very clever way to handle it all. In fact, I think what you did was a brilliant business move. You used your opponent's weakness to your advantage. I wish the men who worked for me could be that insightful."

She laughed, but she was pleased by what he'd said.

When it grew too cool to stay outside, they went into the cabin. Like the cave the day before, the soft firelight made the tiny cabin cozy and, well, romantic.

Miranda glanced at the single bed in the corner. How were they to handle this awkward situation? "How about if we arm wrestle for the bed?"

Frank was kneeling by the stove, poking the inside of it. He'd had an idea that she'd come up with a reason for why he should take the bed and her the floor. He stood up. "Let's toss for it." He pulled a coin from his pocket. "Call it."

"Heads."

He flipped the coin and caught it on the back of his hand. "Heads it is. You win."

"I didn't see the coin," she said.

"Next time." He was pulling sleeping bags from the packs, but struggling with the cast. "Damn thing!"

Miranda moved beside him to help, their shoulders together, the warmth of their bodies shared.

He turned to look at her and, smiling, Miranda faced him. He kissed her. It was a sweet, gentle kiss, tentative, but it was very nice.

He pulled away. "Sorry. I'm overstepping my bounds." Abruptly, he stood up, but he didn't look at her. "I'm . . ." He didn't seem to know what else to say. He left the cabin.

With a sigh, Miranda unfurled the two sleeping bags, putting one on the hard floor and one on the narrow bed.

So much for being seductive, she thought.

She could get a man to ask her to marry him because she looked like "a fertility goddess" but she certainly didn't inspire passion. The years she'd spent with her ex-husband had never been like what she'd read about in books. She'd been a virgin when they'd met and for years she'd thought the two kisses and four strokes were normal.

She knew the books she read were fantasy, but sometimes she wished a man would look at her with eyes blazing fire.

The thought made her giggle. She used the time Frank was outside to undress. Thanks to whoever had tampered with her luggage, the only nightgown she had was the thin one — but she hadn't brought it with her. Instead, she'd sneaked in one of Frank's big long-sleeved pull-on shirts. It fell down to the top of her thighs. Her legs would be bare but she thought she'd be warm enough in the sleeping bag.

She slipped inside the bag and meant to stay awake until Frank returned. But the long walk up a mountain had worn her out. She was asleep as soon as she lay down.

Thunder loud enough to split her eardrums woke her. As she sat up, lightning lit the cabin, and she gave a little involuntary scream. She wasn't used to such storms.

Frank was beside her instantly, just sitting

there, not touching her, but at the next flash of lightning she flung herself into his arms.

She had almost forgotten how good a man could feel. His big, strong body enveloped hers, and before she could breathe, he pulled her head back and kissed her.

It wasn't a kiss like the first one. There was no sweetness to it. It was a kiss of raging passion, of desire as strong as any she'd ever imagined. The sensation was new to her, but at the same time it was as old as time.

He moved down to kiss her neck. The cabin was lit with lightning and the roar of the thunder seemed to echo within her.

"Yes," she whispered as his hand went to her breast. "Yes, please."

He took her face in his hands, his eyes searching hers. "I have no protection with me."

For a moment she held her breath. She felt sure he didn't have a communicable disease. All that mattered was here and now and this man.

"Yes" was all she said, then he was on her.

He was as hot in bed as he was cold out of it. He'd made a few jokes, but she'd never seen him leering at her. And yet he seemed to have noticed all of her body and to want her very much. Her shirt and underpants were off in seconds. His hands were everywhere, caressing her, touching her.

Miranda had never felt the way he made her feel. He seemed to know what she liked, seemed to find places she didn't know she wanted him to touch.

By the time he entered her, she was nearly screaming with desire. She held him inside her for a moment, loving how he filled her. When he began the velvet strokes in and out, she thought she might die with the pleasure.

He seemed to know when she was ready to peak, then he thrust into her until she thought she might faint. Waves went through her body. Afterward, still shaking, she snuggled in his arms, feeling safe and secure and at home. She could feel herself dozing off. "That was lovely," she whispered.

"Not for me," he said.

Her eyes opened and she saw in the firelight that he wasn't anywhere near sleep. "There's more?"

He smiled in a wicked way. "We haven't begun."

"Really?" she said with such enthusiasm that he laughed.

They made love all night. Frank seemed to be insatiable — but then, so was she. For her, there'd been a lifetime of suppression, of reading about, but never experiencing, uncontrollable passion.

He never said so, but he seemed to be shocked that she didn't know about positions and what to do with your mouth besides kissing. "I've read about these things but haven't done them," she said.

"Your husband — ?" Frank began but stopped.

"He thought wives should be good girls."

"Me too," Frank said as he moved down her body.

Sometime during the night she thought she heard him say, "I love you," but she wasn't sure.

Miranda slowly woke up, and she was smiling before she got her eyes open. She could feel that the old cabin was empty. She even remembered Frank getting up and going out. Right now all she wanted to do was lie still and think about last night, to remember every second of it.

She'd never thought she could be so . . . well, so abandoned. Her legs around his neck, his hands cupping her behind, was an especially vivid memory.

The door opened and Frank came in carrying a load of firewood.

"Good morning," he said. "Sleep well?"

"Like a rock," she said. "I did have some odd dreams, but nothing significant."

Frank smiled as he put the wood down. "I was going to stop at the little French café and get us some croissants, but they're closed. How about cold corn bread and bacon?"

"It sounds divine."

He brushed off his clothes and looked at her for a moment, then went to sit beside her on the old bed. Her bare arms and shoulders were exposed, and he ran his hands over them. "I enjoyed last night," he said softly. "And you?"

"Very much."

Bending, he kissed her, then sat up to stroke her hair. "We can go down the mountain or stay here for another day."

"Stay," she said without hesitation.

"Sure? We didn't bring a lot of food."

"I think I can survive. How did your shirt get wet?"

"It isn't," he said, then smiled. "You're right. It's soaked and I think I should take it off."

"My thought exactly." She pulled back the top of the sleeping bag, showing that she was nude underneath.

They spent a whole day at the old cabin. Neither of them said so, but they seemed to have reached a mutual agreement to talk of nothing of the outside world. No business, no ex-husband, not even children. Frank didn't come close to telling her about any women in his past, certainly not the one who was expecting an engagement ring.

They laughed and ate and made love. Everything and every place seemed to become erotic to them. They stripped and went swimming in the icy pond. Miranda nearly turned blue from the cold water, and it took Frank thirty minutes of kissing and long, slow, deep strokes to warm her up.

When her skin was at last pink again, he collapsed beside her in exhaustion.

"Let's do it again," she said and got up and headed toward the frigid water.

But Frank caught her ankle and pulled her back. "If you want more, you have to revive me."

"Is that a challenge?" she asked.

"If it encourages you, yes. If not, how about a bribe? Half my kingdom work for you?"

Laughing, she kissed him. "Let's see if *this* works." She moved her lips downward on his body.

"I feel nothing. Try harder. No. No. Ah."

At night they put their sleeping bags together and, naked, snuggled close, watching the fire in the little stove.

"I never want to leave," Miranda said.

"Me neither," Frank said. "I'd like to shut out the world."

"What about your houses with the perfect towels?"

"You make me want to buy new ones in lots of colors."

"And throw them on the floor?"

"I'm not quite to that point yet."

She kissed him thoroughly.

"Maybe a hand towel on the counter," he said.

Miranda rolled on top of him, her bare body against his, and kissed him again.

"Okay, wet towels across the tub. But no purple or pink."

"Done," she said, and kissed him again.

The next morning, they made their way down the mountain, taking their time. They stopped for lunch and lovemaking, then continued on to the cabin. After where they'd been, it seemed too big and too clean.

They had dinner by candlelight and afterward she started to pull down the blanket that separated their beds. Frank made her laugh by pretending to blow a trumpet. She knew what he meant. In the movie *It Happened One Night,* Clark Gable said the Walls of Jericho were coming down so he blew a toy trumpet.

They fell into bed laughing.

Early the next morning they were at the stove, with Frank helping Miranda make pumpkin scones, when they heard the helicopter above the cabin. Frank reacted instantly. He ran to the door, and to her consternation, he flung open a door hidden in the log wall and withdrew a rifle. "Stay here," he ordered.

"Okay," she whispered, feeling a bit like a heroine in a Western movie.

Seconds later he was back. He put the rifle away, then went to the table. He was frowning. "Is breakfast ready?"

She heard him only by reading his lips, because the sound of the 'copter overhead was deafening. His attitude and whoever was arriving piqued her curiosity. Quickly, she flung food onto a plate, sloshed coffee into a cup by his hand, and ran out the door.

The helicopter was directly overhead. A couple of duffel bags had already been lowered, and a tall blond man wearing a dark suit, briefcase in hand, was descending. His foot was hooked into a loop of cable. Miranda couldn't help smiling at this version of Wall Street coming down through the tall trees, the mountains in the distance.

As he got closer, she started laughing because she could see that while holding on to the briefcase and the cable, he was also eating an apple.

He landed in front of her. He was quite good-looking: very blond, very white skin, blue eyes so bright they dazzled. Holding the apple in his mouth, he motioned the helicopter to go away, and Miranda saw that the briefcase was handcuffed to his wrist.

"Hungry?" she asked, as he stood there staring at her.

"Starved." He was looking at her in a way that made her feel quite good about herself, and she smiled back warmly.

"You here with Frank?" he asked.

"I am. I was hired to be his nurse. That turned out to be a joke, but I'm still here because . . ." She trailed off, not wanting to explain something so private. With her hand shielding her eyes, she watched the helicopter disappear over the horizon, then looked back at the man.

"Mike. Or was it Kane?" he asked.

"I beg your pardon?"

"If a joke was played on Frank, it would have to be either Mike or Kane." When she didn't respond, he held out his hand. "I'm Julian Wales. Frank's assistant. Or actually, glorified gofer. And you are?"

She put her hand into his large warm one. "Miranda Stowe. I'm a nurse, but I'm also the cook-housekeeper."

He gave her a look that made her blush. "Perhaps I'll find myself becoming ill and have need of your services."

She withdrew her hand from his — after two tugs. "Mr. Taggert is in there, and I have pumpkin scones for breakfast."

"Gorgeous, and you can cook too. You wouldn't like to marry me, would you?"

Feeling like an eighteen-year-old, she laughed. "Frank's already asked." She was horrified at what she'd revealed. "I shouldn't have said that." She had no idea how to cover herself, so she went back into the cabin. Julian, his eyes wide in disbelief, stared after her for a moment before following.

Frank's only greeting was "You're early."

Julian's reply was to remove the briefcase from his wrist, unlock it, and turn it over to Frank.

"Unfortunately," Julian said, "I arranged for the 'copter to pick me up tomorrow morning. I'd planned to stay and do a little fishing, but I didn't know you had a guest. If it's not suitable for me to stay, I can walk out."

Buried in the papers, Frank didn't look

up. "Take the couch."

"Yes, sir," Julian said, then winked at Miranda as she put a plate of scones and scrambled eggs in front of him.

"Have you had breakfast, Miranda?" Julian asked. When she shook her head no, he said, "How'd you like to join me outside? A morning like this is too beautiful to waste in here."

She looked at Frank but he was absorbed by the papers. Smiling, plate in hand, Miranda followed Julian out the door.

He put his plate on a stump and began to remove his suit jacket and tie. "Hallelujah!" he said, unbuttoning the top of his shirt. "Twenty-four hours of freedom." Sitting on the stump, the plate on his lap, he looked up at her. "There's room for two."

She smiled graciously but sat down on a rock a few yards away.

"Did Frank actually ask you to marry him?"

She nearly choked. "I truly should *not* have told you that. Sometimes I have an inability to keep my mouth shut. It wasn't a *real* marriage proposal, just sort of a business arrangement."

Julian cocked one blond eyebrow. "I see what he gets, but I can't see what you get. Except the money, of course."

His attitude and his words sent anger coursing through her veins. Miranda stood up. "You know, Mr. Wales, I think you and I are going in the wrong direction. I find Mr. Taggert to be a very likable man, and I won't allow you or anyone else to disparage him."

For a moment Julian looked too shocked to speak. He too stood up. "I apologize. It's just that you are such a surprise that I don't know how to react. Please stay and finish your breakfast. I promise I won't be offensive."

When she sat back down, he did too, but she didn't say anything.

"You and Frank get along, do you?"

"Quite well," she said and could feel herself blushing.

While he was eating, Julian couldn't take his eyes off her. "Please forgive me for staring, but you aren't what I'm used to seeing with Frank."

The man was beginning to annoy her. "Mr. Wales, I am well aware that I'm not some romantic heroine from a novel. I am rapidly approaching middle age, I'm overweight, I'm a single mother, and I'm sure that suit you have on cost more than I earned last year. If any other woman on earth were here, I'm sure neither of you men would notice me."

He was smiling at her. "Miranda, you know what you are? You're *real*. I knew it the moment I saw you. Usually, the women near Frank are so perfectly beautiful they look as though they were manufactured. And you know that if he lost his money, they'd never look at him again."

"Really, Mr. Wales, I —"

"Julian."

"Julian, I am a perfectly ordinary woman."

"Oh?" He took a big bite of his scone. "Ever been married?" When she nodded, he said, "When you divorced your husband, did you take him to the cleaner's?" He didn't wait for her answer. "No, of course not. Looking at you, I'd say you 'understood' his need to run off with some empty-headed Barbie doll."

She looked down at her food. "You seem to be rather good at figuring out people."

"That's what Frank pays me for: to look into people's eyes and keep the deadbeats and con artists away from him."

At that moment, the cabin door opened and Frank came outside, a fishing rod over his shoulder. "I'd like to do some fishing myself. Shall we go?"

Miranda stood up. "I think Julian should change his clothes, and I'll need to pack a lunch for you two. You can't leave without something to eat."

Frank turned his back to Julian. "Mrs. Stowe, I'd like for you to come with us, as you're rather good with fish."

His words were cool, even businesslike, but he was smiling at Miranda and once winked at her. She knew that he didn't want his employee seeing what was between them.

With his face again serious, Frank looked back at Julian. "Sort out what is needed and follow us." Turning away, Frank started walking down the trail, Miranda inches behind him.

Julian stood where he was, staring in openmouthed astonishment after his boss. He'd worked with Frank Taggert for over ten years. During that time Frank had never once told Julian — or anyone else for that matter — about himself, but Julian had been able to piece together a great deal. He knew his boss very, very well.

"He's in love with her," Julian whispered as he watched them walk away. By all that's holy, he's madly in love with her. Only deep love could make Frank leave corporate merger papers and go fishing. Julian watched as they disappeared down the trail. Of course Frank knew so little about women that he'd mess this up — as he'd destroyed every relationship he'd ever had with a woman. But Julian had to admit that Frank had never thought any woman was worth missing a meeting for or even postponing a call. And when the women's complaints become intolerable, it was always Julian who had the task of telling them to leave. He'd had dishes thrown at him and heard curse words in four languages as he removed women from Frank's life.

It was this part of his job that was making him begin to wonder if there was more to life than just doing whatever Frank Taggert wanted done.

Julian went into the cabin to change his clothes. But now Frank had asked a woman to *marry* him. And knowing him, he'd presented the proposal as he would present something to a corporate board. No passion, no fireworks, no declarations of undying love. Just "I have a proposition to make you: Will you marry me?" As usual, everything Frank acquired came easily to him.

As Julian changed into jeans and a sweater, he couldn't stop thinking. While it was true that Frank kept rigid control over himself, his loyalty was unbreakable.

When Julian had smashed a Ferrari, it was Frank who'd flown in doctors from London and New York. When accounting's Mrs. Silen's husband had nearly taken her children away from her, it was Frank who'd secretly stepped in and got the decision of the court reversed. Frank often helped people; he just hated anyone knowing he'd done it. He liked his image of ruthless negotiator.

In his dealings with his employees and his relatives, he was always fair. Never warm, but always fair.

Two years ago something had changed Frank, had made him even more remote, but Julian didn't know what had caused it. And this broken arm seemed to have made him pull back even more. He'd been playing handball as fiercely as he worked at business and he'd slammed against the wall, pinning his right arm under him. It was a nasty break, and Frank had been in the operating room for two hours. The next day, Julian had been there, along with most of the Taggerts. They were a loud, happy family, exactly the opposite of Frank with his cool reticence. They'd teased him mercilessly about his injury proving that he was as human as other people.

As far as Julian knew, Frank had never so much as flinched from the pain, but that day something seemed to have happened inside him. Days later Frank canceled some very important meetings and announced that he was retreating to his cabin high in the Rockies and he was not to be disturbed. Julian didn't dare ask Frank why, but one of his brothers did, and Frank had said he'd wanted to heal and to think.

Julian might not know what was wrong with his boss, but his intuition told him that Miranda Stowe was part of it. Whether she was a cure or part of what was wrong with him, he didn't know — but he meant to find out. He grabbed a fishing rod and headed out the door.

4

The three of them spent a very pleasant day beside the lake high in the beautiful Rocky Mountains — and Frank was so different from the man Julian knew that he wondered who he was. Identical twins ran in the Taggert family and it crossed his mind that Frank secretly had one of them.

He and Miranda laughed and chatted and teased and shared inside jokes with such ease that a person would think they were long-term friends. There were no outward displays of affection but Julian was sure they were sleeping together. Glances, quick eye contact, lingering touches gave them away.

They talked about a gold miner's cabin, of returning to it and combing the surrounding area in search of treasure. There was talk of almond oil. It didn't take much for Julian to understand the sexual undertones to their words.

As the day wore on, Julian stepped back

into the shadows — and they didn't notice. But then, they only saw each other.

And the more they smiled, the more Julian frowned. He knew that what he was seeing wasn't *real.* Frank Taggert in his denim and flannel wasn't the man who did corporate mergers before breakfast. The man pulling fish off a hook wasn't ruthless — as you needed to be in the real Frank Taggert's world.

Most of all, Julian looked at Miranda. This pseudo-lumberjack was the only man she knew. He doubted if she'd even seen the real one.

Julian remembered the tears of the women Frank had sent him to. The questions! "I did everything he wanted," they said. "I ran his entire social life. He *needed* me. So why is he dumping me like I'm some high school girl?"

Julian never had an answer for them because he didn't know. He felt bad for them but at the same time he knew they'd land on their feet. They were all so perfectly beautiful, so educated, so competent, that they'd have another man in no time.

But Miranda was different. Standing away from them, he saw the looks she gave Frank. If she wasn't in love with him, she would be soon. Then what? Some megabucks wedding that would be expected for Frank's status? Julian couldn't imagine Miranda in a wedding dress with a twelve-foot train walking down the aisle of some cathedral. And didn't she say she had children? Would they be her attendants?

And after the honeymoon, would Frank go back to being . . . well, to being Frank?

Miranda made lunch for them, serving perfectly cooked fish and potatoes roasted over a campfire. As Julian watched the two of them, he saw that they were lost in the here and now, that the outside world didn't exist for them.

But Julian was very aware of what awaited them. Their worlds could not be more different from each other. His fear was that Frank would survive at the expense of Miranda. She would go into a marriage expecting the man she'd spent time with in the glorious mountains, but she'd get the Frank Taggert that Julian knew.

It was almost sunset when they walked back to the cabin. Miranda served them a lovely dinner of fish and vegetables flavored with wild herbs, and Julian sat in near silence as he continued to watch them. He felt like he'd interrupted two people on their honeymoon. As the meal ended, he could see that they wished he weren't there.

Miranda made up the couch for him, and as he lay there, he listened to the two of them whispering to each other from their separate beds that were so close together.

It was a long time before Julian could sleep.

In the morning, as Frank helped Miranda make bacon and eggs, Julian knew he had to talk to his boss. Even if it meant losing his job, he had to say his piece.

When Frank took his coffee outside, Julian went with him. On purpose, when they weren't too far from a window, he began to talk. To give himself courage, he took a deep breath. "Have you told Miranda you want her in your life?"

Frank didn't say anything.

"You might be able to fool the rest of the world but not me. When you look at her, it's the same way you look at corporate papers."

Frank took a while to answer. "When I first met her, she didn't like me."

"Frank, a *lot* of people don't like you."

He gave a one-sided smile. "They don't like what I stand for or that I have money and they don't. It's not *me* they dislike."

Julian snorted. "Don't kid yourself, Frank, it's you people don't like. Freezers are warm compared to you."

Frank smiled. "Women don't think so."

"True. Women do make fools of themselves over you when they first meet you. I've always wondered why."

"Money and power equal sex."

"Miranda is different, isn't she?" Julian waited for Frank to answer.

"She is everything that I'm not. She loves easily while I find it difficult to conjure that feeling. If Miranda were to love a man, she'd do so unconditionally, with or without money. I need that . . . that security. Women change toward a man. They love him today, but if he forgets her birthday, she withdraws her love."

"Miranda wouldn't like a man to forget her birthday."

"If I forgot it on the true date, I'd take her to Paris a week later and she'd forgive me."

"Probably," Julian said. "For the first seven or eight times anyway, but how would someone like Miranda fit into your life? If I remember correctly, your last love interest — the one before Gwyn — had a doctorate in Chinese poetry and spoke four languages."

"She was a bore," Frank said with contempt. "Julian, something's happened to me in the last two years. I've had a change of heart. Many people have asked me what I'm earning money for, but I've never had an answer. I think it's been the challenge and the goal. You above all people know that I haven't wanted to buy anything. I've never wanted a yacht that costs a hundred grand a day to run. I've just wanted to —"

"To win," Julian cut in. Sometimes he was sick of seeing Frank win.

"Julian, you know how I make money? I make money because I don't care. I don't care whether I win or lose. If there is a deal I really truly want, then I step out of it. You can't be ruthless if you care."

"What happened two years ago?"

"I met a kid, and it was like looking into my own eyes. He was so ambitious, so hungry for achievement." Frank chuckled. "He steals office letterhead and writes letters to people on it."

"That's illegal."

"Yes, but he does it to help people. I looked at him and thought, 'I wish I'd had a son just like him.' It was the first time in my life that I ever wanted a child of my own."

"The Taggert bug," Julian said. "Bitten at last."

Frank smiled. "Ah, yes, my prolific family. They seem to be born with the urge to procreate. I don't want the mother of my children to be anything but a mother to them."

"And a wife to you, I take it."

"Yes. I . . ." He took a deep breath. "When this happened" — he nodded toward his arm — "I had some time to think and to remember. If I'd broken my neck, not one of those billion dollars I own would have missed me. Not one of them would have cried in misery at my death. And worst, when I got out of the hospital, there wasn't a soft, sweet woman whose lap I could put my head on and cry."

At that Julian raised an eyebrow in disbelief.

"I *could* have cried that day. The Chinese-poetry lady called me and you know what she wanted to know? She asked me if breaking my arm and being in that much pain was arousing. Was my pain sexually exciting?"

"Tell her," Julian said fiercely. "You *must* tell Miranda what you feel."

"Tell her what? That I've been looking for a woman like her, someone who'd get on a horse and ride into the middle of nowhere to nurse an injured man? As far as I can tell, she asked no questions. She was told she was needed, so she went. For a ridiculously low sum of money."

"Then tell her you need her."

"She'd never believe that. What do I need her for? I have a cook. Sex is easy to come by, so what else do I need?"

"Frank, no wonder women come to hate you."

"Women hate me when I refuse to marry them and make them part of my community property."

"What are you going to change for her? The life you have now doesn't favor a woman like Miranda."

"I don't know what you mean. I have to earn a living and now I'll have a reason for what I do. If there's a house, or anything she wants, of course I'll give it to her."

Julian was quiet for a moment. "That's not what I meant. In spite of what you say, some women have genuinely cared for you. You, not your money. But without exception you dropped them. If Miranda got a nudge from you, I think she could actually love you. But then what? You drop her somewhere and see her when you aren't too busy to stop by and say hello to her and the kids?"

Frank was frowning at him.

From the corner of his eye, Julian saw that Miranda's shirttail was by the window. She was listening. "Are you sure this is the right thing to do? Does Miranda know the business, Frank? It's easy to see that she's dazzled by you. But she's half in love with an unshaven guy who lives in a cabin, wears flannel, and catches his own dinner. But you're that man what? Two weeks a year? The rest of the year you're in a ten-thousand-dollar business suit or a tux. I can't see her in a Dior gown at one of your charity events, with two hundred paparazzi bulbs flashing in her face."

"So we won't go."

"That's a concession, but how else are you willing to change your life? Are you going to put her in a house in Connecticut and leave her there? Do you plan to go home at six every evening?"

"Miranda is an understanding woman."

"Yeah, well, so were most of your women. I don't want to see Miranda hurt. I don't want to call her six nights in a row to tell her that her husband is staying in the city because he has to go to Tokyo, or that he has to attend some charity event that she would hate. Miranda doesn't deserve that. She doesn't deserve *you*. The *real* you. Not the woodchopper, but the Frank Taggert who focuses on work — and everyone and everything else be damned."

He turned to look at Frank. "I can't do this. I don't want to have to try to explain you to Miranda. I don't want to be sent to her to dry her tears with a box full of emeralds." He paused. "In fact, I don't want to do any of this anymore."

Julian gave Frank time to reply, but when he was silent, Julian stood up straighter. "I've worked with you for ten years. I've admired and respected you and at times envied you. But at this moment I feel nothing but pity for you." As he turned away, he halted. "Seeing you and Miranda together has made me remember what I'm missing. Unlike you, I'm willing to make some changes. This weekend I was supposed to go on a date with a wonderful woman, then you called and told me to bring you the papers. You didn't ask; you just told. So I left a message on her machine and came here. I doubt now that she'll ever speak to me again."

Overhead was the sound of an approaching helicopter. As Julian started back into the cabin, he halted. "You will have my resignation on Monday. I left the papers about that kid, Eli, on the kitchen countertop."

For a moment he hesitated, waiting for Frank to call him back, but Frank said nothing, so Julian kept walking.

As soon as he stepped inside the cabin, Frank saw that Miranda knew. She was at the counter reading the papers about her son. When she spoke, she couldn't keep her voice from rising. "What do you want with my son?"

"Not what your tone is implying," he said stiffly.

As she began to figure out what was going on, her eyes widened. "I'm not sure what these documents are saying about my son using your company's letterhead, but I think maybe he and his friend Chelsea planned all this." She waved her hand to include the cabin. "And you knew about it — even though you've pretended that you don't know my son. Did you and those children decide to take care of dumpy little Miranda? Give her a weekend like one of those silly books she reads? Big, strong billionaire makes love to her in a cabin? Is the payoff that my son does something with your computers?"

With every word she spoke, Frank's shoulders went farther back. The softness she'd seen in his face was leaving. *This* was the man the business world saw.

As for Frank, everything Julian had said

was ringing in his head. If he did this wildly romantic thing and took on this woman and her child, was he willing to change every aspect of his life? Give up everything he knew to live in suburbia and invite the neighbors to Sunday barbecues? No matter how he looked at it, he couldn't imagine doing what it would require if he were to stay with this woman.

Or was she to change? Would she set aside her pie baking to walk down a red carpet?

All in all, the two of them were almost different species.

He *had* to end this. He *had* to be the villain. He gave her a little smile. "I've had a great time these last few days. Please tell your son thanks from me."

It took Miranda a moment to understand what he was saying, then it was as if all the blood left her body, along with thoughts and feelings. "Me too," she said. "Truly great." Turning, she went to the front door. When she'd arrived, she'd dropped her handbag onto a little table. She picked it up, draped it cross body about her, and ran to catch the helicopter before it took off.

5

The outside offices were decorated for Christmas, and in the distance was the sound of laughter and glasses clinking at the annual party at the Montgomery-Taggert offices. But inside Frank Taggert's office there were no decorations, no lights, just Frank sitting alone, staring unseeing at the papers on his desk.

In the weeks since he'd been at the cabin and met Miranda, he'd lost weight and there were dark circles under his eyes. During that time, his life had changed. Not that he'd wanted it to, but he seemed to have lost his edge in the business world. He'd certainly lost his hunger to achieve more and more.

"Hello," said a tentative voice from his doorway, and he looked up to see young Eli Harcourt. They hadn't seen each other since that first meeting two years before. Their entire friendship had been conducted solely by letters, all correspondence going through a PO box in Denver. Eli was taller now and he looked less like a child. There was an adult look in his eyes that Frank thought shouldn't be there.

"Eli" was all that Frank could say, and the first hint of a smile in a long time appeared on his face. "Come here," he said, standing up and holding out his hands.

Closing the door behind him, shutting out the sounds of the other people, Eli walked over to stand in front of his friend.

"You look as bad as I feel," Frank said, and opened his arms to the boy.

Eli would have died before he admitted it, but part of his anger at his father was defiance, telling himself that he didn't need a dad. He threw his arms around Frank and the man held him close, and Eli found how much he'd missed the solid touch of another male.

Much to his horror, Eli found himself crying. Frank didn't say a word, just led him to a small leather couch and sat down with him. When Frank offered him a clean white handkerchief, Eli blew his nose.

"You want to tell me about it?" Frank asked.

"My mother is unhappy and so am I. Everything has changed and I don't like it.

Chelsea and I —"

"Do you need money? I can —"

"No!" Eli said sharply. "I don't want you to give me money."

"Okay." Frank pushed Eli's head back down to his shoulder. "Tell me about you and Chelsea."

For a while Eli didn't speak. "Why haven't you told me what happened between you and my mother?"

"I don't think you'd understand."

"That's what adults always say. They think kids are too stupid to understand anything."

"You're right. We adults do tend to put children into difficult situations, then mistakenly think they can't understand them. But we're trying to protect you."

"From Chelsea?"

"Tell me what's going on."

Eli took a while before answering. "I guess you know it was Chelsea and me who . . . who . . ."

"Sent your mother into the woods to take care of me? Yes. I found out all about how you talked to my brother and he made the arrangements."

"Are you mad at me?"

"No," Frank said. "I had a wonderful time with your mother. We went up to an old cabin where a prospector lived. There's a legend that he hid gold up there."

"Did you do something to make my mother so angry?"

"Not then, no." Frank knew he was evading that question. "What's happened with you and Chelsea?"

"Mom won't let us see each other. She said our lie about going on a yacht and about . . . about all of it was too much and it had to stop."

"To be separated from the person you care about the most is awful."

"Yes. I miss her. We understand each other. We *help* people."

"True," Frank said, "but your mom is right and some of what you two do needs to stop. Lying is bad, and using corporate letterheads is illegal, and —"

"I know!" Eli moved to sit up and look at Frank. "I know all of it. My mom has told me over and over and over. She made me tell her everything. Since she came back from meeting you, she's been different. What did you *do* to her?" He was nearly yelling.

Frank got up and opened a door to a little bar area. He didn't have much for kids but he poured Eli a glass of seltzer water and handed it to him. "I fell in love with your mother. I even asked her to marry me."

Eli, eyes wide, drained the glass. "Did she tell you no?"

"Yes," Frank said slowly, "but she should have. I would have made her miserable."

"No you wouldn't!" Eli said. "You're the best man in the world."

Frank sat back down on the sofa. "You're the only one who thinks that. Since your mother walked out on me, everyone I know has told me what a jerk I am."

"I'd like to tell *them* that they —"

Frank put his arms around Eli's scrawny shoulders and kissed the top of his head. "If you and Chelsea swear to stop sending illegal letters to people, maybe your mom will let you get back together."

"We did. We wrote contracts and signed them in blood."

"Ouch!" Frank said. "That was a bit dramatic, but what did your mother say?"

"No. That's all she says anymore. My dad . . ." He trailed off.

Frank's jaw hardened at the mention of the man. "What did Leslie Harcourt do?"

"He said that Mom had turned into such a witch that he was going to go to court and make me live with him and his new wife, Heather. I don't like her and she doesn't like me."

He was glad Eli's face was down so he

couldn't see the smile on Frank's face. "Tell me everything that's been going on."

Eli began talking in a steady, quick stream and Frank listened. What he heard was the story of an angry woman. When Miranda had returned from her time with Frank, she'd declared that she was going to quit being a naive, gullible woman who believed in romance.

"She gave all her novels away," Eli said. "And she changed our house. She threw out all the pretty little things she had. It's all . . . I don't know, cold now. Does that make sense?"

"Yes," Frank said and thought of his own houses, where he'd outlawed anything that made them different from one another.

"Right after she got back, Dad came over and she was mad."

"What did he say?" Frank was frowning.

"He called Mom a slut, and said she was spending nights with men in bars and that he was going to get a lawyer and take me away from her."

"Have you ever heard him say that before?"

"Only once when I was little. That time I got scared and so did Mom. But this time she wasn't scared. She wasn't even angry. You know what she did?"

157

"I have no idea."

"She told me to pack my bag, that I was going home with my father. She said she'd deliver all my computer equipment to his house that afternoon and that she'd send Heather a list of foods I won't eat."

"What did your dad say?"

"I was really, really scared. I held on to my mother, but she pushed me to my father. He said Mom was crazy and he left. He hasn't been back to our house since then."

"Good for her," Frank said. "You know, don't you, that she wasn't going to give you away?"

"I'm not sure, but I think you're right."

Frank held Eli to arm's length and looked at him. "Your mother loves you very, very much. You are her whole life."

"Not anymore," Eli said. "Now she doesn't talk. She says she has to work more and she needs to go back to school and . . ." He looked at Frank. "Did you really ask her to marry you?"

"Yes, I did." Frank took a deep breath. "I did a very stupid thing: I fell in love. No, don't look at me like that. It was all right to fall in love, but I was afraid and I let her get away from me."

"Why were you afraid? I love my mother, but I'd never run away from her."

He shook his head. "I don't know how to explain it. In all my life I've never needed anyone. Maybe it was because when I was growing up, I had so many people around me. It was a huge family and I always had a lot of responsibility. I think maybe at an early age I decided I wanted to be different and separate. Or maybe it was just that I didn't want to be like them. Can you understand that?"

"Yes. I'm different from other kids."

"You and I are misfits, aren't we?"

"What about my mom?" Eli urged.

"I loved her. I just looked at her and loved her from the very first." Frank smiled. "Actually, at first I thought she was something other than what she was, and that made her angry. But then I saw that she was a sweet, gentle woman." He smiled again. "Well, not too gentle."

He paused. "You know what I liked best about your mom? She judged me on my own merits, not on my money or even on my looks. She just told me she didn't like me and didn't want to be near me. She even ran out the door of the cabin and tried to walk back to Denver."

"She has no sense of direction."

Frank looked surprised. "That's true, but how did you know that?"

"It's women. My mother has none and Chelsea has none," Eli said.

"Better not let any woman hear you make such a generalization. Anyway, I wanted her to stay and cook for me, so I offered her a great deal of money. But do you know what she asked for?"

"Something for someone else," Eli said.

"Exactly. That's just what she did. How did you guess?"

Ignoring the question, Eli said, "What did she ask for?"

"An education for her son at the finest school in the world, from freshman to PhD."

"Yes," Eli said softly. "She would." He spoke louder. "But what happened?"

"We, ah, we . . . Later we . . . We got to know each other a great deal better."

"So why didn't you stay together?"

"I hesitated and she saw it."

"I don't know what that means."

"You know how scared you were when you thought your life might change drastically if you went to live with your dad and Heather? That's what I saw. A man who worked for me made me see that if I stayed with your mother it would be the end of my life as I knew it. I wasn't ready for that. I guess I thought the things I'd worked for were what I wanted."

He looked at Eli. "I think I wanted it *all*. I wanted the lights and the accolades, but I also wanted a home. I wanted someone to wait for me and be glad when I showed up."

"Mom would be glad if —"

"Yes," Frank said, cutting him off. "Your mother would have waited for me, but she would have been very unhappy."

"Like she is now?"

"Worse," Frank said.

"What are you going to do now? About my mom, I mean."

Frank went to his desk, pulled out a leather pouch, and dumped the contents onto the little coffee table. They were unopened letters, all of them addressed to Miranda Stowe, all of them labeled *returned to sender.* "I've written to your mother every day since a week after we parted. It took me that long to realize what a mistake I'd made. You want to hear what happened?"

"Yes," Eli said.

"When I got back to town, my girlfriend, Gwyn, was waiting for me. She is really beautiful. She's been on the cover of some magazines. She's also smart and educated, talented and quite likable. When I got home, I told myself I was really glad to see her, glad to get out of a world of having to catch my own meals, and back to my own personal kingdom where people jumped to do my bidding."

Frank got up to pour himself a drink, and he gave Eli more seltzer. "I was really happy for about four days, then . . . I don't know what did it, but I became restless. I missed my right-hand man, Julian, but I was too proud to say so. I had to hire three people to do all the work he did. But it was okay because I had Gwyn. She was great. Perfect."

He looked at Eli. "I'm not sure why, but I began to not be able to bear the sight of her. Trust me on this, but perfection is a highly overrated attribute in a human being."

"My mom is perfect," Eli said, sounding as though he was offering a challenge.

"She is, but in a different way," Frank said. "Anyway, it was a bill for a Dior gown that sent me over the edge. I thought of something Julian said, then . . ."

Frank shrugged. "Anyway, I went to spend time with my cousins in Maine. I stayed there for about three days, listened to all the screaming children, went out on a boat with them. It was all the things that had bored me in the past."

"It sounds good to me," Eli said.

Frank smiled at the boy. "I thought about

you a lot. You know what I decided? That I liked you and your mom better than all the Dior dresses in the world."

"Is that good?"

"Very good," Frank said. "When I got back to Denver, I had a whole new purpose in life, and I began downgrading."

"You mean your computers?"

"No. I downsized my entire *life*. I delegated." He smiled. "I *shared.* I turned over a lot of my businesses to my little brothers and to one of my sisters. And I began to write to your mother."

"You never told me any of this in your letters to me," Eli said, sounding hurt.

"I know. I didn't want to get your hopes up. The letters I wrote to your mother told her what I was doing."

"But she didn't read them." Eli nodded to the unopened letters piled on the table.

"No, she didn't," he said sadly. "I don't think she wants me, and there's nothing else I can do. By now, she's probably forgotten me."

Eli lifted his head to stare at Frank. "I don't think she has. Sometimes I hear her crying at night. What if that's because she misses you?"

Frank raised one eyebrow. "I don't think so. A woman scorned, that sort of thing. I found out a long time ago that if you leave women, they never forgive you. They might say they have, but they get you back in other ways."

"But what if she's not like that? What if she loves you too and she would understand if you explained to her that you were frightened and a coward?"

Frank made a sound that was half chuckle, half a scoff. "You're making me feel worse. Okay, so maybe I was a coward. I'd fall on my knees to her and declare my undying love, but based on these letters, I'm sure she'd turn me down. You have any suggestions?"

"Let me think about it. We need something Mom can't refuse."

"All right," Frank said, "let's change the subject. What do you want for Christmas? Computer equipment?"

"No," Eli answered. "I haven't done much work lately." Suddenly, his eyes widened. "Can you ride a horse?"

"Rather well, actually."

"Do you own a black one? A big black stallion?"

Frank smiled. "I think I can find such an animal. I didn't know you liked horses."

"It's not for me. My mother was paying the bills last week, and she said that we had to face the facts. No handsome man was going to ride up to the front door on a big black stallion and rescue us, so we'd have to make ends meet another way."

"And you want *me* to ride up on a black horse and beg your mother to forgive me?"

"Yes," Eli said with such conviction that a light came into Frank's eyes.

"A black stallion, eh? And I guess I should do it tomorrow, on Christmas Day?"

"Yes, definitely. But maybe you're busy with your family on that day."

"Somehow I doubt they'll miss me. Besides, the idea of me humiliating myself would greatly amuse them." He paused to think about the idea. "Shall I wear a black silk shirt, black trousers, that sort of thing?"

"I think my mother would like that."

"Okay, tomorrow at ten a.m. Now that that's settled, what do you want for your birthday?"

"The password to tap into the Montgomery-Taggert data banks."

At that Frank laughed harder than he had in months. "Come on, let's get something to eat. And I'd have to adopt you before I let you tap into that."

"Would you?" Eli asked as they left the office. "Adopt me, I mean?"

"It would be my greatest honor." Before

them was the raucous office party and they stood there staring at it. Frank looked at Eli. "I know a great hamburger joint. Want to go?"

"Yeah . . . Dad," Eli said, and Frank put his arm around Eli's shoulders and they got on the elevator.

"My brothers will want to put some muscle on you. Think you can stand that?"

"Yes," Eli whispered as the doors slid shut, and he slipped his hand into Frank's.

6

"Eli," Miranda said, exasperated, "why are you so nervous?" Since early that morning, while Miranda was up to her elbows in cranberry sauce and pumpkin pie, every few minutes Eli had been going back and forth to look out the window. "If you're searching for Santa Claus, I don't think he remembers where this house is."

She'd meant to make a joke, but it fell flat. This year she hadn't been able to afford much in the way of gifts, and she was constantly worried about how she was going to support them in the coming months.

She stopped herself from thinking of the bad things, such as money and where and how. She also wouldn't allow herself to think of Frank Taggert, the rotten —

Calm down, she reminded herself.

"Is Chelsea coming over?" she asked. She felt some guilt over having separated them for so long, but after she'd returned from the cabin, she'd been so angry she hadn't been coherent. It hadn't taken a lot of work to find out what her son and Chelsea had been up to. Eli kept files on everything — and she'd read them in horror.

Yes, he'd done good things, but the danger of his illegal acts was frightening. She'd separated the two kids, not allowing them to continue. She'd also shredded all the stationery they'd collected and had forbidden anything like it to be done again.

And in one harrowing, terrifying episode, she'd at last confronted her terrorist of an ex-husband — and won. No more giving him money to pacify him. And no more fear that he was going to take Eli away from her.

For all that she had accomplished some things, the last months had been hell. But on the other hand, they'd also been good for her. Sometimes she thought she was at last growing up. The things she'd talked about to . . . him — she couldn't even bear saying his name — made her see how vague her life had been. Because of him, she'd decided to take charge of her own life.

She was sorry for the unhappiness she saw in Eli, but she knew the changes she was making were for the better.

As for "him," she'd returned his letters unopened. She wasn't even curious as to what was in them. An offer of money to assuage his guilt? Apologies for taking advantage of her?

Whatever he had to say, she didn't want to hear it.

The fact that she now bore the consequences of their "meeting" was beside the point. That she dreamed of him at night and remembered him during the day meant nothing.

"Not now," Eli said, and Miranda almost didn't remember what she'd asked. "Later —" He broke off as his face suddenly lit up in a grin. In fact, his whole body seemed to light up. He gained control of himself, and doing his best to appear calm, he went to sit on the sofa and picked up a magazine. Since it was a copy of *Good Housekeeping*, Miranda knew something was up.

"Eli, would you mind telling me what is going on? All morning you've been looking out that window and —" Halting, she listened. "Are those hoofbeats? Eli, what are you up to? What have you and Chelsea done now?"

He gave her his best look of innocence.

"Eli!" Miranda said. "I think that horse is coming onto the *porch*!"

When her son just sat where he was, his head down but looking as though he were about to burst into giggles, Miranda smiled too. She had an idea that she was going to open the door to find pretty little Chelsea on her pony, her hair streaming down her back, a Christmas basket in her hand. Miranda decided to play along with the game.

Wiping her hands and putting on her best stern face, she went to the door, planning to look surprised and delighted.

She didn't have to fake the look of surprise. Shock would be more like it. She didn't see Chelsea's pony but an enormous black horse trying to fit itself onto her little front porch. A man, dressed all in black, his face turned away from her, was on its back, trying to get the animal under control without tearing his head off on the low porch roof.

"You have any mares around here?" the rider shouted above the clamor of the horse's iron-shod hooves on the wooden porch.

"Next door," she shouted back, thinking that she knew that voice. "Could I help you find your way?" She stepped back from the prancing hooves.

After a few powerful tugs on the reins and some healthy curses muttered under his breath, the man got the horse under control, then turned to look at her. "Miranda," he managed to say.

She could say nothing. Turning, she went inside the house and bolted the door behind her.

Frank was off the horse in seconds, not bothering to tie the animal but leaving it where it was and going to the closed door. "Miranda! Please listen to me. I need to talk to you."

Miranda, with her back to the door, squinted at her son, who was bent over the magazine as though it were the most interesting thing he had ever seen. "Eli! I know you are somehow involved in this and I demand to know what's going on."

Outside, Frank spoke through the glass-paned door. "Miranda, I must talk to you."

"Over my dead body," she shouted back. "And get your horse off my porch!" She looked at her son. "When I get through with you, young man, you are going to be very sorry. This is an adult problem and *adults* are handling it."

Eli bent more closely over the magazine, fascinated by what was going on around him, and straining to hear every word that was being said. How he wished Chelsea were here!

Maybe it was the clothes, maybe it was

because it was Christmas, or maybe it was because Frank was sick of doing things the proper way, but he picked up a flowerpot from the porch and threw it through the glass of the door, then reached inside and opened the lock.

"Get out!" Miranda said when he was inside. "Or I'll call the police."

He caught her before she reached the telephone. He was sure there were words he should say, but he couldn't think of them. All he could think of was how glad he was to see her again. He grabbed her in his arms and kissed her. When he stopped and she started to speak, he kissed her again.

When he stopped kissing her, Miranda was leaning against him, her full weight borne by him. "Now listen to me, Miranda Stowe, I may not know how to be a hero out of a book, but I know that I love you."

"Our lives . . ." she whispered.

"I know," Frank said, "but if you'd read my letters, you'd know how hard I've worked to change things so we're more alike."

"Are you referring to my boring, middle-class life?"

"Yes," he said. She tried to pull away but he wouldn't let her. "I am going back to who I am, to my family. I realized that what

I want is what I once had."

"I heard what Julian said." It was hard to think with his arms around her. "I don't fit in your life. I doubt if they make designer ball gowns in a size twelve."

Frank laughed. "I have missed you. When Eli —"

This time, she did pull away from him. "You and Eli *again* did this?"

"Mom!" Eli said as he jumped up. "He loves you, he told me so."

"I don't think this —"

Frank caught her hand. "I want you to listen to me. I love you and I love Eli, and I have for a long time. I may not be any good at being a father or a husband, but I'll do my best and that's all I can promise. And I —"

Suddenly all the bravado left him, and he held her hand. There were tears in his eyes. "Marry me, Miranda. Please, please marry me. I'm sorry for how I acted when I first met you. Sorry for what I said later. The truth is that I thought I could forget you, that maybe it was all due to the moonlight and the trees and your strawberry pancakes."

"What was it?"

"You made me see what I was missing and what I truly wanted."

Before Miranda could say a word, Eli yelled, "Yes! Yes, she'll marry you. Yes, yes, yes."

"I can't —" Miranda began, but Eli, behind her back, started kissing the back of his own hand. Frank was so fascinated with this pantomime that he almost didn't understand what the boy was trying to tell him to do. He took the boy's suggestion and didn't let Miranda say another word but kissed her again. "Think of your son," he said.

"But I'm not sure this could work between us. Our lives are so different."

He kissed her again. "I'm changing mine and I love you. Don't you love me some?"

Miranda smiled. "Yes, I do. You don't deserve it, but I do." She leaned back away from him. "What about Julian? You weren't very nice to him."

"I think that was my first taste of jealousy. You smiled at him too much. He was bored to death after weeks without me, so I hired him back at half again his salary. But now he likes me even less than he did. Miranda, please marry me."

At that moment a siren went off in the next block and scared the horse, which ran inside the house for safety. It collided with Frank, Miranda, and Eli, who all tumbled into a startled heap on the couch.

"Stupid animal," Frank muttered as the horse nudged his pockets, looking for apples.

"Whose idea was the horse?" Miranda asked.

"Mine," the two males said in unison.

And it was that unison that made Miranda know what to do. From the beginning Frank had reminded her of someone, and now she knew who it was: Eli.

"Yes," she said, her arms going around his neck. "But I think I should tell you that I'm going to have a baby."

"Oh," Frank said. The horse was pushing at him.

"If you don't want this . . ." Miranda began.

Eli flung himself on top of both of them. "It's okay, Mom, he's a coward, but if you give him a chance, he can become your hero on a black stallion."

Frank was recovering. "I do. You can't be angry at a man for being slow-witted, can you? In fact, I think it may be illegal."

Eli hugged them both. "I got exactly what I wanted for Christmas and my birthday," he said. "And I'd rather go to Cambridge than Princeton." But his mother and Frank didn't hear him because they were kissing again.

Smiling, Eli untangled himself from the two adults and the horse and ran to his room to call Chelsea and tell her the news.

Robin and Marian Les Jeunes had struck again.

■ ■ ■ ■

PART TWO

■ ■ ■ ■

7

Edilean, Virginia
Twenty years later
2014

"And get some bottles of champagne," Eli said as he put his hands on the bar and bench-pressed six reps with over two hundred pounds.

His assistant, Jeff, tapped the note into his phone. "What kind of champagne?"

As Eli sat up and wiped the sweat off his face, he gave him a look.

"Right," Jeff said. "You have no idea. How about the kind that has pretty flowers painted on the bottle?"

"Keep it up and I'll make you hold the pads."

Jeff groaned. The gym they were in was big and smelly and full of people who were so physically different from him they might as well have been another species. In the boxing ring was a woman with a fantastic body wearing red boxing gloves and hitting the hand pads held by a kid who made grizzlies look small.

Those were the pads Eli was threatening him with. All 130 pounds of him would have to stand there with those things on his hands while Eli hit them very hard. Once was enough!

He watched Eli do more reps while lying under a bar that could come down and crush his neck — something Jeff was sure would happen to him so he never touched it. But Eli said that a man didn't join the Taggert family and not get into iron. "Iron" as in picking it up and putting it down.

"Okay," Jeff said, "what else should I get for the beauteous Chelsea? Flowers? Candy? Condoms?"

Again, Eli gave him a look to stop it.

"Got it," Jeff said. "Chelsea the Pure. Chelsea the Innocent." He lowered his voice. "Even if you haven't seen her since she was a kid, and you know she's had a lot of boyfriends, you still think she is an angel come to earth."

Eli took a couple of forty-five-pound dumbbells from the rack and went to an incline bench to do three sets of flies. When he'd finished, he sat up and looked at Jeff. "I know I'm being ridiculous, but I want this visit to be a good one. Get whatever you think will make her feel comfortable. I'm doing abs, then hitting the shower. I'll meet you at the car."

Gratefully, Jeff started for the front door, while mumbling, "And the objective in all of this is to persuade her to stay for the entire summer. Or maybe a lifetime." He didn't mean to be so negative, but he thought Eli was putting too much hope into the coming meeting. And he feared that Eli was going to be seriously hurt when it failed. He'd worked for Eli for seven years, and while his boss had had a few girlfriends, none of them had stayed around for long. But then, when there was a choice between work and a girl, Eli always chose work.

For all that Jeff was only five foot eight, skeletal skinny, and had a face like a mischievous boy's, women liked him. He said his secret was that he made them laugh.

But Eli was shy around women. If Jeff got him to go to a bar, Eli would sit there drinking his beer until he'd eventually take out his ever-present notepad and start creating something. There were times when Eli had excused himself and later Jeff had found him outside in the car doing calculations while his pretty date waited inside. Only women who were very determined made it past Eli's work barrier. But eventually they all left because, although he'd often grow fond of them, he never came close to giving them the love they wanted.

But about a year ago things had changed. One morning Jeff had shown up at his boss's small apartment as usual, and Eli said, "I'm going to take next summer off." Jeff had nearly choked on the bagel he was eating.

"Take *off*? As in, not work?" Jeff was shocked.

"Yes. I've been thinking about it. When my biological father died, his will said he wanted to be buried near his father's family in Edilean, Virginia. When I went to the funeral, I saw that it's a pretty little town, and it's just outside Williamsburg. I think I'll go there."

"Ah. Right," Jeff said. "It's near Langley." He went back to eating. Eli might be planning to do the unthinkable of taking time *off,* but he wouldn't be far away from government offices if he was needed. If the president called him — which had happened several times — and asked him to, you know, save the world — something else that Eli had done a few times — he'd be nearby.

"Then what?" Jeff asked.

"I'm going to get a house there and invite Chelsea to visit."

"The excitement is making my heart flutter." He couldn't remember which one was Chelsea.

But it turned out that she wasn't someone Jeff had met, and as the weeks passed, he decided to discover who she was. It took a lot of beers before Eli told him, but when he started talking, he wouldn't stop.

According to Eli, Chelsea was smart, clever, a daredevil, afraid of nothing, the best companion a person could have, etc. It took Jeff a while to realize that Eli hadn't seen her since they were sixteen years old. He told Jeff how even though his mother had married a fabulously wealthy man, they'd stayed in the same neighborhood so Eli could still go to school with his beloved friend, Chelsea. He postponed college, but he didn't mind. He said it was part of the "Great Compromise" his parents had settled on before they got married.

Eli said it had been traumatic for both kids when, a few years later, her father said they were moving. The kids had promised to write each other every day.

Eli told Jeff that that's what he'd done, but a year later, his letters were returned with *no forwarding address* stamped on them. After that, he and Chelsea lost contact.

By that time Eli was going to college and turning the computer world on its ear. Many companies had approached him about a job and had offered him money and luxuries. But then somebody from the US government showed up and said, "Would you like to work for us? We'll pay you practically nothing and keep you so busy you won't have time for a life. But then most of what you'll be doing is Top Secret so you can't share with anyone and that's hard on every relationship. So how about it?"

Jeff still couldn't understand why Eli had said, "Yes! Love to do it. Where do I sign?"

After the first five years of working for the government, Eli wrote a few software programs and some games for the real world — and that's when he'd hired Jeff to help with everything outside of work and programming. Not that Jeff wasn't handy with writing code himself, but he couldn't compete with Eli. But then, when it came to brains, nobody could. However, even though the programs were 90 percent Eli, he still cut his assistant in for a share of what came to be huge profits.

One time Jeff asked Eli why he'd hired him over the many other applicants. Jeff had hoped to hear that it was his magnetic personality or his speed on a database. But no. Eli said, "Because you look like me. Makes me feel comfortable."

That statement made Jeff laugh, for Eli was one good-looking man. Six feet two, dark hair, a body the Navy SEALs would envy, and rich. He was the whole package.

Smiling, Eli had pulled a photo album from a bookcase and showed a picture of himself at fourteen. Yes, Eli had once been as thin as Jeff. But after years with the family his mother had married into, he had physically changed.

Maybe it was because of a past physical resemblance, but they became friends as well as coworkers, and it was a shock to Jeff to hear about a girl who was so important to Eli. Maybe she was why Eli wasn't interested in the beautiful girls who leaned over him and slipped their phone numbers into his pocket.

The day after hearing Eli's story, Jeff went online and found photos of Miss Chelsea Hamilton and was stunned. She was beautiful. Like have-a-fantasy beautiful. "Is this her? She's a stunner."

"Yeah," Eli said. "She's always been pretty."

Jeff laughed at the understatement. A few

days later, he began to search for houses for sale in Edilean, Virginia. By the time spring began to arrive, Eli owned a modest house on the outskirts of the little town, and they'd contacted Chelsea. She'd replied, saying she accepted.

On the drive from the Edilean gym, Jeff kept glancing at Eli. He'd never seen him like this: nervous, excited, unable to concentrate on his work. Several times in the week they'd been here, Jeff had looked at the phone ID and said the caller was "General Weber" or "Agent Blackburn." Or it was Eli's secretary: "Pilar says it's urgent." Each time, Eli had waved his hand. "I'm busy. Call them and see what they want."

What they wanted was for Eli to return and do the work of five people — like he usually did. But all he seemed able to think about was the coming visit.

"Did you get —" Eli asked.

"Yes!" Jeff said before he could finish. "Whatever a person can eat or drink I've put it in the house." But with another glance at his boss, pity took over. "Why don't we stop at the grocery and have lunch? I'll order while you sit and work on" — he glanced at Eli's ever-present notebook — "whatever." And after lunch, Jeff thought, he was going to leave his nervous boss at home and go into town to look around. He needed some time away from Eli's skittishness. I hope she's worth it! Jeff thought as he pulled into the parking lot.

Chelsea stopped at the big grocery store just outside Edilean to get lunch — and to think. What she wanted to figure out was how to get out of seeing Eli.

That she'd even accepted his invitation was all her mother's fault. When it arrived, Chelsea had been at her parents' home and using her mother's big desk computer to check her email. If she'd just used her phone like normal, she wouldn't have been caught.

"You got an email from Eli?" her mother said as she looked over Chelsea's shoulder. Her voice was nearly breathless with excitement. "Have you two been corresponding long? Have you seen him? Are you two dating? Is it serious?"

Chelsea was sure her mother asked more questions but she didn't listen. All she could think was, So *now* you find me? All these years of being apart and at last you find me? What happened to make you seek me out now? Some girl drop you? Or did the world run out of secrets for you to untangle?

"Yeah, it's him," Chelsea said as she got

up from the desk. "I guess. Who knows?"

"May I?" her mother asked, but she was already in the chair and reading. "He has a home in Edilean, Virginia, and he'd like for you to visit him. How delightful!"

Chelsea wanted to leave the room. She wanted to put her nose in the air, flip her long hair, and leave. But she didn't. She plopped down on the sofa and picked up a magazine she'd already read and opened it. No matter how she tried to soothe herself about it, it still maddened her that her parents dismissed all she'd done in her life. Years of modeling, magazine covers, the people she'd met. What seemed to matter to them most was her childhood with Eli. "I can't imagine why he'd ask me to visit him. If he wanted to see me, he could have shown up at my door."

"And which door would that be?" her mother said. "You move every six months." She took a breath. "Eli was always shy and you're the one who stopped writing him, remember?"

"Yes, Mom, I do remember. But then, you've reminded me every day since I was what? Seventeen?"

"Yes. But then, you stopped writing your best friend when you discovered big, strapping boys who could barely talk." Her mother turned around to look at her daughter. Chelsea was home because she was hiding from her latest boyfriend — and she was in a bad mood because he hadn't found her. "Are you going to go see Eli?"

"Of course not." Chelsea got up to go to the kitchen.

Her mother was close on her heels. "I think you should go. Eli was always the nicest, most considerate boy I ever met. And you two had so much fun together."

"Mother, the things Eli and I did were illegal. Don't look so shocked! It wasn't like that. It was —" Chelsea put up her hand. "It doesn't matter now. If Eli wanted to keep in touch, he would have."

Her mother, usually so sweet tempered, glared at her. "Yes, Eli failed your test. You dropped him and he didn't pursue you. You played a little-girl game and lost the best friend you ever had. And now you're losing him again. And for what? So you can sit around here and wait for another one of your brainless boyfriends to find you? Is this one the Brazilian polo player?" She took a breath. "You're my daughter but I'm beginning to think you don't deserve a young man like Eli." With that, she turned on her heel and left the room.

Chelsea made a face at the doorway and

said, "He's Venezuelan, not Brazilian." She picked up her phone and reread Eli's email. It was very plain, just saying he'd purchased a house in Edilean and asking if she would please visit. That's all. No dates, no mention of where she was to stay, nothing.

But then, Eli wouldn't think of those things. He was the genius; she was the practical one.

The next few days were miserable! Chelsea's mother hardly spoke to her and her dad looked at her with big, sad eyes. He too had liked Eli.

Chelsea couldn't take it. Her parents' disapproval combined with the fact that no boyfriend came after her broke her. She'd thought this one was different, that she was seeing a future past looking good. She'd been involved in his business. She'd set up a website for him. *She* was the one who'd found out his accountant was embezzling from him. Didn't any of that count? And the truth was, as exciting as her life was, it wasn't fulfilling her. She wanted to *do* something, but she didn't know what. "Okay!" she yelled at breakfast. "I'll go!"

Immediately, her father put down his newspaper and smiled at her, and her mother asked if she wanted blueberries in her pancakes.

Chelsea had a whole day of being the best-loved daughter in the world, then the next day she awoke to see her mother in her bedroom packing a suitcase.

"I think you should take this." She held up a little black dress with a low neckline and spaghetti straps.

"Mother, what are you doing? It's six a.m."

"Your father and I thought you should get an early start. And we think you should drive so you'll have your own car with you." She opened the chest of drawers. "You should definitely take this." She held up a black-and-red corset with matching panties.

"Mother!" Chelsea said in shock. "I can choose my own clothes."

"Of course you can. Shall I make a lunch for you to take on the road? I bought Eli some of those sugared almonds he always liked so much. Remember how he used to eat them by the handful? It always puzzled me why that child was so thin. But now he's all grown up so I'm sure he's better."

"Mother," Chelsea said as she threw back the covers.

Her mother was at the door. "Don't take too long to pack, dear. Your breakfast will get cold."

Chelsea knew when her welcome was

over. After all, it had been her parents who'd listened and sympathized after every breakup she'd been through. No matter how many times she tried to explain to them that she was searching for . . . for . . . She didn't know what, just that she'd know when she found it. But they never seemed to understand.

She took two days to drive to Virginia, and being alone in her car gave her time to think. And what she tried to plan was how to get out of this meeting with her childhood friend but at the same time placate her parents.

Never once did she consider that it might work between her and Eli, not as a friendship and certainly not as anything else. Too much time had passed and besides, they were two different people. It had worked when they were children because they were both outcasts, different from the other kids. But now . . .

Now Eli was some kind of big-deal government genius — she'd met a general's assistant who'd told her that — and she was . . . Well, she hadn't yet decided what she was, but she liked adventure in her life. If they met now, they'd just sit around and stare at each other, with nothing to say. And of course Eli would look at her with those eyes that penetrated and want to know why she hadn't continued to correspond with him. No matter what lie she made up, he would be hurt — and it would be her fault.

So now she was sitting at a little table at the back of the grocery, sliced turkey and raw carrots before her, and an open map in her hand. She had on a floppy-brim hat that nearly covered her face and a trench coat that concealed the rest of her.

She was about to take a bite when in walked a man who looked exactly like Eli had as a kid. He was the same height and his face was nearly the same.

Smiling, she looked down at her plate and again wondered what Eli looked like now.

"Eli!" she heard and looked up as the man stopped to look down an aisle. Not possible! she thought. This couldn't actually be Eli! She put a menu in front of her face and looked around it.

He's happy, she thought, and was glad of it. As a child, before his mother remarried, he'd been quite morose — which was understandable considering his home situation.

Chelsea watched him go to the deli counter. For all that he was very thin and looked like he could play Huckleberry Finn, there was a swagger in his walk that was kind of appealing. Maybe it was his adoptive father who'd done that.

As Eli stood there waiting to give his order, he looked around the store. There was a pretty red-haired girl to one side, and he smiled at her in such an inviting way that Chelsea nearly giggled.

When his wandering eyes got near Chelsea, she put the menu up in front of her face. He had changed! she thought. Maybe his looks were the same and he'd never be someone who'd set a woman on fire with lust, but he might be good company. The intensity of the young Eli that she'd been dreading seemed to be gone. Thank you, Frank and Miranda Taggert, she thought, and started to stand up. *This* was a man she could say hello to.

But when a second man walked up to stand beside Eli, Chelsea sat back down.

Hot! was all she could think. He was tall, towering over Eli, had longish dark hair, and a beautiful, chiseled face. He had on a black T-shirt that clung to a muscular, perfectly shaped body, then jeans that showed well-toned legs, down to a pair of heavy boots. Unfortunately, *he* — not skinny Eli — was the kind of man she always went after.

Chelsea couldn't help staring at the man

in the black T-shirt. Who was he? Eli's body-
guard?

She watched Eli say something to the
man, then he went to sit at a table, where
he opened a leather notebook and began to
write. He was two tables away from her, but
the one separating them was empty. He
really was one of the most beautiful men
she'd ever seen.

"Eli?" the skinny guy at the counter said.
When there was no response, he said louder,
"Eli!"

The dark-haired man looked up.

"Do you want mustard or mayo?" the thin
one asked.

"Mustard," he said in a deep, rich voice,
then went back to his notebook.

Chelsea's mouth dropped open. Eli? This
gorgeous creature was *Eli*?

When did he — ? How did he — ?

She couldn't collect her thoughts. Vaguely,
she remembered that long ago Eli had told
her how weird his new father's relatives
were. "They spend so many hours in a gym
they look like draft horses." The two of them
had laughed in that way children do because
they know everything.

But it looked like somewhere along the
way he had visited a gym. Often.

When Chelsea stood up, she found that

her knees were weak and her hands were shaking. She could hardly pick up her bag. She didn't dare look around for fear one of the men would see her.

Somehow, she managed to get out of the store. As soon as she was outside, she paused to take a few breaths. Coming toward her was a big man in a tan uniform and a leather jacket. There was a sheriff's badge on his chest.

"Excuse me," she said and he stopped.

"Welcome to Edilean and how can I help you?"

She smiled at him, the flirty smile she'd learned to use when she wanted something from a man. But this man didn't so much as react, just waited for her to continue. His badge said Colin Frazier. "I was wondering if you might know someone named Eli Harcourt."

"I do." His voice was cautious.

"I don't mean to pry, but I haven't seen Eli since we were teenagers, and I just saw . . . Well . . ." She didn't know how to ask without sounding like a stalker. Pulling her wallet out of her bag, she removed an old photo from the hidden compartment. It was of her and Eli on their bikes. She was on her way to being the beauty she'd become, while he was scrawny and nerdy-looking.

Sheriff Frazier took the photo and looked at it. "This is Eli? He looks like Jeff."

"Who is Jeff?"

Sheriff Frazier frowned. "I don't give out information about Edilean residents."

"Okay then, who's the best gossip in town?"

For the first time, the sheriff smiled. "I'm not about to tell you that. Why do you want to know?"

"Eli invited me for a visit and I just saw him in the grocery, but then he called the other guy Eli. I found it all quite confusing."

"I see," the sheriff said. "You want to know who is who. Eli's the pretty one. His assistant, Jeff, is the skinny one who makes everybody laugh. That answer your question?"

"Oh, yes. But please don't mention to either of them that I asked."

"I wouldn't think of it," he said and went into the store.

Eli had a wheelbarrow full of gardening tools and was using the loppers to cut away a big shrub at the corner of the house. He'd bought the place completely furnished. A couple had built it about twenty years ago, thinking they'd live there forever. But as they got older, the two acres of grounds had been more than they'd wanted to handle, so they'd bought a condo in Florida. As always, Jeff had befriended them and ended up buying everything in the house — which is why the garage was full of old garden tools and inside was worn, but comfortable, furniture.

It was early in the season but it was a warm day so Eli had removed his shirt. He should have been inside at his computer but he was too nervous to sit still.

Chelsea would be here soon and he needed time to think about what he wanted to say to her. Originally, first on his list was to ask why she'd stopped writing him.

But Jeff had vetoed that. "You can*not* start an interrogation of her the second she gets out of the car!" he'd nearly yelled.

"I would just like to know —"

Jeff had thrown up his hands in frustration. "She was sixteen and beautiful and rich. That's all the excuse she needed not to keep up some deep, philosophical letter-writing campaign with the kid she used to ride a bike with."

"We did more than that!"

"Yeah, yeah," Jeff said. "I've heard all about it. But it was a different time back then. If you illegally used corporate letterhead today, you'd be facing charges. You two were white-collar juvenile delinquents."

"I guess we were." Eli said. "Robin and Marian Les Jeunes."

"I want you to swear that you will not question her. Just have *fun.*"

"Fun?" Eli asked.

"Tell me you've heard of it."

"Of course. Chelsea and I always had a good time together."

"Figuring out about a kid's dental health care is *not* a 'good time.' " Jeff was glaring at his boss. In the last months he'd done a lot of research on Chelsea Hamilton. It hadn't taken much to learn about her penchant for polo players, race-car drivers, and Olympic skiers. Lots of excitement. Not a computer nerd anywhere to be seen.

He looked at Eli, standing in his jeans and T-shirt, and thought that he certainly looked the part of the man Chelsea would like — except for his expression. He was scowling in a way that was almost scary. "Too bad you couldn't be me on the inside," Jeff mumbled.

"What?" Eli asked.

"I said it was a shame you and I couldn't do one of those *Freaky Friday* exchanges. If I had your looks and body along with my humor and way with women, I'd have a harem in minutes."

Eli grimaced. "Then you'd have a dozen women complaining that you never pay any attention to them."

"No," Jeff said. *"You* have heard women say that, but not one of them has said it to *me."*

Eli smiled. "Then I wish we could trade. I'd do most anything to get Chelsea to stay, even if it's only for a few days."

Jeff shook his head. "You do have it bad, don't you? Okay, my advice is to lighten up. Act like you haven't compared every girl you've ever met to her and found her to be lacking. Pretend that seeing Chelsea is nice but not some monumental event that you hope will change your entire life." His head came up. "You haven't bought her a ring, have you?"

"I thought we'd go together to look at —"

Again, Jeff threw up his hands. "That poor girl. If I were her, I'd never get near you again. I wonder why she agreed to this visit?"

Eli frowned. "Maybe she wants to see me as much as I do her."

"I doubt it," Jeff said and was glad when his phone rang. "It's Pilar and she says she needs to talk to you."

"Tell her I'll call her back later."

Jeff relayed the message, but after he hung up, he said, "You ought to be nicer to Pilar. If Chelsea falls through, your secretary is a great backup. I don't know why she stays around you."

Eli shrugged in dismissal. "I'm going to get a beer. You want one?"

"No thanks," Jeff said. "I'm watching my figure."

His joke cleared the air and they were back on good terms. Actually, Chelsea was their only real bone of contention.

That had been days ago and with every minute since then, Eli had become more apprehensive. He spent hours in the local gym, doing some sparring with the owner, Mike Newcomb, and being spotted on the weight bench by Colin Frazier. With Mike being a retired police detective and Colin the town sheriff, Eli had felt very comfortable in the gym. In fact, just a couple of weeks ago, Eli had used his contacts to help on a case Mike had taken on. "*Retirement* is a relative term," Mike had said.

As for Colin, when Jeff and Eli first arrived, he'd asked them questions about why they were here, who they knew, where they worked. Eli had answered all that he could. He couldn't tell much about his job, and he knew little about his father's family, the

Harcourts.

"My wife, Gemma, and I will have to have you over for dinner and introduce you to some people," Colin said.

Eli said that sounded nice. Maybe he and Chelsea . . . He had to force himself not to think like that.

Now, he moved on to a row of bushes and began to trim them. He really should find out what kind of plants they were and when they should be pruned. But his mind was so full of Chelsea that he couldn't concentrate on anything else.

Chelsea didn't pull into the driveway. She was afraid that Eli would hear the gravel crunching and suddenly open the car door and say, "Why did you stop writing me?!"

She had no idea what her answer would be because she had no legitimate excuse. On the long drive to Edilean, she'd thought of lots of answers to give him. There was the therapist way — something she'd had experience with — of explaining how she'd been young and frivolous and didn't understand the value of friendship. Or she could get angry and yell at him. Or she could laugh and say, "And hello to you too, Eli." She came up with dozens of ways to confront him, ways to answer him, but every scenario ended with her getting back into her car and leaving.

But then she'd seen Eli in the grocery store. She knew she was being shallow, but it was a lot harder to say no to a drop-dead gorgeous man than it was to a man-boy whose ears stuck out.

Since seeing him, her answer to his question of why she hadn't written had changed. One of them was to shoot back at him, "Why didn't you tell me you'd grown a foot and put on forty pounds of muscle?" The thought of throwing her arms around him and French-kissing him hello was another answer she rather liked.

But all in all, she wasn't sure what she was going to do.

She closed the car door quietly. She'd seen the assistant, Jeff, drive away, so it was her guess that Eli was in the house alone. She wasn't sure if that was good or bad.

As she quietly walked across the lawn, she wished she hadn't worn heels. If Eli got too bad, she'd need flats for running away. Maybe she should give a quick knock on the door, then leave before he answered. She could tell her parents that —

She didn't complete her thought because Eli was outside. He had his back to her and his shirt was off. From his thick dark hair to his feet, he was beautiful. His shoulders were broad and his waist was small. He was using big cutters to trim some bushes and the action made the muscles on his back move like waves in an ocean.

For a moment, Chelsea closed her eyes. I am in trouble, she thought.

If only this weren't Eli, a guy she had so much history with — and knew so very well. She had no doubt that he was going to make her feel disloyal and superficial, and he was probably going to point out that she had no clear direction in life. Yes, she was the one who hadn't written. No, she hadn't given her life over to helping her country, as he had done. But she had . . . What? Well, actually, she'd had a damn good time in her life. Could Eli say *that*?!

She took another step forward, ready to take her punishment for past offenses, but then an idea came to her. Why not turn some of that Robin and Marian Les Jeunes onto themselves? Save the two of them, so to speak. His muscles were still moving under his skin, and Chelsea thought how much she loved surfing.

She took a breath. Courage! she thought. I need all of it that I can muster.

"Is he gone?" she asked.

Eli turned toward her, and for all that his

face and body were different, those were the same eyes — and she could read the accusation in them. She knew she'd better talk fast or he was going to start with the questions about why she'd broken contact with him so many years ago.

"That was Eli driving away, wasn't it? Someone told me he's your boss and I don't mean to disparage the poor guy, but I really can't take his doom and gloom right now. I only came because my parents threatened me into it. Maybe I can just leave a note saying I'm sorry I missed him. That will get my parents off my back without having Eli's guilt dumped on me. Oh! I'm Chelsea, and you're Jeff, is that right?"

She watched him use his prodigious brain to try to understand what she was saying.

As Chelsea spoke, Eli watched her — and it was as if time fell away. She might be an adult now, but when he looked into her eyes, he saw what he'd seen when he'd met her in elementary school: fear. When her family moved to town that summer, her father had caused a local sensation. He'd bought a big, historic mansion, tore down the newer houses surrounding it, and moved into what was an ordinary, middle-class neighborhood. People with his kind of money didn't usually live in that area.

When his youngest daughter entered the local elementary school that fall, everyone had gathered around her. She was pretty and rich and they all wanted to be her best friend.

Eli, always a loner, hadn't paid any attention to her. But one day in the cafeteria she'd asked him what he was reading. He'd told her — it was a book on artificial intelligence — then he'd looked up at her, expecting to see the usual bored expression the other kids wore. But that's not what he saw. Chelsea's eyes had the look of a wild animal — scared and desperate — plus a look of, well, not belonging. But best of all, she'd understood what he'd told her and she didn't look bored. After that, they were friends.

She'd been an extraordinarily pretty girl and now she was beautiful in that way that tended to make men weak. She was tall and thin, with long, thick hair, the same golden color it had been when they were children. It was easy to understand why people stopped and stared at her.

But none of that mattered to Eli, for right now, that look of fear he'd seen so long ago was again in her eyes. He didn't understand why, but he knew she *needed* him to be someone he wasn't. And if Jeff was who she needed, that's what he was going to give her.

He started to say something but when Chelsea turned, she seemed to get dizzy. "Sorry, I missed lunch," she said, her hand to her forehead.

Eli came out of his trance. "I think we better get you out of the sun." His T-shirt was draped across a handle of the wheelbarrow and he pulled it on over his head.

"Darn!" Chelsea said.

Eli started to ask what she meant but then told himself that Jeff would probably know. With him, it was usually sex. Oh, right. His shirt. Jeff would probably say something self-deprecating. "I don't want to scare the neighbors," Eli murmured.

"I think they may show up with cameras."

At her flattering words, Eli felt warmth flow through him — and oddly, he felt a bit taller. He moved ahead of her to go up two steps toward the porch, then held out his hand to her. It was ridiculous to think that she couldn't climb a few steps by herself but it's what Jeff would do. Eli remembered one time when Pilar had brought some papers to him. Jeff had made a fool of himself over her — and she had giggled like a teenager.

Chelsea didn't seem to be offended. Smiling, she took his hand and walked up the stairs with him.

"I want you to sit here," he said, indicating the big wooden seat. The cushions on it were fatly stuffed and the fabric faded from years of use. "And take off those shoes."

"But they're —" she began, but stopped. "I'd love to, but I don't mean to take your time."

At the thought of her leaving, Eli felt a sense of panic. What would Jeff say? "A beautiful woman and a day full of sunshine. How could that be a waste?" Eli held his breath. Surely she'd tell him his words belittled her as an intelligent being.

But she didn't. Instead, she smiled at him. It wasn't the smile she used to give him after they'd completed some quest together. It was the smile she used to direct toward the boys who were wearing some absurd uniform for sporting events. When he'd seen that look in high school, he'd told her it was false and didn't suit her. But right now, when it was directed at him, it felt quite good.

He went into the house to the kitchen and, with extraordinary speed, made her a sandwich and poured a glass of lemonade. Minutes later, he pushed open the screen door and went back onto the porch. She had taken off her ridiculous shoes — why women wanted to misalign their bodies with them was beyond him — and put her legs up on the cushions. Her eyes were closed.

He stood there for a moment, looking at her. She was indeed very pretty, but Eli had always looked beneath her exterior to the person underneath. Right now he thought she was thin to the point of emaciation and she looked tired.

When he put the dishes down on the coffee table, she opened her eyes and smiled. "Look at all this food! It's more than I eat in a day."

You're too thin, he started to say, but caught himself. That's what Eli would say. Jeff would say . . . "Personally, I think women should look like they were meant to. Curves in the road and curves on women make them both more dangerous."

Eli held his breath. Surely that remark would offend her — or send her into hysterics of laughter.

But Chelsea gave a sigh. "What a nice sentiment. Maybe I will try just a bit of something." She picked up the plate with the tuna-salad sandwich and bit into it. "This is great. I haven't tasted mayonnaise — or, for that matter, bread — in about three years."

"You have an allergy?"

"No," Chelsea said. "The style for women now is to be as thin as a broom handle. And that's what modern men like. Or at least the ones I know do."

"The polo player?"

"Yes! How did you — ?" Chelsea put up her hand. "Don't tell me how you know about him. Yes, Rodrigo the polo player." She glanced at Eli sitting there in the chair, his face a study in concentration. One thing she'd always liked about him was the way he listened. "We had a big fight," she said.

Eli wanted to say that since she'd never been an animal aficionado, of course she'd quarrel with a man whose livelihood dealt with horses. But Jeff wouldn't say that. He'd say . . . "So what was it? Another woman?"

"Yes!" Chelsea said, her voice almost fierce.

Eli saw that she'd finished her sandwich and all the corn chips he'd put on her plate. He stood up. "What was she like?"

"Which one? Minnie, Esther, Firebrand, Hector?"

Eli had a moment of confusion. "Oh. The horses."

"All twenty of them."

Eli went into the house and quickly returned with a tray. In the center was a chocolate cake thickly covered with chocolate frosting. Two plates, two forks, and two glasses with full-fat milk were beside it.

"Chocolate cake?" Chelsea said. "I haven't eaten dessert in years. And no dairy at all."

Eli cut two big slices of cake and put them on the plates, then settled back in the chair with one of them. "He couldn't possibly have liked his horses more than you."

"He did," Chelsea said as she picked up the other plate of cake and closed her eyes in ecstasy at the taste of it.

It was after she'd told some about living on the polo circuit — which sounded pointless — that he said, "You don't want to see Eli?"

Chelsea took a moment before opening her eyes. This was it! This was when he'd start his sad diatribe about how she'd abandoned him, left him to face the world alone, how she had —

"I don't blame you," Eli said.

Chelsea looked at him.

"He's a pain to be around. He does nothing but work. Day and night. He neglects his family and he has no friends. Girls come on to him but he ignores them."

Chelsea was eating her cake and listening in wide-eyed astonishment. Maybe she'd mixed this up. The sheriff said Eli was "the pretty one" and Jeff was the "skinny one." But compared to the bulk of the sheriff, this man was thin. "Was he looking forward to seeing me?"

"Are you kidding? You are his obsession. It was so bad I was tempted to call you and tell you not to come. Do you know that he's thought of you incessantly since he was a kid?"

"I guessed that," Chelsea said as she put her empty plate down and picked up her glass of milk. "Does he talk about me often?"

"I never heard of you for the first six and a half years I worked for him, but in the last few months you're all he's talked about. I told him that if you had any sense, you'd not show up. How did your parents threaten you?"

Chelsea felt a little guilty for that lie. "It was more implied than really said. My parents always liked Eli a lot."

"He said he liked them too."

"My dad used to talk to Eli about the stock market. Actually, he made a fortune from Eli's advice. If he ever needs money my dad will gladly give him some."

"He has his own income. How about some more cake?"

212

"I couldn't possibly do that," she said as Eli handed her another slice. She was beginning to relax. She hadn't realized it, but she'd spent two days in the car with her body tense and tight from dread of what was coming.

"So what are your plans?" he asked. "You want to stay in Edilean or leave as soon as possible?"

"I hadn't thought past saying hello and good-bye. I figured I'd show up, endure Eli's lecture, snap a photo of the two of us together so I could show my parents that I tried, then drive away at about a hundred miles an hour. I'd be very sad when I told them we weren't going to get together." She shrugged.

"I won't let him do anything you have to work to survive," Eli said.

"He's your boss. You can't stop him from anything."

"He knows he needs me. Before me, no assistant lasted longer than a few months. But then, he expects people to anticipate what he wants before he thinks of wanting it."

Chelsea laughed. "He hasn't changed at all! When we were kids he'd call me in the middle of the night. I don't think he paid any attention to the time. And he couldn't have cared less about a social life. I used to try to get him to go with me to parties and dances, but he always said no. He wasn't like a regular teenager wanting to drink and make out. Eli wanted to save the world."

He was doing his best not to let her words hurt him. He'd thought that back then they'd been in agreement about everything. "You must have been dying to get away from him."

"Oh, no! Not at all. When I was with Eli, I felt that I was part of the whole world. It was all very exciting. Did he ever tell you of the things we did?"

"Dental care?" Eli's voice was contemptuous. "That couldn't beat a drive in the moonlight or skinny-dipping on a dark night."

"But it did," Chelsea said. "I remember looking down my nose at the other kids and feeling superior to them. Eli and I were working on saving the world, while all they thought about was how to get beer for Saturday night."

Eli smiled. "Beer can be a lot of fun."

"Oh, yes," she said. "Beer and wine and fast cars and beautiful men — they've all been glorious."

"And men who love polo ponies," Eli said.

"Maybe not *him*," Chelsea said. She put

her plate down. "I better go." But she didn't move. She sat there, her long legs stretched out, and looked at the garden. "It's very nice here, isn't it?"

"I like it. I haven't lived in a house for years."

"Me neither," she said. "It's been apartments and hotel rooms, and . . ." Her voice began to trail off. "It's very warm here and I haven't been sleeping well."

As he watched, she fell asleep.

Eli took the empty glass out of her hand and put it on the table. Quietly, he left the porch and went inside to his bedroom, shut the door, and called Jeff.

When Jeff heard his phone, he grimaced. Why oh why couldn't the man manage his own life for even a minute?

Jeff was sitting on a bench under a gigantic oak tree in a little park in the middle of the cute little town of Edilean. Beside him was a young woman named Melissa, and he'd asked her about the tree. She'd told him that it came from a seed brought over from Scotland by the original Edilean.

"So the town was given the name of a woman?" Jeff asked, his eyes wide with interest as she told him the history of the town. She was pretty, with freckles on her nose, and she was a deputy sheriff.

"In your job, don't you risk getting shot at?" Jeff asked.

"There's not much of that in Edilean." She turned to look at him. "You're easy to talk to."

"And you're easy to listen to," he'd answered. "Would you like to have dinner with me tonight?"

"I'd —"

She didn't finish because Jeff's phone rang and it was the theme from *Jaws*. Eli. Jeff gritted his teeth. Now what? Eli wanted him to buy polish for Chelsea's wings? He touched the phone on.

"You have to be me," Eli said, without a greeting. "If she figures out I'm me I think she'll leave. She *needs* me to be you."

They'd worked together for so long that Jeff almost understood what his boss was saying. "She thinks you're me?"

"Yes!" Eli said. "And if she figures out the truth she'll leave."

It wasn't the first time someone from the past had thought Jeff was Eli. After seeing the photos, Jeff had understood the mix-up. But Eli'd had years of being what Jeff called Taggertized. Early on, his new relatives by marriage had pulled Eli into a gym and told him of the benefits of eating protein by the pound. By the time Eli was twenty, he looked completely different.

When the Taggert family had first met Jeff, they'd tried to do the same thing to him, but he'd just laughed at them.

"I think you should tell her the truth," Jeff said and knew he was saying this mainly to impress the young woman next to him. She was unabashedly listening to his conversation. Was snooping part of her law enforcement job? "Just tell her the truth!"

"No," Eli said. "I don't want to be me. I don't want to be someone she has to endure."

Jeff got up from the bench and walked to the far side of the park. "Take her out somewhere nice, have a good time, then surprise her with the good news of who you really are."

Eli sighed. "Yeah, you're right. That's what I should do. I'll tell her who I am, then of course she'll leave, and you and I can go back to Langley. Pilar says DC wants me to fly to some station in Iceland and see what's going on there. You can go with me."

He saw Melissa get up, and he watched her cross the street, her uniform clinging to her. She waved to him, then he saw her hurry after some guy who looked like he should be on the cover of *GQ*. There was a stethoscope around his neck. Jeff was sick of Iceland and deserts and places with bugs bigger than his face. It had been exciting for a while, but lately he'd been wanting something more ordinary.

Jeff went back to the phone. "I'll be there in a few minutes and I'll pretend to be you. But what then?"

"I have no idea," Eli said. "I'm playing this by the minute. I have no long-term plan."

That sentence silenced Jeff. Eli was a master at planning. He had one-year, five-year, and ten-year goals. Eli often astonished people at meetings by quickly outlining a plan of action that would take many years to complete.

"Interesting," Jeff said. "Where is she now?"

"Asleep on the front porch. I think she's in a sugar coma."

"You were alone with a beautiful girl and you put her to sleep?"

"At least I kept her *here,*" Eli said. "She's going to wake up soon and I don't know what to do to make her stay."

Jeff heard the panic in Eli's voice and thought, If I ever fall in love, I hope someone shoots me.

But then he looked across the street.

Pretty little Melissa was talking to a woman with a baby in a stroller. A bit of wind ran through the oak tree and a couple of leaves fell down. No, he didn't want to go to Iceland — or for that matter, to Paris or London. He didn't want to sit at a table full of men in uniforms as they made decisions about the future of the universe.

Right now all he wanted was to take a pretty girl out to dinner and know that he could ask her out on a second date. "I'll fix it. She won't leave," he said, then clicked off his phone.

When Chelsea awoke, she lay still. She'd been dreaming about her last fight with Rodrigo. For weeks she'd suspected that there was someone else in his life, but he hadn't had the courage to say so. But then, she'd thought she'd found something more in her life.

It took her a moment to come back to the present, then she looked around. The big deep porch was lovely and she wondered where . . . "he" was. Based on their talk, she was no longer sure who the man was.

But she liked him. He had a quiet sense of humor and he'd made her feel so good that she'd fallen asleep. Some date you are! she thought, laughing at herself.

She got up and opened the screen door. "Jeff? Are you in here?" When there was no answer, she looked around. Everything in the house was old and faded and worn — and cozy, she thought. It was very different from the places she'd lived in for the last few years. Everything had been new and modern, all of it painted white. In her crowd, to be truly sophisticated meant no color was allowed anywhere.

Chelsea went through the house, looking about, then returned to the living room — and there was Eli. Or was it Jeff? Whoever he was, he was just as she remembered him. Thin, serious, without humor.

In the grocery store he'd been wearing a smile, but he wasn't now. He was shorter than she was and as thin as a jockey. And he was scowling with such anger that Chelsea took a step back.

"Why did you stop writing me?" he asked in a low voice that was mostly a growl. "We were friends but you walked away from that. Do you have any idea how much you hurt me?"

He took a step toward her. "Did you think that having a brain makes me incapable of feelings?"

"I didn't mean . . ." Chelsea began, but tears were coming to her.

"You didn't *mean* to tear my heart from me? Do you know what you've done to my life? Because of you, I work all the time. The way you treated me made me feel that I'm not good enough for any woman. I —"

Neither of them saw Eli enter the room. He stood there in shock for a moment, then crossed the room in three strides. With a twist of his body, he pulled back his right arm and let it fly. His fist connected so hard with Jeff's head that the smaller man flew backward and landed on the floor. Like some gladiator of old, Eli stood over him, straddling his body. "You don't talk to her like that."

Jeff put his hand to the side of his face and tried to flex his jaw. Pain was shooting up through his face. "You're fired," he managed to say. "Get out."

"Good, because I quit."

Eli grabbed Chelsea's hand and went to the front door. He pushed it open so hard that it slammed against the exterior wall. He went down the stairs, still holding on to Chelsea, and stalked to her car.

Dropping her hand, he opened the car door but then leaned against the vehicle. His face was flushed from anger and she could see that he was trying to calm himself.

"I'm sorry," he said. "I've never hit anyone

outside a ring." He pushed away from the car. "I have to see if he's all right. I have to apologize."

"Like hell you will," Chelsea said, then pushed on Eli until he was in the seat. She slammed the door and hurried around to the driver's side and put the key in the ignition.

"I have to —" Eli began but broke off when Chelsea sped away so fast he fell back against the seat.

She drove out of Edilean and stopped at a roadside tavern. It was still early and there were only a few cars there. "How about some tequila?"

"Actually, I could use something to drink." He was rubbing the knuckles of his hand, and he looked very upset.

Turning away, she smiled. She liked that he'd come to her defense, but she also liked that he felt bad about hitting someone. Sort of hero meets your best girlfriend.

Inside, they took a seat at a booth and ordered their drinks. Rock 'n' roll was playing on the jukebox.

"So Jeff, what do you do besides beat up nerdy guys who tell the truth?" Chelsea asked over the noise of the music and the people who were beginning to fill the tavern.

He didn't answer her question. "I didn't

like hearing what he said."

"But that's Eli. The way he said that was the exact tone of him. It was like he was a tape recorder and playing back what had run through his head a million times."

He sat there for a moment, thinking about what she'd said. "Unfortunately, I think you're right. You want to dance?"

"I'd love to!" She got up and he put his arms around her. Their bodies fit together well, and his movements were well timed to the music — and seductive. "So why hasn't some woman snatched you up?" she asked.

"Women can't tolerate my life. I'm gone most of the time. They want a depth of togetherness that I can't manage." He didn't add that *togetherness* meant emotional as well as physical. "What about you? Weren't you engaged once? What happened?"

Their hips were close together and moving to the music. Chelsea had her head on his shoulder, her eyes closed. He was so good with the rhythm that she wondered what he was like in bed. Maybe if she stayed around, she'd find out.

He pulled back, looking at her to answer his question.

"Boredom," she said as he whirled her about the floor. "He worked for my dad and I liked the family approval, but he was so much a creature of routine that I wanted to murder him. He came home at the same time, ate the same things. Six months after I met him, I knew what he was going to say before he did."

"Some women like that." He spun her to arm's length, then pulled her back to him.

"Where did you learn to dance?"

"From the relatives I gained by Mom's marriage. So why didn't you find something to occupy yourself?"

Chelsea shook her head. "You're supposed to tell me he should have done exciting things to keep someone as fabulous as me around. Then you should hint that if you and I were together, you'd make every second an adventure."

"If you were so bored with yourself that you were studying him, you weren't exactly fabulous, were you?"

For a moment Chelsea was stunned, but then she laughed so loud several people turned to look at her. Still smiling, she put her head back on his shoulder, her lips against his neck. "Don't you know that beautiful women don't have to *do* anything? To be seen is enough."

"Is that why you starve yourself? So nothing else is asked of you?"

"Of course. Only Eli ever expected me to

be something more than a pretty girl."

When the music stopped, he led her back to the booth, where they ordered some more drinks. Chelsea'd had a few shots of tequila, but Eli had only nursed a single beer. He knew he'd be the one driving home.

He was quite consciously trying to get her drunk. Maybe if she had alcohol in her system he could get her to tell him what was so deeply wrong in her life.

When he'd first seen her today, all he'd been able to think about was how she'd left him. He'd vividly remembered his pain over the years, his deep loneliness, the sense that his life wasn't complete.

It was his stepfather Frank who'd understood the most. Since Eli's mother had been nearly overwhelmed with babies, a new husband, and a home, Eli had worked hard to keep her from seeing the turmoil that was going on inside him.

But Frank had seen it — and he'd told Eli about his own childhood and how in an attempt to do his duty, he'd given up the solitude that he needed. Frank didn't let that happen to Eli. Over the years, the two of them had often gone to Frank's cabin in the mountains and spent days there. When his mother asked him what they did, Eli said, "We spend the time in silence."

At that moment two toddlers were loudly crying because the three-foot-tall tower they'd built had collapsed. His mother had laughed in understanding.

It was only after Chelsea moved away that Eli realized how very important she had been to his life. The ache he felt at not having a person to share everything with had been like a wound — and he'd almost not recovered.

Frank had offered to find her. "No!" Eli had said. "If she wants me, she knows where I am."

After Chelsea left, Frank had moved them from that area. Eli had decided that he wasn't yet ready to leave home to go to college, so Frank sent him to an exclusive private school where he wasn't labeled "the brain" or "the nerd." After the Taggert family got him into a gym, he began to attain that elusive thing called popularity.

But Eli never found anyone who came close to filling the gap that Chelsea had left in him.

Of course he kept up with her, reading about her on the internet. And Frank made sure Eli had access to any information he needed.

In college there'd been a few girls, but not many. And as his studies neared completion, he didn't know what he was going to do with his life. Companies offered him money, cars, houses, vacations in exotic locales. He wasn't tempted. But when the government offered what he and Chelsea used to have, the chance to help people, he said yes. Frank was so proud of him there were tears in his eyes.

Through everything, Eli never came close to telling anyone about Chelsea. But then Jeff, with his sarcasm and excellent brain, came into Eli's life. Other than Chelsea, he'd never had a best friend. Jeff wasn't as adventurous as Chelsea, wasn't willing to take on the world as she was, but at least he didn't run away as so many people who'd worked for Eli did. Morons! he thought. Cowards to the core.

Jeff had nagged until Eli told him of Chelsea. He told of what they did as children and how they'd succeeded so spectacularly in getting Eli's mother with a really good man.

But unfortunately, Eli had also told Jeff about how Chelsea had left him and how it had hurt something deep inside him. It was as though some fundamental part of him had been broken, and it had never come close to being repaired.

Eli had been glad that Jeff hadn't spouted

the currently popular phrase *move on with your life.*

Instead, Jeff had said, "I wonder why she did that?" After that, Jeff's innate ability to turn anything to sarcasm had taken over — and that had been good for Eli. He had enough self-pity for both of them.

It wasn't until Jeff said those horrible words to Chelsea that Eli had seen the truth. Yes, he'd blamed her for so much bad in his life. When some girl left him — usually in a rage — Eli had thought of Chelsea and how this wouldn't be happening if it weren't for her.

But hearing that from Jeff made Eli see himself in a way he didn't want to. The truth was that Eli had never really *liked* any of the young women he'd dated. They were too dull-brained, too uninteresting, too easy to obtain. Something.

In other words, they weren't Chelsea.

In those moments when he heard himself through Jeff, Eli changed. First there'd been a burst of anger at himself — and he'd taken it out on Jeff. Eli had wanted to hit himself, but it was Jeff on the floor with what was the beginning of a black eye.

For a while Eli had been too horrified at his own actions to be able to think clearly, but as he began to calm down, he looked at

Chelsea. But he wasn't looking at her with the eyes of a wounded boy, but as a man. His mind wasn't full of what-you-did-to-me, but of concern.

He looked at her as does that very underrated creature, a true, deep, and loyal *friend.*

What he saw was a woman whose eyes darted around nervously. She seemed to be searching for something, but wasn't seeing it.

She was too thin and her words about her beauty being her only asset haunted him. There were delicate, faint lines at her eyes, and he wondered how her polo-playing, race-car-driving boyfriends were reacting to those lines. He seemed to remember photos of those men with girls in their early twenties. At thirty-two, Chelsea just might be considered too old for them.

When they went back to the booth, he watched her throw back another straight shot of tequila in a way that showed she'd done it many times before.

His life had been missing *her.* But what was missing in Chelsea's life?

She put her empty shot glass down and looked at the dancers on the floor. Her eyes stopped at a man who was moving about with a pretty blonde clinging to him. He was holding her, but he was looking at

Chelsea.

"Am I going to have to fight him too?" Eli said.

Chelsea turned back to him. "Not on my part. I never like men who are too easy to get, and he's a one."

At Chelsea's glance, the man moved him and his date closer to their booth.

Eli stood up, putting himself between the man and the table. Eli was taller, younger, and had more muscle than the man. With a derisive little guffaw, he moved away.

Eli sat down beside Chelsea on her side of the booth and reached across for his beer. "What's this 'one' mean?"

"It's a girl thing. Would you really have hit him for me?"

"Would you like it if I had?"

Chelsea groaned. "You sound like my therapist. But to answer your question, a one is from the Challenge Test. A girlfriend and I made it up. We judge men as one to three."

"On their looks?"

"Heavens, no! That's old-school. It's how hard they are to get. How much you have to work to get a man to notice you — without letting him know you're interested, that is."

"And that guy is a one?"

"More like a point one." As she picked up Eli's beer bottle and drank from it, she smiled at the guy who was dancing.

"So you're just playing with him now?"

"Yes. And I can see that you don't approve."

"Seems like a waste. But the concept is interesting." Eli took his beer back and drank deeply of it. "Any threes in this room?"

She didn't take her eyes off his. "The man at the bar."

Eli was a bit shocked but also impressed that she'd been observing the people so closely. Turning, he saw that every stool at the bar was full.

"The one on the far left," she said. "The big guy with the smoldering good looks. He's a three. Top-of-the-line. He's well built, has a good face, no wedding ring, and he's minding his own business. Since we've been here, two pretty women have tried with him but he's not interested."

That she'd seen all that further impressed Eli. How had he forgotten how she had talents that he didn't? "Maybe it's women in general he doesn't like."

"No, he's checked out every woman who's come through the door." She turned to Eli. "I bet twenty bucks that I can get him to notice me."

"Of course you can. You're the prettiest girl here. Unbutton your blouse and —"

"No. Not that way. That's for college girls. I will get his attention by ignoring him."

Eli didn't like what she was saying but at the same time, he was intrigued. It had been years since any problem he'd encountered didn't involve numbers and a computer — or a firearm. He took out his wallet and put a twenty on the table. "You're on."

Chelsea waited for Eli to get out of the booth, then she got up, picked up the empty shot glasses, and took them to the bar. She stood close beside the man, who was sitting alone, quietly drinking his beer.

"Two more of these," she said to the bartender, then leaned forward and waited. She kept her head turned away from the man. Never once did she so much as glance at the man on the stool.

Eli watched as the man slowly looked her up and down. He reminded Eli of someone. He caught the attention of the waitress and asked who he was.

"Lanny Frazier, the sheriff's brother."

When Chelsea's drinks came, two full shots and two beer bottles with clean glasses over them, she picked them up, but nearly dropped one bottle. The man caught it.

"Thanks," Chelsea said in a brusque way, but she still didn't look at him. She went back to the table. "Is he looking?" she asked Eli.

"Actually, he is."

She sat down, took the twenty off the table, and slipped it into her cleavage.

"Interesting talent," Eli said, "but perhaps of dubious merit." He paused. "In reference to your Challenge Test, may I ask what I am?"

Chelsea downed another shot. She was indeed getting drunk. "You are a one. Beyond easy. You look at me like it's one hundred and ten in the shade and I'm an ice cream sundae."

Before she finished the words, she glanced back at the man at the bar. He had turned away, but that didn't keep her from admiring the way his muscles moved under his shirt.

Eli pretended that her words meant nothing to him, and he changed the subject. "What happened to your interest in photography?" he asked. "You once said you were going to become a great news photographer."

"I think ambition for a career left me when Eli did."

"I was told that you left him."

Chelsea waved her hand. "Whatever. He certainly didn't come after me riding on a black stallion, did he? You want to dance?"

"Sure," he said.

8

Eli pulled into the driveway, turned off the engine, and looked at Chelsea in the passenger seat. She was half-asleep, half-awake, and humming a little tune. He got out and went around to pull her from the car. When she had trouble standing, he put her over his shoulder and carried her inside. He would have put her on his bed but there were too many things in the room that belonged to him and he didn't want her to see them — not if he meant to keep up his charade of who he was.

He carried her up the stairs to the guest room and put her on the bed. He slipped off her shoes but didn't touch her other garments. "Well, ice cream sundae," he said as he looked down at her, "looks like you're about to melt."

He stood there for a moment. She looked good in the barely lit room, but that's not what interested him. Tonight he'd seen that the Chelsea he used to know — and love — was still in there. She still liked a challenge, still liked to prove herself. It was just that somewhere along the way, she'd lost her direction.

Eli turned out the light and went downstairs. He was known for his ability to set goals and make step-by-step plans to reach them. Rarely did they fail. Right now a new plan was forming in his head and this one was *not* going to fail.

Earlier, as Jeff lay on the floor of the house, the side of his face aching, he'd cursed the entire Taggert family. What normal person needed boxing lessons? Who needed to pick up pieces of iron and put them down again? It wasn't natural!

He got up with the help of a chair back. Now what happened? Was he supposed to keep up the lie of being Eli? Fat lot of good that did him. He'd only said what Eli had. Quoted him verbatim. And now his whole head was hurting because of it.

His intention had been to make Eli fake getting angry, then leave with the girl he was trying to impress. He'd never thought that Eli would actually get angry. And certainly hadn't considered that he might *hit* him.

Jeff flexed his jaw. It didn't seem to be broken, but it hurt!

He went to the bathroom in Eli's bedroom and looked in the medicine cabinet for some painkillers, but saw nothing. He'd negotiated for the house to be furnished, but he hadn't thought of things like over-the-counter medicines.

When the cabinet shut, he saw his face in the mirror. It was swelling and his eye was turning dark.

He went back into the bedroom but didn't know what to do next. Since he was supposed to be Eli — at least to Chelsea, anyway — did he take over the house? Or should he pack and leave?

All he knew for sure was that his head was hurting too much to think clearly. He got his car keys from the bowl by the front door and left.

He drove into town, parked, got out, and looked around for a drugstore.

"Hey, Jeff," came a voice behind him.

It was Melissa and he did *not* want her to see his face. Putting his hand over his eye, he turned halfway toward her. "Hi."

But she did see. Instantly, her pretty face went from smiling to being the deputy sheriff. "Who hit you?"

"I ran into a —"

"Who hit you?"

"Eli," he said and Melissa took her phone out of her pocket. "Wait! Please. Let me explain."

"Assault is not an explainable action."

"It is if I set it up so Eli could impress a girl."

"I'm listening," Melissa said.

"Could we go somewhere and get something for pain?"

"Sure," she said. "Then we're going to sit down and you're going to tell me every word of this story. If I don't like it, I'm going to arrest Eli."

"Then I guess I better add Master Storyteller to my many other talents."

She didn't smile. "Looks like you should."

Hours later — after Melissa'd had the local doctor check Jeff's jaw and X-ray it — they were having dinner in a very nice restaurant and Jeff was just finishing telling his life story. They'd stopped talking about Eli and his problems thirty minutes after they got together. Melissa said, "Eli's an idiot."

Jeff agreed. "He's got a dozen gorgeous females after him, but he wants some girl who drinks champagne for breakfast. Why does he think that's going to work?"

"I'm living proof that opposites don't

mesh," Melissa said as she flaked off a piece of trout.

"You?" Jeff said. "I would think you could have any man you wanted."

"Thanks, but men like me until I cancel the third date in a row. When something happens, Colin expects me to be there. I can't tell him, 'Sorry about the three-car pileup, but I have a hot date.' "

"Same with me," Jeff said. "Eli calls me at three a.m. and asks me questions. He works in thirty-hour marathons and thinks I'm a wimp when I fall asleep. When we were writing on *Trafalgar Knights,* I thought —"

"*You* wrote that game?" Melissa's eyes were wide.

"With Eli," Jeff said modestly. "It sold well."

"Are you kidding? I have three nephews and I bought each of them that game. The hugs I got were worth the price."

"Game two, *Trafalgar Warriors,* is about to come out. I can get you some early copies."

"Would you? I'd be such a hero to my nephews that maybe my sister would get off my back about my lack of a life." She looked down at her food. "So where are you staying tonight?"

"At Eli's house, I guess. Unless he's told her the truth. Any motels around here?"

"There are, but there's also an empty apartment above the sheriff's office. It's not great. In fact, it's so gloomy that Colin calls it the Devil's Den. But it has a bed and a kitchen and . . ." She shrugged.

"And it's near you," Jeff said, smiling. "I mean, in case something bad happens, it's nice to be near law enforcement."

"Yeah," Melissa said. "I'm a great shot."

"Good to know," Jeff said. "I'm not. Except with a game, then I can vanquish any demon you can throw at me. But in real life I've never even held a gun."

"A person should know about firearms. Maybe you'd like some lessons."

"I would like that very much," he said. "Did your nephews have any trouble with level six and the underwater battle?"

"Is that the one with the giant squid?"

"Yeah, and the treasure," he said.

"They did. Maybe Sunday you could go with me to my sister's house for dinner and show them a few tricks."

Jeff took out his phone and began to tap out a text.

"Something urgent?"

"I'm telling our editor that I need six copies of the new game sent by express so they get here by Sunday. That okay with you?"

"More than okay."

They smiled at each other.

When Jeff's phone rang and woke him up, he didn't have to look at the clock or the ID. Of course it was Eli.

"Are you okay?"

"Nothing's broken," Jeff said.

"Did you have X-rays to make sure? I hit you too hard. I'm sorry. I've never hit anyone before. Where are you now? You didn't need surgery, did you? You —"

"I'm fine!" Jeff said loudly. "Yes to X-rays, no to surgery, and no hospital. I'm in an apartment above the sheriff's office and —"

"I don't blame you for pressing charges."

"I didn't," Jeff said. "I'm dating the sheriff's deputy. She's pretty and smart and . . . Oh, well. So how did it go with Chelsea?"

"I didn't do as well as you did," Eli said. "She thinks I'm too easy, that I represent no challenge to her."

"I could have told you that. In fact, I *did* tell you that."

"Yeah, well, that's not the problem. She's not happy."

"And you are?"

Eli hesitated. "I need you to do something for me. I want you to buy some camera equipment and camping gear. I'm going to take Chelsea camping and try to renew her interest in photography."

"That sounds really exciting. Camping." His voice was sarcastic. "She likes sleeping outdoors?"

"No. She hates it. Always has."

"Then why — ?"

"I have my reasons," Eli said, but didn't explain further.

"I have just one question," Jeff said. "Are you still in love with her?"

"Absolutely," Eli said. "It's never changed and I didn't think it would." He hung up.

Jeff had trouble going back to sleep and he woke early. One thing he realized during his wakefulness was that it was in his own best interest to make this work between Eli and Chelsea. If it didn't, Eli's broken heart would affect a lot of people. Hell! It could affect the entire country. Maybe the world.

Jeff waited until seven to call Melissa. "Not too early, is it?"

"I've been working out since six," she said.

"That explains why you look so good in your uniform."

"Yeah? So what's on your mind?"

He told her about Eli's planned camping trip and the photography sessions.

"She hates camping, but that's where he's

taking her? That boss of yours is romance personified. Want to meet for breakfast and talk about this?"

"Anything in town open at this hour?"

"My kitchen is."

Jeff drew in his breath. "My favorite restaurant. I'll be there in ten minutes."

Eli was dreaming. He was remembering how he and Chelsea had been best friends, how they'd worked so well together. Then the dream changed and they were both adults and she held out her arms to him.

He pulled her close, feeling her warm body against his, and he kissed her. It wasn't a kiss like any he'd ever felt before, but deeper, reaching down inside himself.

The dream continued and they were in bed together. His leg moved over her hips; his mouth was on hers. Searching, seeking. It was the first time that all of him, his body, his mind, his very soul, had merged with another person. He was holding nothing back. This was Chelsea, the woman he'd loved all his life. If there were ever soul mates, they were it.

Suddenly, the bedroom door opened and light came in. "Do you have any pain pills? Aspirin? Ibuprofen?"

"Kitchen," Eli said as his lips moved to

Chelsea's neck.

A switch was flipped and the two bedside lights came on.

"I don't mean to bother you two, but where in the kitchen?"

It took Eli a moment to realize who was at his bedroom door. He turned sideways to look at her, his eyes trying to adjust to the light. "Chelsea?"

Pointedly, she looked at the woman in Eli's arms. She had long dark hair and sultry eyes that were only half-open. Her lips were full and quite red from kissing.

He turned to her. "Pilar?"

"Mmmm," she said as she snuggled against him. "And good morning to you, too."

Eli started to move away but she twisted one of her long — and bare — legs around his and he couldn't move without a wrestling match.

"Top right-hand drawer in the island," Pilar said to Chelsea. "Maybe you could give us a bit of time together. Oh, by the way, I'm Pilar, and you must be Chelsea. I'm so very pleased to meet you."

Chelsea watched as Pilar stepped out of bed. She had on a man's white dress shirt, her long legs bare. She was almost as tall as Chelsea, almost as slim, and nearly as beautiful. "I'll . . ." She couldn't think what to say. "Kitchen," she added, and left the room, closing the door behind her.

"What the hell are you doing?" Eli said as soon as they were alone, and he sat up in the bed.

"Giving your race-car-loving girlfriend a bit of a competition. You know, Eli, if you kissed other women like you just did me, they'd be all over you. A woman would die for you."

"That's the last thing I want. Would you put on some clothes?"

"Sure." She unbuttoned the shirt and slipped it off. Under it she wore a matching pair of lacy and very small underwear.

"That isn't what I meant," he said, but he didn't look away as she walked across the room to get her clothes off the back of a chair. She had a truly beautiful body. "Did Jeff put you up to this?"

"Yes, and he told me to get some camera equipment. My ex-boyfriend is a professional photographer."

"You have boyfriends but you did . . . did this?"

"Anything for my job." She was pulling on a pair of jeans. "Anyway, he knows someone who owns a camera store so he got in while the store was closed. Everything's in the dining room. And I went to a twenty-four-hour department store and bought us some camping gear. It's in the trunk of your car. Sure that's how you want to try to win her?"

"You can't go with us," he said.

"You're Jeff and we're lovers. There's no way you can go camping alone with another woman."

"I think it's time to start telling Chelsea the truth and drop this idiocy about who I am."

Pilar went to the bed and leaned close to him. "Sure you want to do that? Admit that you've lied to her? Or maybe you want to confess that all Jeff said about her was straight from *your* mouth. How long before she'll leave? Ten minutes? Five?"

"But this . . . you and me, will compound the lie."

"Tell her the truth when you're kissing her like you did me this morning." Standing up, she looked down at him. "I never would have guessed you had such passion in you. I thought all you cared about was the greater good. Nothing personal allowed."

"Passion is passion," he said as he got out of bed. He had on a T-shirt and boxers. "Great love transfers to anything. And good or bad, you are *not* going with us."

"Interesting philosophy," she said as she watched him walk to the bathroom. Smiling, she left the room and went into the kitchen.

Chelsea was standing at the dining table, which was covered with boxes full of high-end photography equipment. She'd opened most of them. "This card says all this is a gift from Eli. Did you bring it?"

"Yes," Pilar said. "He said he wanted to apologize to you for something. Mind if I ask what he did?"

"He said what I knew he thought. I deserved it, but it was nice when Jeff decked him."

Pilar's eyes opened wide. "He *hit* him?!"

"Oh, yes," Chelsea said. "It was rather nice. So you work for Eli but you're sleeping with Jeff?"

"Looks that way," Pilar said.

Chelsea held up a lens that was about eighteen inches long. "Do you know how to work any of this? It's been a long time since I held a camera."

"But Eli said you liked taking photos."

"I did when I was a kid. What's he like to work for?"

"Difficult," Pilar said. "He expects people to read his mind and know what he needs done. 'You handle it' is one of his favorite sayings."

"So he can think about larger things. What's he working on now?"

"Can't tell you," Pilar said. "It's all Top Secret. I don't even know half of it."

"Robots or computers that can think?"

Pilar laughed. "Looks like his interests haven't changed since he was a kid. Here, let me show you how to attach that to the camera."

After Eli showered and put on clean clothes, he hesitated before leaving the bedroom. What would Chelsea think of him after finding him in bed with another woman? Would she be angry? Jealous?

He took a breath before opening the door. Both women were sitting at the kitchen counter, plates of scrambled eggs and bacon before them, their hands full of cameras and lenses.

Pilar was speaking. "I've seen great photos taken from a hundred yards away with this lens. And this one does the opposite. It can magnify the eye of a butterfly."

"When I think of all the pictures I could have taken in my life, I feel regret. But maybe —" Chelsea looked up to see Eli/Jeff in the doorway. "Good morning," she said cheerfully. "Sleep well?" She glanced at Pilar. "Or did you get any sleep at all?" Her innuendo was clear.

"Some," he said, looking from one women to the other.

"We made breakfast," Chelsea said. "Come and join us. I like this woman. Maybe you should buy her a ring, something big and flashy."

Eli stood there for a moment, not sure how to address that. "I'm going out to mow the lawn. When I get back, we'll leave." He seemed about to say something else but didn't. He practically ran to the front door.

Pilar waited until they heard the lawn mower, then she turned to Chelsea. "You know, don't you?"

Chelsea looked up from the camera. "That Jeff is Eli? Of course. Can I assume that you're part of the effort he's making to win me?"

"I am, but I was Jeff's idea. I'm afraid I've shocked my boss."

"Tell me the truth about what it's like working for him."

"I'm tired of it," Pilar said. "There's so much data, so many secrets, and Eli keeps everything in his brain. He's such an introverted person. Only if Jeff is near him does he loosen up. Are you going to tell Eli that you know who he is?"

"Maybe." She looked back at the camera.

"So what's it like to kiss him? And how is he in bed?"

"He's an expert at kissing, but I wouldn't know about the bed from personal experience."

"Good," Chelsea said with a smile. "And just so you know, you ever touch him again, I will hurt you."

Pilar laughed. "I like that. He needs someone. Besides, I just met a guy. At three a.m. this morning I got a flat tire and some big, gorgeous man stopped and changed it for me. On my part it was instant attraction. I thought he was interested too, but when I thanked him, that was it. I figured he was probably married. But when I got here and took my suitcase out of the trunk, I saw that he'd stuck his business card on it. Lancaster Frazier. His family owns the local car dealership."

"Good," Chelsea said. "Stick with him and leave Eli to me."

"A deal," Pilar said, and they smiled at each other.

An hour later Chelsea and Eli were in the car together and driving out of Edilean.

"So where are we going?" she asked. "There are some beautiful resorts around here."

"We're going camping."

"Is this a joke?"

"No. Pilar bought the gear and it's in the trunk."

"I think you should know that I hate camping," she said.

"Do you? Eli never told me that. He told me everything else about you, but not that. Interesting. Well, it's only for one night and you need a place to use all the new camera equipment he bought you, don't you? Sunset over the mountains, that sort of thing. You can —"

"Cut it out, Eli! You very well know that I *hate* camping."

He glanced away from the road for a second to hide his smile. He was glad the charade was over. "Just one night," he said.

"I don't want to go camping!"

They argued all the way to the campground.

Chelsea stood to one side, her arms folded across her chest, and glared at Eli as he quickly put up the tent. Even though he'd agreed to stop at a huge mall and she'd spent hours shopping, she was still angry. He'd driven through a forest and down an old road, and stopped at a locked gate that had signs reading NO TRESPASSING, GOV-

ERNMENT PROPERTY, and KEEP OUT.

Chelsea wasn't surprised when Eli had a key to the lock. As he drove down a gravel path, she was too angry to speak to him. He *knew* how much she hated camping, so why did he bring her here? From the way he'd been kissing Pilar this morning she wondered if he was planning a seduction. But that could have been accomplished at a hotel.

He seemed to know the area well and came to a stop by a pristine lake. It was so clean that it looked as though no human had been near it in centuries.

For a moment, all Chelsea could do was stare at it, but when she glanced at Eli, she saw his little smile of triumph. "We could have come here on a day trip."

"And miss the sunset?" He was at the trunk and unpacking the gear.

She stood with her arms folded over her chest and glared at him while he set up the tent and spread two sleeping bags inside. When that was done, he got out two canvas chairs and a big blue cooler, then handed Chelsea a small backpack.

She stepped back, hands raised. "Oh, no you don't. I don't hike."

"Open it."

When she did, she saw that all the new

camera equipment Pilar had bought was inside.

Eli sat down on a chair. "Think you remember how to use it?"

"The last camera I used — other than my phone, that is — had film."

Smiling, Eli reached into the cooler. He knew that about her, which was why he'd requested a retro-looking camera that would remind her of ones she'd used as a child. He held up a beer. "Want one?"

"No, thanks." Chelsea sat down on a dry place and removed the pretty Nikon Df camera and an 18–200 lens and attached it, then pointed it toward the lake. For all her protests, she instinctively turned the band on the lens to zoom in and out, snapping at every stop.

Eli drank his beer and watched her as she fiddled with the silver knobs and clicked away. When he glanced away for a moment, she quickly turned the camera toward him and he heard the rapid fire of the shutter.

He looked back at her. "So why did your parents want you to visit me?"

Chelsea put the short macro lens on the camera and began adjusting it to photograph arrangements of pebbles. "I'd rather hear why you brought me to this place."

"To get you away from all the distractions.

You hungry?"

"Starving — as I have been since I first saw you. Ow!" She swatted at a mosquito. "Are there large animals around here?"

"Lots of them. Bears and deer. And a few dinosaurs. But the government has them in electrical cages. I hope they hold."

"If you're trying to be funny, you aren't succeeding."

Eli got more supplies from the car and began clearing an area to build a fire. "I want you to tell me about yourself. Hold still."

"What?"

"Don't move."

Chelsea froze her body into place but her face moved into a form that told him what she thought of him.

Slowly, Eli stepped around her, picked up a stick, and flicked a rather fat snake away from her. The two of them watched it slowly move away into the woods.

"I'm leaving," Chelsea said and went to the car. It was locked. She glared at him. "Give me the key."

"Nope," Eli said as he squatted down to tend to the fire. "I have you all to myself and that's where I plan to keep you."

"This is kidnapping."

"Probably," he said, unperturbed. "I had

Jeff get all the things needed to make s'mores. Remember how much you always liked them?"

"When I was eight. I'm grown-up now and I like adult things."

"Do we change?" Eli said as he looked at the fire. "Most of the time I feel like that kid who just wanted to save the world."

"Isn't that what you do?" Her tone was angry and she hadn't moved away from the car, but she knew Eli wasn't going to give in. If he was nothing else, he was stubborn. *Nothing* could make him get off course once he'd made up his mind.

Tentatively, and looking where she stepped, she went to the fire. "What are you working on now?"

"Can't tell you," he said as he put a marshmallow onto a piece of wire. "What about you? Thinking of starting a ladies' polo team?"

"For your information, I help Rodrigo with his business. It takes work to stay on the polo circuit."

"I bet," Eli mumbled. He handed her a toasted marshmallow. "You'd better tie your hair back or —" He broke off when a breeze caught her long hair and wrapped it around the sticky marshmallow.

Chelsea's anger showed on her face. "I

knew this would happen! What next? A family of bears shows up?"

"I hope not," Eli said cheerfully. "How about a sandwich?"

"Only if I can throw it at you."

He smiled at her. "Jeff sent a bucket of KFC. Sound good?"

"Fried?! You want me to eat something that has been *fried*?"

"It's your choice. You'd better get your camera equipment because it's starting to rain."

A fat drop hit Chelsea in the face. "I hate you, Eli Harcourt," she muttered as she grabbed her gear and zipped the lid of the case closed. She started toward the car but as the rain began to come down harder, Eli held the tent flap open.

Grimacing, she went inside.

A moment later Eli entered, a big red-and-white paper bucket in his arms and four bottles of beer.

It was two hours later that Eli looked at Chelsea, asleep in the down-filled bag, and smiled. It had taken work on his part but he'd managed to get her to use the container of wet wipes to remove all the makeup from her face. She'd pulled her hair back in a ponytail and had eaten heartily of the fried chicken.

And in between she'd talked. Over the years, he'd been able to deduce a lot about her life from photographs and tidbits he'd heard from people. But he couldn't know the whole truth from being on the outside. Was she truly in love with her latest boyfriend? Had she found something that occupied her life so she felt as she had when they were kids? Whenever one of their projects worked, they'd put ginger ale in champagne glasses and toasted, "To saving the world."

To Eli's mind, he was still trying to do that, but what was Chelsea doing now?

The rain pounding down on the little tent, the light from the lantern, the closeness, plus the food and beers, had made Chelsea open up as he doubted she had in years — or ever.

As he looked at her sleeping, he didn't lie to himself. His desires were all selfish. He still wanted her for himself. There was something about her that . . . well, made him feel as though the half of him that had been missing for so very long had been returned to him.

As he snuggled down in the bag beside her, he knew the camping trip had worked. Of course he knew she hated camping. One of his favorite memories of their childhood was when Chelsea had climbed a tree to avoid the "creatures of the night" as she called them. Since they'd been in her parents' backyard, there hadn't been a lot of danger.

But to Chelsea's mind, it had always been "one of the worst experiences of my life."

As he'd hoped, this camping trip, short as it was, had made her so angry, had so completely taken her out of her comfort zone, that she'd told him more than she would have if they'd been in some pretty hotel. He'd seen that she tended to dazzle everyone around her and he didn't want that.

Smiling, he went to sleep.

He awoke to a flood of complaints. It was as though their camaraderie of the night before had never happened.

"I can't appear in public like this!" she said as she tried to comb marshmallow out of her hair. As other women before her had discovered, it wasn't possible.

To Eli's dismay, Chelsea pulled a little case out of her big handbag and proceeded to darken her eyelids to the point where he hardly recognized her.

By the time they were ready to leave, it was strained between them.

■ ■ ■ ■

"Is there a bug in my hair?" Chelsea asked as they got out of the car. "Or maybe a thousand of them?"

Eli grit his teeth. "No bugs. No dirt. No mosquito bites anywhere. You are model perfect."

"That was mean," she said. They'd been driving back to Edilean and had stopped at an off-road diner to have lunch.

"Sorry," Eli said. "It's just that your incessant complaining is getting me down."

"I told you I didn't want to spend time in the woods. No bathroom, no —"

"No hairdresser," Eli said. "I get it. It's just that the Chelsea I knew —"

She threw up her hands. "Don't start on me again! The Chelsea you knew was a myth. Something you made up. I became an adult."

"And chose to dedicate your life to your hair," Eli said under his breath.

"I heard that. At least I *have* a life! All you do is stare at a computer screen and make up games that live out your fantasies. Where are the *real* women in your life?"

He turned to her. "Maybe they're dating the men who are no longer in *your* life."

Glaring at him, she stepped around an old car that was parked over the line. She wasn't surprised when the rusty bumper reached out and grabbed the side of her white jeans and held on. She heard the fabric rip. "Perfect," she muttered, then tried to unfasten it, but it stuck.

Eli was holding open the door of the restaurant for her. Not only had she remade her face as though she were about to go on a photo shoot, she'd put on some white outfit he was sure had a designer's name attached. When she kept fiddling with her clothes, he went back and stood there watching.

"You could help, you know."

He unsnapped the leather holder at his side, withdrew a big knife, and opened the blade. Before she could protest, he cut the fabric that was being held by the rusty metal.

"You just cut a hole in my pants. Do you have any idea how much these cost?"

Eli wasn't paying any attention to her. "This would never pass a road inspection."

"You mean my trousers?"

He gave her a look.

"Oh, yeah, right. The car." It really was a dreadful piece of junk. The body was covered in several shades of paint, all of it worn and dirty. The front windshield was cracked and the wipers had no blades. The passenger door was wired shut. "I wonder if it still runs."

"Unless it was towed here, it has to."

Chelsea walked around the vehicle. The trunk was tied down with burlap string and a taillight was missing. She looked around at the road. To the right was just forest. There were four cars besides Eli's parked in front of the diner, and the old junker stood out from the others for the sheer horribleness of it. But something about the car wasn't right. It was almost as though it were disposable, something to be discarded once a job was done. She looked at Eli. "You don't think there's a robbery going on, do you? Or maybe there's someone tied up in the trunk."

Eli started to say that was ridiculous, but he was glad to hear about anything besides her physical discomfort. He went to the back and used his knife to cut the string holding the trunk down. The lid sprang up. Inside was a lot of trash, old food containers, empty beer cans, and a threadbare tire — what would be expected in a junker. But oddly, spread over the tire was a snowy-white linen dinner napkin and on top of it was a briefcase.

"No one's tied up," Eli said.

Chelsea was staring at the contents. "That case is Stefano Ricci and they cost about three grand. Think it was stolen?"

Before Eli could answer, Chelsea reached for the case. "Keep watch," she said as she opened it and looked inside. There were some papers with Longacre Furniture written at the top, and a side pocket was full of business cards. As she took a few cards, something in the bottom caught her eye. Reaching inside, she pulled out a Rolex watch and held it up to the light. "This watch cost about forty-five grand."

Eli blinked a few times, then said, "Someone's coming."

Quickly, Chelsea put the watch back, closed the case, and set it on the cloth. Eli pulled the trunk lid down just as an older couple came out of the diner. They looked at Chelsea and Eli, then at the old car. Something must have looked suspicious because they hesitated.

"My wife caught her pants leg on the rusty bumper," Eli said as he quickly retied the trunk. Since the string had been cut, it was almost too short to tie.

Chelsea went around the side. "Look at this!" She showed off the hole Eli had cut.

"Cars like that shouldn't be allowed on the road."

"I don't think they are," the man said. He was smiling so sweetly at Chelsea that his wife pushed him in the other direction.

Eli went to stand by Chelsea and put his arm around her shoulders as they waved good-bye to the couple.

"Think they'll call the police?" Chelsea asked as the couple drove away.

"Because we looked like we were trying to rob a car that's not worth a hundred bucks? I don't think so."

They went inside the diner, and for a moment Chelsea stood looking around. There were eight tables and four booths along a wall. Only five of them had customers. Who owned the old car? she wondered. Who was hiding a multithousand-dollar watch and briefcase — and why?

Eli caught Chelsea's hand and pulled her to the left. There was another room that sold snacks and maps and toiletries. Grabbing a basket, he led her to the aisle of chips: blue, flavored, corn, potato. There seemed to be a half mile of them.

"Look," he said, "as you have said to me about a dozen times in the last twenty-four hours, you and I aren't kids anymore. Why that man has a couple of expensive items in his trunk is none of our business." He glared at her. "We are not Robin and Marian, certainly not Les Jeunes."

"Are you saying that with all your famous friends you can't find out anything about this man?"

Her words were a challenge to him, and after a moment he sighed. "All right, get something." He pulled out his phone.

"Who are you texting? Pilar?"

"Can't tell you. You don't have the security clearance. What's the guy's name on the business card you lifted?"

"You don't have my clearance to see it."

Eli looked at her in disbelief, but she just smiled. "Okay, I'm sending the license number to a cop friend of mine. He's not supposed to do this but he owes me. Now will you give me the name?"

"Let me type it in."

Reluctantly, he handed her his phone and she tapped in the name Orin Peterson, plus the name of the store she'd seen on the papers.

When a man came down the aisle, Eli and Chelsea grabbed bags of chips and left. Around the corner were drinks.

"What do we do now?" Chelsea whispered as she reached for bottles of water.

Eli put a six-pack of ginger ale in the

basket. "We just wait until Steve gets back to me."

"It's Saturday!" Chelsea said. "Nobody is at work today. Most people are out having fun. But *you* made me sleep on the ground last night so we're not. Did you think that all that outdoors was going to put me in the mood to . . . To what? Be seduced by you?"

He leaned toward her. "I thought maybe you'd be inspired to take some pictures. As for seducing you, I leave that to the sheriff's brother. He's a three. I'm a one, remember?"

When the other customer moved to their aisle, they went to the refrigerator case. Chelsea tossed containers of Greek yogurt in the basket Eli was holding, while he pulled out a couple of ready-made sandwiches.

"What does Sheriff Frazier have to do with any of this?" she asked.

"Not him, his brother, Lanny. The guy at the bar, remember? And how do you know Colin?"

"I don't," Chelsea snapped and moved to the candy aisle. "Wait a minute. Lanny? Is his real name Lancaster?"

"I have no idea," Eli said. "If you don't hurry up, whoever owns that car is going to leave. You do want to see who it is, don't you?"

"I'll get a table while you pay for this. And get a cooler and some ice."

As he watched her walk away, Eli was annoyed — but only for seconds. He was so very pleased that his plan had worked. The Chelsea who'd arrived at his house, the one with the scared look in her eyes, was beginning to disappear — thanks to him. He'd thought she needed a jolt, something that would shock her out of what she'd become, which was a woman who didn't laugh at truly idiotic things that were said about her hair and her eyes being pools of . . . whatever.

At one point last night he'd said, "My dad fell in love with Mom when they were alone in the woods."

Chelsea had narrowed her eyes at him. "I bet that adorable little town of Edilean is full of women who love the forest at night. I bet that town has pie-baking contests. You should do a search to find the winner and ask her to marry you."

Eli had tried to act as though her words displeased him, but he was glad he was finally seeing a glimpse of *his* Chelsea. This clean-faced Chelsea, chomping down on fried chicken, was interested in something

266

besides her hair — and her eye makeup and whether she'd gain an ounce from eating a hot dog. He didn't want her to go back to being the perfectly bland creature she'd been when she arrived.

As for the expensive briefcase and watch in the car, Eli didn't think it mattered much. There was probably a perfectly good explanation for it, but if it put light in Chelsea's eyes, then he'd help her. As long as she didn't get too outrageous and do something they could be prosecuted for, he would back her up.

By the time Eli had paid for their items and put them in the car, Chelsea was seated in a booth in the diner and pretending to read a menu. He took the bench across from her.

"The waitress hates me," she whispered over her menu. "I moved three times because I was near the wrong people, but I think I got it right this time." She lowered her voice. "It's the man we saw in the store. I think he's waiting for someone."

"I think I should remind you that you and I are the ones in the wrong here. We were illegally breaking and entering. I think we should —" When his phone buzzed, he looked at the message. "It's from Steve and there are no records on the guy. The car's had several owners, but nothing's been reported on it. The man and his vehicle are clean."

"They tell you anything about him personally?"

"No. Think we should look on his Facebook page?"

She narrowed her eyes at him. "I know you think this is silly. Maybe his Jag broke down and that car is the only loaner the garage had. Or maybe that's not his briefcase or his watch." She took a breath. "But I have a feeling and I *know* something is wrong!"

Eli was looking at the menu. "If I had a briefcase I cared enough about to keep it on a white cloth, I wouldn't put it in a tied-down trunk. I would carry it into a restaurant with me and not leave it in a place that can't be locked. And watches are to be worn."

When he looked up, Chelsea was smiling at him. "I agree."

The waitress came to ask for their orders.

"What kind of salads do you have?" Chelsea asked.

"Baby greens with fresh-caught Pacific wild salmon with balsamic dressing. We age the vinegar in our own kegs."

"That sounds great!" Chelsea said. "I'll

have that."

Eli rolled his eyes. "Two club sandwiches, mayo on the side for her."

"And what about you, darlin'?" the waitress asked Eli, smiling at him.

"All the mayo you can give me." He gave her a slow, lazy smile.

Smiling, she took the menus and left.

"What the hell was that about?" Chelsea asked. "Were you flirting with her?"

"Actually, I was. My Taggert cousins taught me how to do it. It was a struggle to learn, but I believe I mastered it. What do you think?"

"I think you should stick to who you truly are."

"By that I take it you mean a computer nerd? A guy with no life? To quote you: That guy was a myth."

"I liked him," Chelsea muttered.

"Sorry. Didn't hear you."

"I *liked* that guy," she said through her teeth. "He had an honesty about him that was admirable. He was —"

Chelsea broke off because a woman entered the diner. She was in her late thirties and had once been pretty, but now she looked tired and anxious. She was wearing jeans and a shirt, both of which looked as though they'd been washed too many times.

Her eyes searched the diner.

In the booth behind them, the man got up and went to her.

"Give me your phone," Eli said.

"I need it to —" Chelsea began, but at his look, she handed it to him and he began punching numbers into it. "What are you doing?"

"Watch them and listen," he replied and kept punching. "And remember to never carry an open bag."

They were too far away to hear what was being said, but the woman seemed to be upset about something. The man slipped his arm around her shoulders in a comforting way and she leaned her head against him.

"Whoever he is, she trusts him," Chelsea whispered. He was in his forties, maybe older, and the clothes he had on were cheap: a nearly worn-out cotton shirt, the cuffs frayed. His trousers were old and the belt's edges were nearly raw.

At first glance he looked like he was one step below the poverty line, but Chelsea noticed some other things. "His nails were done professionally."

Eli didn't look up from the phone. "How can you tell?"

She put her hand next to his. Eli's nails

were chipped and stained from garden work and last night's camping, while Chelsea's were a perfect oval, the cuticles evenly pushed back.

"Good observation," he said, then stood up. He started toward the door but when he got near the couple, he tripped and almost fell on the woman. "I'm so sorry," he said, his hand on her forearm as though to steady himself.

Only Chelsea saw him drop her cell phone into the woman's open-topped handbag.

Eli went back to the seat across from Chelsea, took his phone out of his pocket, and began more tapping.

"So help me, if you don't tell me what you're doing, I'm going to start screaming."

"I'm being the nerd you think I used to be. I may look different, but it's still me inside. There. Done." He moved to the bench beside her and held his phone up between them.

They heard a woman's voice through the phone: "It's been a long time."

"Too long," said the man. "How is Abby? She must be what now? Thirteen?"

"Fifteen," the woman answered.

Chelsea pulled back to look at Eli. "You set up the phones to eavesdrop?"

"I did. Learned how from some spies."

"Interesting coworkers you have," Chelsea muttered, then leaned her head close to his.

"How is Paula?" the woman asked so softly she could hardly be heard.

There was a pause, then the man's voice sounded near to tears. "Bad. She is . . . It's not long now."

"Orin, I'm so sorry. This is hard on you, I know."

There were some sniffs as though the man was trying not to cry. "When we met she was so very pretty. To me she'll always be that girl I knew in high school. But now she's —"

"You don't have to say it."

"But I need to," he said. "She's dying and it won't be long until the end. Grace, you're one of the few people who haven't deserted us. Your cards and emails have been a treasure to both of us."

"I'm glad I can help in some way," Grace said. "I feel responsible for so much of it."

"It's not your fault!" Orin said. "What Gil did to all of us wasn't your responsibility. You've suffered as much as Paula and I have. I'm just glad your daughter isn't ill like my dear wife is. The bills, the debt . . ." He started crying again.

"I'm so, so sorry," Grace said. "If I could help in some way, I would."

"The money from the sale of the house?"

"I gave you that," she said, her voice alarmed.

"Yes, yes, of course you did," Orin said. "I'm sorry. I spend my life with bedpans and IV tubes. It's hard for me to remember things. Yesterday . . . Oh, never mind. Tell me something happy about your life."

"I don't know what to say. Abby has grown into a very pretty young woman. She's rather shy, but one of the football players has taken a liking to her and he invited her to the prom. Next Saturday we're going to buy her a dress."

"How wonderful," Orin said, but there was a bit of an edge to his voice. "How different our lives are. Yesterday four big men came to repossess the mechanical bed Paula lies in. I can make it go up in the back so she can see out the window. It's one of the last pleasures she'll ever have. Oh, Grace! I was begging them to give me another week. Just one more week with the bed and I swore I could somehow raise the three hundred dollars they wanted. Paula was there in the room and she heard me pleading. She was so humiliated that there were tears running down her cheeks. She only weighs eighty-four pounds now, and to see those tears broke my heart. She —" He began to sob loudly.

"I'm so very sorry," Grace said.

"I know you are." His voice grew angry. "But sometimes, I remember what Gil did to Paula, me, and to you and sweet little Abby, and I want to . . . I want to . . ."

"I know," Grace said. "I do too, but he's gone now."

"Yes, he is. Did you ever find any of the money he took?"

"Not a penny of it. Orin, please. You know I sold everything and I shared it all with you. The house, the cars, the mountain cabin. And I signed the stores over to you."

"I know," he said. "It's my fault that I couldn't keep them running. But Gil had taken even the deposits on the orders. No one would send me furniture I couldn't pay for, so I had to give the deposits back to the customers from my own pocket. I owned three stores but I ended up massively in debt. Ironic, isn't it?"

"Yes," Grace said, her voice tired. "And that's why I gave you what I made from the sale of the house."

"Yes, of course you did."

"Orin, I need to get home. You said you had something you had to ask me."

"I just wondered if you'd ever found the papers from the last sale."

"No, I haven't. Everything is stored away and I work long hours. Besides, those things are hard for me to look at. I . . ." She trailed off.

"Gracie, I apologize. The papers were just an excuse to see you again. You and Abby are like family to Paula and me. I wish we'd been blessed with children. How wonderful it would be to think of buying a dress for a dance instead of facing creditors. Maybe after Paula is . . . is gone I can get a full-time job and help your little family some. Maybe I can give you —"

There was some noise of papers and keys as Grace rummaged in her bag. "Here!" she said. "That's the three hundred I was going to use to buy Abby a new dress. Take it and pay some on Paula's bed."

"I shouldn't, but since it isn't for me, I accept. Thank you, Grace, thank you very much. You don't know what this means to Paula and me. Three hundred dollars is like a million to us. And I promise that after she . . . she leaves this earth, I'll pay you back."

"Sure, of course," Grace said. "I have to go. Good luck to you both."

In the next second the woman was hurrying out of the diner.

"My phone!" Chelsea said.

"I'll get it." Eli got up and left behind the woman. Minutes later, he returned, put Chelsea's phone on the table, and sat down by her. In front of them were empty plates. While they'd been listening, their sandwiches had been delivered and they'd eaten them. Eli wondered if Chelsea noticed that she'd eaten the one with a lot of high-calorie mayonnaise on it.

"She was sitting in her car crying," Eli said — and Chelsea saw the blaze in his eyes. She well remembered that when they were children, Eli's father had constantly hit his mother up for money. The man didn't need the money, but it made him feel powerful to take it.

"He went to the restroom," Chelsea said, "so you can talk."

"I tapped on her car window and told her I thought I'd accidently dropped my phone in her bag. She gave it to me." Eli was looking at his hands, which were clasped on the table, his eyes downcast, a muscle in his jaw working.

Chelsea put her hand over his. Eli had always had the softest heart in the world, but then he'd had to watch his mother being misused. "Déjà vu?" she asked.

"Yeah," he said. "She reminds me of my mom and how my dad used to con her out of money. He did it just to see if he could. One time he told me that the only thing that really mattered in life was winning."

"You think that's what this guy Orin is doing?"

He looked at her. "Why doesn't he sell the watch and briefcase to pay his bills?"

"I wonder if they belong to him," Chelsea said. She lowered her voice. "Or maybe he's saving them to sell to pay his wife's funeral expenses. What do you think the husband, Gil, did?"

"Sounds like he embezzled company funds."

They looked up as the waitress returned. With a wink at Eli, she put two big slices of lemon meringue pie on the table, then left.

"Why did she bring these?" Chelsea asked, frowning.

"I asked for one. Guess she misheard and delivered two slices. She said they were homemade by a local widow who has two kids in college."

Chelsea knew that story would get Eli's attention. She took a bite. "Not bad." She took another one. "Is that guy back at the table yet?"

Eli leaned around the end of the booth, and when he turned back, his face showed disbelief. "He stole the tip. When I left I

277

saw three dollars and change by the tab, but it's gone now. I'll be back." He left the table.

It was about ten minutes before he returned and by that time Chelsea had finished her pie and started on Eli's. "He's in there shaving — and smiling. He looks like he won the lottery. He told me I was with a really hot chick and asked if we were having a good time in bed."

Chelsea's eyes widened. "What did you say?"

"All you have to do with men like him is smirk." He looked at her. When they were kids, they often understood each other's mind without words.

"Let's go," she said.

That's all Eli needed. He put money on the table — leaving a twenty-dollar tip — and they hurried out to the car. They were just inside when they saw the man Orin leave the diner and go to the ratty old clunker. For a moment he stood there looking around the parking lot.

Eli and Chelsea slid down in their seats so he couldn't see them. Their heads were close together.

"This is like when we were kids, always hiding from the adults," she said.

Eli was looking at her. "Except that I never

used to have an almost overwhelming urge to kiss you." He lifted up to look out the window. "He's looking at the trunk as though he's trying to decide whether or not to open it."

Chelsea was still down on the seat. "What did you say?"

Eli slid back down. "He didn't open it." He looked back up. "He's driving away. Mind if I follow him?"

Chelsea sat back up. "Of course not. What did you mean that you want to kiss me?"

Eli was looking in his mirror and backing the car out. "Just that. Primal instinct. Once I find out where he's going, I'll take you to back to Edilean."

"I want to know more about the kissing."

"No one taught you how?"

"Stop it! You know exactly what I mean."

Eli gave a little one-sided grin. "You're beautiful, but you know that. Truthfully, beauty in a woman has never been a serious turn-on to me. My cousins make fools of themselves over —"

"Eli!" she said.

"Right. You want to know about you and me. What's to say? Your interest in whatever is going on with ol' smiling Orin and generous Grace and her daughter, Abby, has sparked something in me. Made me want to kiss you."

"Oh," she said. They were back on the highway and Eli was easily moving from one lane to another as he followed the ratty old car. Sometimes Eli let it pass them, then he slowed and moved back behind him.

"Learn this technique from another spy?"

"No, from a cousin. My stepfather is part of the most extraordinary family. When a child is found to have a talent, they all work to cultivate that ability."

"They worked on you and numbers?"

"Not personally, but they got me into any schools I wanted. What I was good at was absorbing what the others could do. Uncle Adam taught me to row a boat, and Uncle Kit showed me how to appear invisible. Aunt Cale gave me lessons on plotting novels. A new branch of the family has been found on Nantucket and I look forward to learning from them — but Aunt Cale said they mostly seem to know about ghosts, which I don't believe in."

"And someone taught you how to follow cars?"

"Ranleigh. He's had some experience in evading the authorities and he taught me his technique. However, in retrospect, his first lesson was a bit harrowing. At the time, I didn't understand that it was real and that we were in an actual car chase trying to escape some drug dealers."

Chelsea's eyes widened. "I assume you two got away."

"We did. Look. He's turning off the highway." Eli slowed and allowed two other cars to get in front of him, then he followed the old car down the off-ramp.

They ended up in a neighborhood that was very run-down. Small houses with falling gutters, peeling paint, and yards full of weeds surrounding them. As Eli slowly drove down the street, some young men wearing black leather jackets and looking under the hood of a car stopped to frown at the silver-blue BMW.

"I think we're in the wrong car," Chelsea said and instinctively leaned away from the window. "Did you, by chance, learn self-defense moves from any of your cousins?"

"I took years of classes with them. And Todd taught me about firearms."

When she looked at him in alarm, Eli shrugged. As he drove down the streets, she stared at him. He had on a T-shirt that clung to his muscular body. His dark hair curled about the back of his neck. This is *not* what she'd thought Eli would grow up to look like — or that he'd know the things he did. Dancing, car chases, firearms. When they were kids and they'd talked of their futures, she'd imagined him emaciatedly thin, living alone on delivered pizza, and sitting in front of eight computer screens.

"There," Eli said and slowed the car. They saw Orin pull into a driveway of one of the worst weed-infested houses. The windows were dirty and two of them were cracked. The old car fit perfectly with the shoddy house.

Eli parked across the road under a big tree that looked to have been struck by lightning. A heavy branch hung dangerously low over the crumbling sidewalk, but it hid Eli's car.

They saw Orin get out of the car and go into the house.

"Wow!" Chelsea said. "If that's where he lives, he was telling the truth about being broke. Think his invalid wife is in there?"

"Only one way to find out. Stay here while I —"

"Like hell I will!" She had her hand on the door handle when he stopped her.

"If you so much as step out of this car, you'll create a crowd. Look at you! Hair, clothes, all that makeup. You look ready to be on the cover of *Vogue.*"

"Thanks. Maybe. You have a baseball cap?"

"In the bag in the back."

282

Chelsea got onto her knees and bent over to reach through the bucket seats to the back. She knew that doing so put her derriere close to Eli and she couldn't resist checking to see if he was looking. He was.

Smiling, she unzipped his duffel bag, rummaged inside, and pulled out a dirty T-shirt, an old baseball cap, and a package of wet wipes. She'd had a lot of experience in quickly making up for photo shoots so she could just as quickly unmake herself.

She sat back in the seat and quickly removed all her carefully applied cosmetics.

Eli was watching her. "Why did you go to all that trouble when it's just you and me?"

"To make you see that I've grown up. To impress you. To show you that I'm no longer a girl with skinned knees." As she spoke she pulled her designer shirt over her head, exposing her breasts in a lacy bra, and slipped on the big T-shirt. She wrapped her long hair in her hands and stowed it under the cap. "So?" she asked, turning to him. "How do I look?"

"Like an actual woman. I am impressed, and by the way, I liked your skinned knees." Bending, he kissed her cheek. "Right now I can see a bit of *my* Chelsea in you. Didn't think that was possible." He stepped outside.

Smiling, she got out of the other side and hurried after Eli as he crossed the street. "You know, if you had a tattoo or two, you could fit right in with these guys around here."

Without pausing, Eli lifted his shirtsleeve and twisted his arm about. On the underside of his upper arm was a tattoo of a symbol for infinity with some words in another language under it.

"What does it say?"

" 'Time has no meaning,' " he said. "I think. That was on a case and . . ." He shrugged, then began to run.

Chelsea was nearly as tall as he was so she could keep up with him. They went to an adjoining house and stopped behind a fence with missing boards. She started to pull off a board so they could get through.

"What are you doing?"

"Don't you want to go to the other house?"

"Yes, but not at the destruction of other people's property. We need to go over the fence." He put his hands together and cupped them. "Put your foot here."

"I like this better than sliding through splintered wood." She put her foot in his hand and he hoisted her up.

"Thought you would," he said, then gave

such a thrust upward that she almost went flying over the top. She caught on to the board ridge and tried to throw her leg over. Eli put one hand firmly on her round behind and pushed her up and over. "Too bad your polo-player boyfriend isn't here to give you a boost up."

She started to protest what he was saying but changed her mind. "Yeah, it is a shame, isn't it? A sleek, black pony to — oh!" She lost her grip and fell over the side.

Eli caught her.

In his arms, she looked at him. "How did you get over here so fast? I didn't see you climb."

"I walked around the front of the fence," he said as he put her down. "Come on, let's go."

Silently laughing, Chelsea ran behind him. It felt good to know that he had done all that just to get his hands on her backside. They went to the back of the house and looked inside. It was as barren and threadbare as the outside. They were squinting through the dirty window into the kitchen, with its old appliances, a few cheap cooking pans on the counter.

Beyond the kitchen was a small room with an old couch and chair.

Chelsea moved away from the window.

"Maybe she's in the bedroom."

"I doubt it. He's leaving," Eli said and they ran around to the front of the house. He crouched down behind a bush that hadn't been pruned in years and motioned for Chelsea to join him. She got between his legs and it seemed natural when his arms went around her shoulders.

They heard Orin open and close the front door, then lock it.

"He's leaving her in there alone?" Chelsea asked.

Eli put his hand out to part branches of the bush so they could see.

The man they saw didn't look like the same one who'd entered the house. He had on a suit of perfect fit, the dark fabric having no gloss to it. There was nothing synthetic in that material!

"London. Savile Row," Chelsea said. "Custom-made."

"Exactly," Eli replied.

They watched him open the car door.

"Come on, let's go," Chelsea said. "We have to follow him."

But Eli's arms held her in place. "Wait. I think I know what he's going to do."

They stayed hidden and watched as Orin reached inside the car, pushed a button, and the garage door went up. He drove the car inside, then there was silence.

"Think he's getting the briefcase and watch out?"

"Yes," Eli said. "What's that smell on your neck?"

"Charred wood, fried-chicken grease, and probably lemon from the pie you made me eat. I really need to take a shower."

"I think you should start a perfume line."

She turned her head toward him, his face close to hers.

But then they heard a car engine start and Eli stood up so fast Chelsea sat down hard in the dirt. By the time she got up, dusting off her behind, the car was gone. "What was it?" she asked.

"Mercedes E63."

"That's about a hundred grand," Chelsea said.

"Do you know the price of everything?" he asked over his shoulder as they ran across the potholed road to his car. Her silence made him suspicious. He stopped at the car door. "You didn't have to buy your boy-friends gifts, did you?"

"Of course not," she said and hurriedly got into the car.

As Eli got behind the wheel, he gave her a glance as he started the engine.

"Don't look at me that way. There were

extenuating circumstances. Besides, what's the difference? I'm sure you handed out a few sparkly stones to your girlfriends."

"No," he said. "Never."

"And that's why they're *past* girlfriends."

"And your boyfriends are present?"

"Okay!" Chelsea said. "So we're even."

"I always thought we were," he said in a way that made her smile.

As Eli drove along the highway, the black Mercedes not far ahead of them, Chelsea leaned back in the seat. They were heading west and as far as they could see, Orin wasn't planning to get off the expressway anytime soon.

"How's your mom?" Chelsea asked. "And all your sibs?"

"Mom is great." Eli's voice softened. "She and Frank are an excellent match. They agree about everything. Frank is so happy he turned a lot of his business over to Julian. Remember him?"

"Sure. I thought he was half in love with your mother."

"Probably, but he married a cousin of Frank's and they have three kids. And all my half siblings are fine. The oldest is nineteen now."

"Any of them as smart as you?"

Eli couldn't fully suppress a smile. "No. I'm the odd man out. But they never made fun of me. All of them are quite physical and they insisted that I participate with them. I had a hard time adjusting to that."

"It looks good on you," she said.

For a few seconds he took his eyes off the road to give her a glance up and down. "And your parents?"

"Very well. But not long after we left Colorado Dad had a mild heart attack. It changed him. He gave up trying to have the biggest and the best. Mom and I were glad as we got to see him more."

"Did I hear that you didn't finish college?"

"So you did snoop about me?" When he didn't reply, she shrugged. "I was 'discovered.' You know, playing volleyball on the beach and some guy was taking photos and the next thing I knew, a New York modeling agency was calling me. I was so young and it was all so dazzling that I said yes without saying the actual words. It all just sort of happened."

"How long did it last?"

"I don't remember." She looked out the window. She wasn't about to tell him of the haze of drugs and booze and men. Sometimes it seemed that one day she'd been playing volleyball on a beach, wearing her new red bikini and trying to get the attention of some basketball player, and the next she was being sent down a runway in Milan. And *all* of it seemed like just a week ago.

Eli reached across the console and took her hand in his. "It's okay now. You're with me."

"What does that mean? You're going to give up your government job and stay home with me? We'll have a couple of kids? I'll become a housewife?"

Eli pulled his hand away.

"I'm sorry," Chelsea said. "That didn't come out the way I meant. It's just that . . . Well, I . . ."

"You have a low boredom threshold," he said. "You always did. You loved the excitement when we were kids. The football players used to threaten me about you. Why would a hot babe like you run around with a skinny nerd like me?"

"Did they? I never knew that. They didn't bully you, did they?"

"Oh, yeah. But after Frank married Mom they only did it one more time. After I came home one day with a couple of black eyes and a cracked collarbone, a gang of my big Taggert cousins went to school and talked to a whole lot of people."

Chelsea didn't laugh. "Why didn't you tell

me about being bullied?"

"You were what kept me sane. Look! He's getting off the highway."

They left the expressway and drove for another thirty minutes and began to see signs for a lake.

"Interesting," Eli said, looking at the GPS. "This place seems to be equidistant between Richmond and Charlottesville."

"The cities where the two Longacre Furniture stores are," Chelsea said. While Eli drove, she'd looked them up on her phone. From what she could see, the stores were big, carried high-end merchandise, and were thriving. "Too bad Orin sold the stores," she told Eli.

As the road narrowed and the traffic thinned out, Eli had to stay far behind the black Mercedes. "I wish I could have rented a more anonymous car. This one is too recognizable."

"We can do that tomorrow."

He looked at her sharply. "I thought you'd want to go back to Edilean or at least to the nearest airport. Rural Virginia isn't exactly exciting, certainly not like a polo field."

"Cut it out!" she said. "He's turning down that road."

Eli held back as the black car went down a narrow road.

"He'll see us," Chelsea said. "He'll recognize —" She broke off when Eli backed up and returned to the main road. When she glanced at the GPS screen, she knew what he was doing. The map showed a big lake that had fingers of water. There were several carefully planned lanes following the lake, with wider roads leading to them. They were heading into a planned community, all of it laid out for easy access.

"Take a right," Chelsea said.

Eli glanced at the map, then looked at her in question.

"Trust me, I know what I'm doing. Go right. There are always service roads in these places, but they won't show up on the GPS."

He followed her directions and within minutes they were on a gravel road that led them beside a huge house. It was a perfect McMansion, with great windows that looked out at the pretty lake.

Chelsea got out of the car before Eli turned off the engine.

"Wait a minute!" He caught her arm. "We're trespassing."

"We're a young married couple looking to buy. Besides, it's too early for anyone to open their lake house." She was looking across the water. "Is that Orin's car? I wish I had binoculars."

Eli went to his car, got a pair, and handed them to her.

"Part of your spy kit?" When he didn't answer, she looked at him and Eli shrugged. "You don't carry a firearm, do you?"

"Of course not," Eli said, but he was grinning.

"I think you and I should have a talk about your life since you began working for the government."

"Nothing to tell. You know us nerds, we just sit at a desk all day and look at computer screens."

She put the binoculars up to her eyes. "Last time you went out of the country, where did you go?"

"Antwerp."

"Ever been shot?"

"Just twice."

She could hear the amusement in his voice. "That all?" Chelsea said. "How often do you see the president?"

"Whenever he calls me to come."

"Like his kids?"

Eli laughed. "I've helped a bit with homework. Isn't that ol' Orin?"

Across the wide finger of the lake was a big house, mostly made of stone, with tall windows looking out over the water. There was a sprawling patio with furniture, a big barbecue pit at one end. A man in a white shirt and black trousers came out and stood there looking at the water.

"Is that a drink in his hand?" Eli asked.

"Yes." Chelsea lowered the binoculars. "Good eyesight. Open the trunk, would you? I think I'll get some of that camera equipment you got for me."

"I wanted it used for sunsets but you're going to use it for spy work."

She ignored his comment. As she pulled a camera and a 400 mm lens out of the back, she said, "What happened to your glasses?"

"I had a new type of eye surgery. It should be on the market in the next five or six years, but Russia wants to get a cut every time the surgery is performed anywhere in the world. That request is being fought."

"So you're one of the first to try it out?"

"It's hard to wear glasses when you're running away from bullets."

She walked back toward the lake. "You're joking, right? You haven't really —"

"Who is that?"

They watched as a woman came out of the house. She had on dark trousers and a blue blouse and she too held a drink. She was short and plump in a curvy, appealing way. Orin put his arm around her waist and pulled her close to his side.

Chelsea propped the camera on a stone planter and began shooting. "What do you think? Mistress or wife?"

"My guess is wife. And if she is, then he still owns the two furniture stores."

"How did you deduce that?" she asked, then put up her hand. "Wait. Don't tell me. The stores . . ." Her head came up. "This house is halfway between both stores so he can get to them. And if he's here in what is usually a resort house so early in the season, it's because he has to be here year-round to take care of the stores. Orin Peterson may have managers, but it looks like he's a hands-on businessman."

Smiling, Eli took the binoculars from around her neck and looked. "That's a wife. She's pointing at the paving and he's nodding, which means that she's nagging him to *do* something."

"And since he hasn't done it, that means he's a husband."

As they were laughing, Orin began waltzing his wife around the patio, then led her into the house.

"He's using the distraction technique to get out of doing it," Chelsea said. "My father is a master at it." She looked at Eli. "Now what do we do?"

"I'm going to take you back to Edilean.

We can get there in a few hours and you can have a good night's sleep. Tomorrow Pilar can make reservations for you to go anywhere in the world." He held the car door open for her.

But Chelsea sat down on the side of a stone planter, the camera on her lap. "What he's doing is serious, isn't it?"

"Maybe. I think that after I drop you off, I'll run some deep background checks on him. Come on, the faster we get back, the sooner the guys can start on this."

Chelsea didn't move but looked across the water to Orin's big stone house. There was a nice motorboat beside a little dock and a cute little canoe beside that. It looked like it was possible that he and his wife *did* have children.

"He took three hundred dollars from her," she said, her voice barely a whisper.

Behind her, Eli closed his eyes, and for a moment his hand tightened on the car-door handle. He walked to stand behind Chelsea. "I'll have a government check sent to her. It'll say tax refund on it."

"You can do that?"

"Sure," Eli said. "Now I think we should go. There's not much daylight left. Hey! We didn't eat what we bought. Did I tell you about the trouble I had with that cooler?

It's actually a rather funny story. I —"

She looked up at him. "You're going to come back, aren't you?"

"Back *here*?" He looked out at the lake. "It is rather pretty. I saw signs that say there's a little town nearby. But I know small towns bore you. Tell you what. We'll go back to Edilean, pack some of your clothes, then we can return to this area. I bet there are resorts around here with massages and . . . and the other things girls like you like."

"Girls like me," Chelsea whispered.

"That wasn't a put-down. I just meant pretty girls. Beautiful ones. Like you. With hair and all that."

When she stood up, she looked him in the eyes for a moment, then she went to the car and got in.

Letting out a sigh of relief, Eli got into the driver's seat. "We'll be there very soon," he said as he backed the car onto the little road. "Tell me about your modeling career. It sounds really interesting. My cousin Ranleigh tried that but he caused too much chaos so he left. What do you think —"

"Go left," Chelsea said.

"Edilean is to the right."

"We're not going there." When she looked at him, her eyes held no humor. "We are going to drive into the town and get a couple of hotel rooms. I think that over the years that odious man has cheated Grace and her daughter, Abby, out of a lot of money. Tomorrow we're going to start finding out if that's true or not."

"Chelsea, this is not any of our business. I told you that I have friends who are law enforcement agents. My cousin Todd —"

"They would have to get search warrants and to get them, they'd need more proof than an illegally heard conversation. By the time an arrest could be made, Orin will be living where he can't be extradited. You know all this and it's why you're planning to return without me."

Eli's eyes nearly shot fire — a look she'd never seen before. "We aren't kids anymore, and yeah, it looks like there's a lot of money involved in this." He turned the car toward Edilean.

Chelsea didn't say a word.

He drove half a mile, then pulled over to the side. "You plan to return by yourself, don't you?"

She took a moment before answering. "Eli, I don't expect you to understand this, but I have to do this. I *need* to do it! I . . ." She couldn't go on, but she knew something was happening to her. With every minute she spent with Eli, she felt herself regressing, going back to who she once was, to someone she barely remembered. "I need this," she repeated, this time in a whisper.

Eli made a U-turn and headed toward the nearby town. "No separate rooms. You're not getting out of my sight."

"Poor me," Chelsea said.

In spite of his fear of where this could lead, Eli gave a bit of a smile even as he shook his head in frustration.

9

Chelsea stood in the doorway of the B-and-B room and looked around. The old house was cute and homey. There had been fresh muffins on the counter when Eli checked them in. The room had two big beds covered in spreads with blue and white flowers on them. Homemade quilts were at the foot of each bed.

Eli stepped past her to set their bags on the floor. They hadn't spoken much since he'd turned the car around, and it was beginning to annoy her.

"How long are you going to be angry at me?" she asked.

"Until you swear that you're going to go home and not think of this ever again."

"I don't have a home!" she blurted out, then was shocked that she'd said that. She turned away so he couldn't see her face as she was close to tears.

But Eli put his hands on her shoulders

and turned her around to look at him. When she kept looking away, he pulled her into his arms and held her.

"I don't know what's wrong with me," she said, her face against his shoulder. "Ever since we went" — she swallowed — "camping, I don't seem able to think clearly. It's like I'm not myself." She pulled back to look at him. "You're doing something to me, but I don't know what it is."

The light in the room was quite dim. Atmospheric, really. Not quite candlelight, but almost. She was very aware that they were alone in a bedroom, and she remembered Pilar saying what a good kisser Eli was. And that he'd said he wanted to kiss her.

She lifted on her toes a bit and put her lips up for him to kiss.

But Eli didn't take the opportunity. Instead, he stepped away, no longer touching her. "You're right. Your hair is a mess. I think it has tree sap in it and some twigs. Shampoo won't get that out. How about if you sit down and I brush it out before you shower?"

"Sure," Chelsea said, frowning.

"First, I —" He nodded toward the bathroom and hurried inside and shut the door. He put his hands on the counter and his head down. Refusing Chelsea's offer had been difficult. Actually, nearly impossible. But in an instant, he'd seen the consequences of such an action. He would never have been able to stop at one kiss. The two of them alone in the pretty room, the beds crying out to be used . . . No, he wouldn't stop.

And then what? he thought. He would become one of Chelsea's men? Just one of a list of them who she'd used, then left?

No. He wanted a great deal more than that from her.

Tomorrow, he thought, he'd step out of this thing they'd accidentally become involved in and they'd return to Edilean — Then what? How did he win her?

When he left the bathroom, Chelsea was unpacking her bag.

"I swear everything in here smells of burnt wood."

"My favorite. Come on, sit down and let me fix your hair."

She sat on a little bench, her back to him, and he began to try to disentangle the rat's nest her hair had become. He'd never done anything like that before and he found the softness of her hair erotic. It seemed to wrap around his arms. There were curls at the end and they held on to his wrists, as though they were pulling him to her.

"You do like girls, don't you?" she asked.

Eli paused as he tried to remove a piece of tree bark. If she'd turned around, she would have seen how much he "liked" girls. "I do, yes," he said.

"But just not me. Except you said you wanted to kiss me."

"I don't want to be Rodrigo or Clive or Thomas or Nigel. If we become more than just friends, I want you to see *me,* not just a body that's been built by sweating in a gym."

She ignored the last part of what he said. "So you have kept track of me to the point where you know the names of my exes. You didn't just discard me because I quit writing letters."

"No, I didn't." He was smiling. She'd managed to twist what he'd said to being about his never-ending . . . What? Obsession with her? "There, I think I got most of it out."

Chelsea stood up and turned toward him. With her eyes on his, she pulled her shirt over her head, exposing her breasts, encased in a very pretty, very skimpy bra. "Eli," she said, "trust me, I know who you are."

She picked up her toiletries bag and went into the bathroom.

Eli stood still for a moment. As far as he

could tell, he hadn't won even one round with her.

When he heard the shower water running, he got his phone and stepped outside to call his father.

"Eli!" Frank said. "How are you doing? How's Chelsea? Where are you?"

"Dad, I need you to do something for me."

"Anything," Frank said, then began to make notes while Eli told him all he knew.

"I don't know what this guy is doing, but I'm pretty sure it's illegal," Eli said.

"Anybody who'd go through that much subterfuge of different houses and cars should be looked into. What I would like to know about is the woman Grace's husband."

"Me too. I thought I'd see what I can find out about him."

"Can you use any of your government sources from there?"

"Yes," Eli said. "I can key into most of them."

When Eli stopped talking, Frank knew his son hadn't called only about some guy's shady business practices. "I talked to Jeff and he said you took Chelsea camping. Did you forget what happened when she was a kid?"

Eli couldn't repress a laugh. "I carry the

photo with me. It's one of my favorites."
After their first campout, Eli had crawled
out of his tent to what looked like a bear
cub. Chelsea was on her stomach on a big
branch, arms and legs hanging down. Eli
had used Chelsea's camera to take a picture
before he ran to get her dad to get her down.

"I guess you had a reason for taking her
camping a second time," Frank said.

The question unleashed something in Eli.
Since they'd met, he and Frank had been
kindred souls. "Dad, you should have seen
her when she showed up at my house in
Edilean. She had on so much makeup I
hardly recognized her. Her eyelids were
nearly black and she had on clothes so tight
they were like tourniquets."

"Some men like that," Frank said.

"I like *my* Chelsea better than who she
was pretending to be."

"So what did you do when you saw her?"

"Actually, I pretended to be Jeff."

"Ah," Frank said.

"Right. The truth is that it hurt that she
didn't recognize me."

Frank was smiling, proud of what his son
was saying. Like Eli, he'd kept track of
Chelsea over the years. She'd been on three
magazine covers before she dropped out of
the fashion world. The string of boyfriends

she'd had afterward had dismayed him, and he'd tried to get Eli to go to her. "She's not ready to be rescued yet," Eli had said, but he wouldn't elaborate on his meaning.

"So you took her camping?" Frank asked.

"Yeah." Eli was nearly laughing. "She really hated it! It was just one night, but I got her to take that black stuff off her eyes, and she pulled her hair back. She looked great. Like a real person. And she talked to me. I thought things were going well, but then the next morning she started complaining again, then we overheard this man and . . ." He trailed off.

"You're afraid for her to get involved," Frank said.

"Yes."

"Good. I think you should leave this to me. I'll have my people look into it. If he's pulling a scam like this in his business, I doubt if he's honest with the IRS. You and Chelsea should go back to Edilean and spend some time together. Take her shopping. Women love it when you go shopping with them."

"Is that why Mom buys all your clothes for you? Why she oversees the tailor when you have suits made? Why she —"

"I get your point," Frank said. "Maybe shopping is too much to deal with. You don't want Chelsea involved with this lying scumbag, but I don't want *you* around him either. Two times I've had the authorities at my door saying you'd been injured. That's my lifetime limit."

"Both times it was my own fault. I shouldn't have —"

"Stuck your nose where it didn't belong!" Frank said. "I've heard all that. I want you to promise me to get out of there. Both of you! Got it?"

"Yeah, I do." Eli hesitated. "Dad, do you have any hints on how to make a woman love you? I mean, really and truly *love* you?"

"Lord no!" Frank said with feeling. "If it hadn't been for two interfering kids, today I'd be —" He let out his breath. "I don't even want to think where I'd be. But it sounds like you're doing well. You and Chelsea used to be master sleuths. Too bad you can't find something less dangerous to fix than a crooked businessman."

"You know, Dad, I think you might have come up with a good idea. I wonder what girls today wear to a prom?"

"From what I've seen, they dress like thirty-year-old hookers. But I think Chelsea would be able to answer that better than me."

"I agree. I have to go. Tell Mom and the

kids I love them. And you," Eli added.

"Yeah," Frank said. "Love doesn't cover it. I owe you and Chelsea my life. Good night."

When Eli got back into the room, Chelsea was sitting on a bed, her face clean and shiny, wrapped up in a bathrobe, her long legs bare and a computer open on her lap.

He knew he'd never seen anything more delicious-looking in his life.

"Was that a call to Frank, your mom, Pilar, or Jeff?" she asked without looking up. "Or was it the prez?"

"Dad. Jeff seems to have a girlfriend and the president is busy. Pilar is —"

"Is sick of you."

"Is she?" Eli asked. "Is that why you weren't jealous of her? By the way, Jeff fixed all that up, not me."

"Of course he did. You have the hot body but a lack of interest in the mating ritual, while Jeff is the opposite."

What she'd said was so ridiculous that Eli laughed. "You and Jeff would get along well. He wants to do a soul exchange and put himself in my body. But of course my body would deteriorate without consistent exercise — which he hates. Move over."

He sat down on the bed beside her and leaned over to look at the screen.

"You should take a shower," she said. "You smell like smoke."

"What artificial scent does your polo player use?"

"I'm not telling. Look what I found." She turned the screen around. There was a newspaper article about the suicide of Gilbert Ridgeway, one of the partners of Longacre Furniture.

"Suicide?" Eli was frowning. He took the computer from her and began typing. In minutes he'd brought up an official coroner's report on Gil Ridgeway.

"You have access to files like this?"

"Yes. He hanged himself and his wife, Grace, found him." Eli set the computer back on Chelsea's lap, put his arms behind his head, and leaned against the headboard.

"Out with it," she said. "I can see the wheels in your brain working. What did you and your dad talk about?"

"Besides you? He's going to have some people look into the finances of the two furniture stores."

"And the other businesses?"

He looked at her.

"You're not the only one who can use a computer. Longacre Furniture is a subsidiary of a larger corporation. They own several businesses around Virginia. A car wash, a couple of motels that look pretty sleazy, six liquor stores, and a few other things. And poor Orin and his dying wife — you know, the babe in the blue blouse — own an apartment in New York on Central Park South and a house in the Caymans."

As she spoke, Eli's eyes grew wider. "You didn't find this on Google."

Chelsea shrugged. "I have contacts too. So what are we going to do about this?"

"Nothing. Dad will take care of it through legal channels. It's not for you and me."

"Okay," she said as she put the laptop on the bed, and started to get off it.

Eli caught her arm but Chelsea didn't look at him. "I thought maybe we might go back to Edilean and see if we could help Grace and Abby."

"By doing what?"

"I don't know, but maybe Robin and Marian could figure out how to get a dress for Abby. You have any idea what teenage girls wear to a prom?"

Chelsea turned halfway toward him. "What about Grace?"

"I bet we could find her a better job than whatever she has now."

"Maybe when Pilar quits, Grace could take over."

"That would take a year or more of security clearance. And if her husband committed suicide because he was involved in something illegal, and his business partner is a criminal, that's going to take even longer."

Chelsea had turned all the way around and was glaring at him. "Do you have any romance in you at all? Or have you become some muscle-bound, soulless machine?"

Eli didn't reply to that, but slowly sat up straight, then reached out and pulled her down to the bed. Before she could reply, he put his lips on hers.

He'd meant it to be a sort of demonstration kiss, but the moment his lips touched hers, he knew this was what he'd been waiting for. This woman was the reason he'd paid little attention to other women.

Her mouth opened under his, her arms went around his neck and pulled him closer. Their tongues met. Years of longing, of understanding, of memories, flowed through them.

It was Chelsea who broke away, turning her head to one side. "Go," she whispered. "Leave me."

Eli rolled off the bed and got in the shower — a cold one.

The next morning, by the time they'd had

breakfast and packed — and Chelsea had taken a second shower and blow-dried her hair — it was late when they got to the furniture store. Frank had texted one word, RICHMOND, and that's where they went.

They had to park at the back of the big lot because the rest of it was full of vehicles with FBI and IRS painted on the side. Men and women in lettered jackets were carrying file boxes and computers out of the furniture store.

"I think we should go," Eli said. "We don't want to get mixed up in this."

"Your dad certainly knows the right people. Do you think they arrested Orin?"

"They can't until they find some evidence against him."

She looked at Eli. "Did you tell your dad that we have proof of what he's been doing? There's the old house and the beat-up old car and how he took three hundred dollars from his former business partner's wife."

"Not one of those is a criminal activity. A jury would see him as a sleaze but you can't put a man in jail for that."

"So Grace is on her own?"

" 'Fraid so," Eli said. "Let's go back and see what we can do to help her. I bet Abby could use a makeover. You could put black stuff on her eyelids."

Chelsea glared at him. "Why are you trying to get me away from here?" Before he
could answer, she hurried forward, making
her way toward the storefront.

Eli went after her, but he was hindered by
half a dozen men who stopped to stare at
Chelsea. But then, she was smiling her way
through the crowd so that no one questioned her.

A few feet from the front door, she
stopped beside an IRS van and stood there
watching.

Just as Eli feared, Orin Peterson was there
talking to two men wearing FBI jackets. He
had on one of his hand-tailored suits and
looked very different from the down-and-
outer they'd seen in the diner.

"He's not being arrested," Chelsea said
when Eli got to her. "And he doesn't look
afraid at all."

"My guess is that if he has incriminating
evidence, it's hidden. Or maybe there is
none. Maybe he only lies to his ex-partner's
wife. Maybe she turned him down and he
wants to get her back." Eli was standing
behind Chelsea and put his hands on her
shoulders. "We need to go."

"What are you —" She broke off because
Orin looked up and saw the two of them.
At first his face showed only appreciation

for a pretty girl, but when he saw Eli, recognition came to him.

For a split second, his dark eyes glowed with such hatred that it sent chills through both of them.

"He's guilty," Chelsea said.

Eli's hands clamped down on her shoulders and led her away. At the end of the van, he took her hand firmly in his.

"What a great poker player he must be," Chelsea was saying even as Eli pulled her at a near run. "He did that act with poor Grace with such sincerity. His tears! Remember them?"

Eli nearly pushed her into the passenger seat, got in the other side, and drove out of the parking lot.

"Why do you think he went to such an elaborate scam with that old house and the story of his dying wife? What does he want from Grace? Or what is he afraid she'll find out?"

"I have no idea," Eli said. "I think we need to stay out of this. You can get a dress for the girl and send it to her."

She looked at him. "So what's spooked you?"

"A gut feeling," Eli said. "And the look in that man's eyes when he recognized us. He knows we had something to do with this raid."

She looked back at the road. "I'm sure you're right. You're going to let law enforcement handle it, aren't you?"

"Yes," Eli said. "I am."

"That's a good plan. I'll find a dress for Abby and send it as a gift from Orin."

"Better not use his name. I'll find out more about Grace and we'll send it from another relative. That will be nice for her."

"That sounds wonderful," Chelsea said, her voice rising. "Mind if I buy her some jewelry and shoes too? I mean, after all, that's all I'm good for, isn't it? To paint eyelids black and pick out clothes. That's what I do. You're the brains while I'm only good for dressing people."

"And hair," Eli said softly.

Chelsea's face was red with her anger. "What?!"

"You're good with hair too. Yours is clean and shiny today. It's really pretty."

"You're a bastard."

"Actually, I'm not. I have two fathers. There was a time when they fought over me, but Frank won."

Chelsea was looking out the side window. Her anger was fading. Unlike every other man she knew, Eli always knew how to calm her down. It didn't take a genius to see that he was trying to protect her from what could possibly be a dangerous situation.

"Why did you contact me?" she asked, all trace of anger gone.

He took a moment before answering. "I saw a photo of you online. You were with your polo boyfriend. Two young women were pouring champagne over his head and you were in the background. You were smiling but I knew you weren't happy."

"You felt sorry for me?"

"I thought that maybe it was time that you'd give *me* a chance."

Chelsea sighed. "Are you saying you were hoping I was ready to get married, have a couple of kids, and stay home to wait for you to return? Would I be one of those wives who makes sure you packed clean socks when you fly off to Antwerp?"

"I didn't think that far ahead."

"Eli," Chelsea said, "I'm not like that. Do you know the truth of why I stopped writing you?"

"No," he said and the word caught in his throat. That had been a long time ago, but the pain was still there.

"Right after my dad said we were going to leave the state, leave *you,* I thought my heart would break. But then one day I showed up at your house unexpectedly. Your mom let me in and said you were in the nursery. I saw you there holding the new baby and Frank was leaning over both of you. There was such love and . . . I don't know what — contentment, maybe — in that room that it scared me. I left without telling you I'd been there."

She looked at Eli. "I'm not like your mom. Miranda never wanted more than a family and a home. All of you are her whole life. But that's not me."

"So what do you want?" Eli asked.

Chelsea let her head fall back against the seat. His tone was saying that he'd try to give her whatever it was that she wanted. But she knew enough about life to know that wouldn't work. "I don't know," she said at last. "I'm still trying to figure that out."

"More race-car drivers?" There was no anger in his voice, just a deep desire to know.

She gave a little laugh. "I'm not sure that what the man does matters. It's taken me a long time to learn that. Would it make any sense to say that I'll know it when I find it?"

"I guess so."

When she looked at him, she saw the sadness in his eyes. "What if I said that if you'd quit your government job, I'd agree to spend my life with you? We could see the world. Would you do it?"

"No," Eli said, "because then you might be happy but I'd be miserable. It wouldn't work."

"I like your honesty." She reached through to the backseat. "Does your laptop have an internet connection even on the road?"

"Of course."

"You have some special hookup that the rest of us don't have?"

When he glanced at her, the sadness was gone from his eyes. "I do. It's from Japan and it's going to make a fortune. Planning to find Grace and Abby?"

"Yes." She started tapping keys. "Eli, just so you know, I may not be in this for the picket fence and family dinner on Sunday, but sex is fine with me."

"Nice to hear," he said, but he made no further comment.

When they got back to Edilean, it was growing dark and Eli drove past the house. He parked some distance away, under some trees.

"Why aren't you using your driveway?" Chelsea asked.

"I want you to stay here in the car and wait for me."

To Chelsea's astonishment, he leaned across her, opened the glove box, pressed a button, and a little tray fell down. There was a pistol attached to it. Eli took the firearm and tucked it into the waistband of his jeans.

"Someone's in the house," he said.

"You think it might be something to do with Orin the thief?" When she looked at the house, she saw no evidence that anyone was inside. All the windows were dark.

"I have no idea, but I'm not taking any chances." He got out of the car, then leaned back to her. "If I flick the lights three times, then it's safe to come in." He closed the car door soundlessly and slipped away through the trees and shrubs.

Chelsea stayed in the car, her eyes wide. *This* was a side of Eli she'd never seen before!

In just minutes the lights flashed three times, then stayed on. The house was lit up like daylight.

Feeling a bit shocked from seeing Eli with a gun in his hand, she walked back to the house and opened the back door.

The first thing she saw was Eli and his assistant, Jeff, in a quiet argument. Jeff seemed to be talking rapidly, and by his gestures he was apologizing. Not far from them was a pretty young woman who seemed to be in the process of refastening her clothes.

On the end of the granite kitchen countertop were two pistols. She recognized the smaller black one as Eli's, but whose was the silver one?

She got her answer when the woman picked it up.

It looked like Jeff and his girlfriend had been making out on the living room sofa. And everyone was either angry or embarrassed.

Chelsea decided to step in before emotions took over. "Hi, I'm Chelsea," she said loudly. "Is there any food in the house? Eli nearly starved me on the way here so maybe we could find something to eat. Or order carryout?"

"I have to go," the woman said, her face red. "I need to —"

Chelsea put her arm around the woman's shoulders. "You can't leave now. I've had days of Eli's morose company and I need some girl time. What are you that you carry a gun?"

"Deputy sheriff." From her look, she seemed to be worried that she might be fired after tonight.

"How wonderful," Chelsea said as she ushered her toward the refrigerator. "Look in there and see what you can find. And Jeff, do you know where the plates are? Of course you do. You probably bought them. Heaven knows Eli wouldn't bother with them. He used to use the leaves from my mother's elephant-ear plants for plates."

They were all standing there staring at her. "Eli! Get some wine. No, make that champagne. You do have some, don't you?"

Eli's face changed from glowering to twinkling eyes. As Chelsea walked past him, she said under her breath, "Put your gun away and lighten up!"

Thirty minutes later the four of them were sitting in the breakfast room around a table loaded with food and drink. Chelsea had found out that the deputy's name was Melissa.

"I thought the two of them were going to kill each other," Jeff was saying as he waved his glass around. "There Lissa and I were, snuggled down on the couch, and suddenly this big, dark man is holding a gun over us."

Melissa was smiling but Chelsea could see that she was still embarrassed over the whole thing. Chelsea decided to change the subject. "Tell me about Lanny Frazier. Does he often change the tires of ladies in distress?"

"He has done. How do you know that?"

Melissa asked.

The men stayed quiet while the two women figured things out. Pilar and the sheriff's brother, Lanny, had been out on a date — one that lasted all night.

"What's he look like?" Chelsea asked.

"He's the number three in the bar," Eli said.

She knew who he meant. The man they'd had the wager on. She looked at Eli. "In that case, you're going to lose your secretary."

He didn't smile. "A woman doesn't have to give up her life, her very identity, just because she falls for some guy."

Jeff threw a piece of bread at Eli. "Stop with the heavy! Did he make you miserable on your little trip? How was camping?"

Eli finally smiled. "I have a picture I want to show you."

Chelsea groaned. "Please tell me you don't have the bear-cub photo. My dad still shows that to people. Hey! I still want to know why you insisted that I go camping."

Eli started to reply, but then he just waved his hand to indicate the table of food that Chelsea was eating, her clean face and hair, and the big smile on her face.

"You're taking credit for all this?" Chelsea said as Eli got up, went to a cabinet, and pulled out an old photo album.

Across the table, Jeff and Melissa looked at each other. He'd told her a lot about the attachment of Chelsea and Eli, and it looked like everything he'd said was true.

It was later, after they'd all laughed over the photos in the album — all of them agreeing that now Jeff looked more like the young Eli than Eli did today — that Chelsea asked about Grace Ridgeway.

Melissa wasn't fooled. She went from laughing to serious in a second. "How do you know her?"

Chelsea started to prepare her words but Eli stepped in.

"We met her in a diner. Very nice lady who talked about little else but her teenage daughter, Abby. Grace said she was meeting someone, and later we saw some guy who looked like a bum come in. And we saw Grace hand him some money. She didn't look rich, so we were concerned."

Eli said all this without the least flicker of his eyes at his distorted truth. He just smiled and refilled everyone's wineglass — except his own, Chelsea noted.

"Does the guy drive a beat-up old car?" Melissa asked. "Weeks ago I ticketed him for a broken taillight, but I haven't seen that vehicle since."

"That's him," Chelsea said. "You remember his name?"

"Yeah. The car was registered to Chester Arthur. I remember because it's a president's name."

"And the driver's license matched his name?" Eli asked.

"Sure," Melissa said. "If it hadn't, I would have reported it. But then, I couldn't imagine that anyone would want to steal that old car. Don't tell me it's still running."

"Yes," Chelsea said before Eli could reply. "Actually, it runs quite well."

"That's because a new engine's been put in," Eli said. "The outside may be a wreck, but the inside's out of Daytona." He didn't look at Chelsea.

That he knew that but hadn't mentioned it so annoyed her that she kicked him under the table. He didn't even wince. "What about Grace? Where does she work?"

"Frazier Motors. My boss's family's dealership. If you buy a vehicle, you go through the paperwork with Grace."

When Eli and Chelsea leaned toward her, Melissa continued, "She's a nice woman, been in Edilean about four years."

"No problems?" Eli asked.

"What's this about?" Melissa asked.

Jeff took her hand in his. "I told you that

Eli can't tell what he's working on. Top Secret and all that."

Melissa seemed to consider that for a moment. "The first year she was in town, she called us out in the night three times. She has a concrete block shed in the backyard, and she said it's why she bought the house. Someone kept trying to break into it."

"Did they succeed?" Eli asked.

"No," Melissa said. "It has a heavy metal door on it. The old man who built it had a collection of old toys. His wife threatened to divorce him if he didn't get rid of them, so he built the shed to house them. It's pretty strong."

"Alarm system on it?" Eli asked.

"Not that I know of, but the sheriff and I suggested she put up some lights around it. What's in there?"

"I have no idea," Eli said as he got up. "Anyone want more pie? What about you, Chels? It's not lemon meringue but it's still good."

"Eli is determined that I gain weight."

"I wanted that when I thought we had a future together," Eli said. "But since I don't play polo or drive a race car, I'm not in consideration." His words were laced with so much anger that Melissa and Jeff looked at him with wide eyes.

But Chelsea knew that he was using a distraction technique. They'd done it when they were children. It looked like he wanted them to be alone. She got up to stand in front of him. "You flirted with every woman we saw." She turned to Melissa and Jeff. "The real reason for all this interest in Grace Ridgeway is that he drools over her. His dream girl. Eli wants a woman who is chained to the stove. One who'll wait at home for him, pop out umpteen babies, and pack his suitcase when he goes somewhere exciting."

"Better than wasting my life living in hotels like you do. Aren't you worried that you're getting too *old* for those young men?"

"You think I'm old?" she said, her voice low. In a quick move, she put her hand at his neck and kissed him with all the passion that had been building inside her.

Eli drew her into his arms, his mouth opening over hers and nearly devouring her.

Melissa and Jeff stood up. "We . . . uh, we better go," he said.

"Uh, yeah," Melissa echoed.

In seconds, they were out the door and hurrying toward the car.

Chelsea and Eli broke apart and stood there glaring at each other.

"Are they gone?" Chelsea whispered.

Eli turned just slightly. "Burning rubber." He looked back at her and they began to laugh so hard they fell on each other.

"Did you see their faces?" she asked.

"They were shocked. You certainly broke up the party with that kiss," he said.

"I had to stop her from asking questions. I guess I could have slapped you, but I was afraid Melissa might draw her gun on me."

Eli stopped laughing.

She pulled back to look at him, and when she saw his eyes glowing, she flung her arms around his neck and kissed him, but this time for real. His body was pressed against hers and he felt so very good.

His tongue, his full lips, the strength of him, were all causing her to lose herself.

He moved to kiss her neck. "No commitment, understand?" he whispered.

"None." Her head was tilted, giving him access to her throat. His hands were roaming over her back.

"I want that white picket fence," he said. "I want kids and a wife in an apron, and a casserole in the oven. And you want none of that."

"That's right," she said, "I don't." Her eyes were closed as she gave herself over to his lips, his hands, to the feel of his mouth against hers.

When he took a step forward, she went with him. He put his hands under her behind and lifted her to the back of the couch. Within seconds, he'd unbuttoned her blouse and his face was on her breasts.

Chelsea knew she'd never wanted anyone as much as she wanted this man. This was Eli. Friends forever.

She opened her jeans-clad legs and held him to her, her ankles clasped at the back of him. Her hands were in his hair, her head back.

His hands slipped under her shirt, moved over her smooth skin, and deftly unfastened her bra. He took a pink tip in his mouth, his tongue caressing in a way that sent waves through her body.

She was hardly aware that his hands were unfastening her jeans. When his fingertips touched the skin below her navel, she caught her breath.

His head came up to her lips, encasing them, devouring them, as his hands held her head.

"Eli," she whispered. "Make love to me."

"I mean to. I —"

Suddenly, he stepped back from her. "Damn! I can't."

She glanced downward. He was ready for her. "Yes you can. I believe in you."

He looked at his watch. "It's late and I have to sleep." He took another step back. "I didn't tell you, but I got a call from the office and tomorrow I have an early duty." Another step back. "But I must say that you look really good, Chelsea. Really, really good. Maybe next time."

With that, he took a few more steps backward, then went into his bedroom and shut the door behind him.

For a long moment, Chelsea stayed seated on the back of the couch. Her shirt was open, her bra loose and exposing her breasts. Her jeans were open down to her tiny thong.

Her first thought was to pound on Eli's bedroom door and demand . . . What? An apology? That he continue?

If Rodrigo had done this to her, that's what she would have done — and he would have loved it. But Eli just might give her that quizzical look of his and ask what had upset her.

She slid off the couch and refastened her clothes. The unspent energy running through her made her feel like her whole body was vibrating.

The breakfast table was covered with dirty dishes and she started to clear them away. But after just two plates, she stopped. Damn him! she thought. Who did he think he was? Who was *she*? Some strumpet he could pick up, then toss aside?

She sneered at the dirty table. Eli would probably wake up expecting the whole house would be clean. His mom was a great housekeeper — unlike Chelsea's mother, who barely knew where the kitchen was. Housework would interfere with her charity work and her tennis. Or at least that's how it had been until her husband had the heart attack.

Chelsea put her hands to her sides. Today in the car she'd been right to tell Eli that she couldn't stay with him, that she didn't want the same things as he did.

As she headed for the stairs, she paused by his bedroom door. Was he in there snoring away? Dreaming about his Top Secret work? Or maybe about Pilar's dark beauty?

She flipped the door a one-finger gesture, then went up the stairs. There were two bedrooms at the top and one of them had her empty suitcases. Since she hadn't unpacked them, she wondered who had. Probably Jeff, she thought.

She didn't bother to shower, just stripped off her clothes, and nude, she fell across the bed.

Sexual frustration was not a good thing!

She flopped around on the bed, looked at the clock, then turned over. Three minutes later, she looked at the clock again.

At 1:00 a.m., she gave up trying to sleep, got up, and took a shower. As she got out, toweling her hair, she saw her laptop on the bedside table. When she'd run off in such a hurry on Eli's dreadful camping trip, she'd left it behind.

From there, they'd gone to the diner and had heard the conversation between Grace and Orin. Tonight, Eli had asked Melissa questions about Grace, but what he'd seemed to really want to know about was the shed in back.

What was it that Grace had said? Chelsea tried to remember.

"I just wondered if you'd ever found the papers from the last sale."

"No, I haven't. Everything is stored away and I work long hours. Besides, those things are hard for me to look at. I . . ."

"Interesting," Chelsea said as she looked at her computer.

When they were returning from Richmond, she'd searched for Grace Ridgeway's address in Edilean. She didn't mention it to Eli, but she'd emailed all that she'd found to herself.

She tossed the towel onto the side of the

tub, gathered her robe around her, and opened her computer.

Twenty minutes later, she'd found Grace's house on an aerial map. She could see the shed in the back corner of what looked to be a very plain brick house set back off the road. There was a wall running along the back, but from what she could see, it wasn't very tall. Chain link enclosed the rest of the property.

She wondered what kind of lock was on the shed door.

As she got up, she looked at the messy bed. She knew she wasn't going to sleep tonight. Maybe if she went to Grace's house, she could see the shed and examine the lock.

She and Eli hadn't talked about it, but she assumed that tomorrow he planned to visit Grace. The question was whether or not he'd take Chelsea with him. The truth was that right now she felt like packing her bags and leaving. In fact, she wasn't really sure why she'd come in the first place. If her parents hadn't bullied her . . .

Okay, so that was their past. Right now, she could either continue being angry or she could *do* something.

She opened the closet door. Someone had hung her clothes inside, and the wire drawers on the side held her knits. She pulled out a black turtleneck, her black yoga pants, and a dark bandanna for her hair.

Couldn't hurt to go and see, she thought.

Chelsea hadn't told Eli, but in the years since she'd seen him, he wasn't the only one who'd had a bit of experience in espionage. Hers was on a much smaller scale, but several times she'd managed to bat her lashes at men on other teams — whether cars or horses — and find out information she shouldn't know. Out of necessity, she'd developed computer-hacking skills that might even impress Eli. And, unfortunately, she'd become an expert on finding signs of when a man was cheating.

In minutes she was dressed in all black. She tiptoed down the stairs, past Eli's bedroom, then out to her car.

Grace's neighborhood was quiet. There were streetlights, but no sign of life anywhere — not even the blue-gray light from a TV showed from a window. The air was still and there was little moonlight.

She parked four houses away and was glad she'd disconnected the interior light in her car so that when she opened the door, it didn't come on.

There were few barriers in the neighborhood, so she moved quietly through the trees and shrubs to Grace's house. The fact that it was completely enclosed was unusual. Chelsea wondered if Grace had done it or if the house was fenced when she bought it.

Toward the back of the chain-link fence she could see the concrete wall of the shed. It was about eight feet square and looked as solid as a bank vault. But then, it wasn't as though she planned to break into it. She just wanted to . . . Actually, she wasn't sure why she was here.

As she got closer to the shed, she wondered where the lights Melissa had mentioned were. She could see two tall poles but they were dark.

Her first thought was that if Orin's files had been confiscated, that might make him work harder to get whatever papers Grace had in storage. Maybe he'd sent someone and that's why the lights were out. If so, Chelsea knew she should call the police.

She pulled her cell phone out of her pocket, but before she could even turn it on, a hand went over her mouth and another around her waist. Her phone fell to the ground.

Chelsea kicked backward, her heel contacting hard with a shin. At the same time, she jammed both elbows back and hit a rib cage on both sides.

There was a grunt of pain, then in a deft move, her attacker's leg went around her knees. In the next moment she was on the ground and he was on top of her, his hands pinning her arms above her head.

"That hurt," Eli said.

Chelsea took about a quarter of a second to register her astonishment that he was there and on her, then she started thrashing about under him, trying to get away.

"I hope you keep this up," he said. "It feels quite good, actually."

Chelsea went still. It was very dark but she had an idea that he could see her face. She was glaring at him with all the anger she felt. He'd left her on the couch! "I thought you wanted to sleep." Her teeth were clenched shut.

"Eventually," he said. He was still holding her hands above her head, but he moved one hand down to touch her hair. "You should have covered this more. The moonlight on it makes it shine like liquid gold."

"*Now* you get romantic? Now?!"

With a chuckle, Eli rolled off to lie beside her, but he didn't let go of her hand. "Want to tell me why you're here?"

"Oh, no, you don't," she said. "You're not going to turn this around so you're the one who gets to ask the questions. Why are *you* here? And why did you leave me sitting on the sofa with my clothes half off? I could have murdered you."

"Since you've been in town, I've taken about twenty cold showers. I think I could fill a bathtub with ice and step into it and turn it all to steam."

"Really?" she asked, sounding interested. But then she sat up and looked down at him. "You're trying to distract me, aren't you? Why did you lie about sleeping? Why are you here?"

"I didn't lie. I just —"

"Eli!"

"Okay, I left you because I had to call Jeff. I wanted him to come over here and find out what kind of lock was on the shed and get me a duplicate."

"You made him leave Melissa?"

"Funny you should mention that because he said he'd rather not do what I asked."

"Curse you out, did he?"

"Oh yeah," Eli said. "He sent Pilar over here. But then, she's better at sneaking than he is. She was on a date with your number three."

"Lanny?"

"You sound like you know him."

"Just wishing," Chelsea said. "What else did you do?"

"Packed a bag with what I need. Called a few people. I think —" He lifted one side of his body and pulled her cell phone out from under him. "I believe this is yours. Do *not* turn it on. You weren't planning to call the police, were you?"

"Yes, I was. The lights over the shed are out and — Did you put them out?"

"I think Pilar did. She'll reconnect them tomorrow."

"What in the world do you three *do* in your job?" Even in the darkness, she could see his shrug.

"If I told you to wait for me in your car, what would you do?"

"You mean you'd tell me to be a good girl and wait for big shot you? How about if I turn on the car lights and the alarm and blow the horn while I wait for the police, who I plan to call immediately?"

"That's what I was afraid of," Eli said as he sat up. "I did bring some duct tape. Maybe I should . . ."

"Funny," Chelsea said as she stood up. "Remind me later to laugh. So did you find out about the lock or not?"

"I did. Pilar will get a duplicate tomorrow morning and replace the one I have to cut away tonight." He picked up a black back-pack from the ground and put it on.

"I'm surprised she didn't break into a hardware store tonight."

"Me, too," Eli said.

Chelsea was being sarcastic, but he was in earnest. "I don't know how you're not in prison."

"I've only been arrested three times," he said proudly as they reached the corner of Grace's property. "Do you think you can get over the fence? If not, you can wait for me on this side."

"You remember all those ballet lessons I used to complain about?" She didn't give him time to reply. There'd been no toehold when she'd gone over the fence at Orin's house, but the chain link gave her a place to put her feet. She'd worn soft, supple shoes that allowed her feet to flex. In a graceful move, in an instant she was up and over the fence and on the other side. "Want some help?" she whispered to Eli through the metal.

"No, but I wouldn't mind seeing you do that again." He easily vaulted up and over the metal.

"After the way you left me tonight," she hissed, "I'm not doing anything for you ever again. I — Oh!" Eli had grabbed her about the waist and swung her over a few feet.

"Dog," he said and nodded toward the

side. Lying on the ground was a big German Shepherd, sound asleep. Chelsea had almost stepped on him.

"Pilar?" she asked.

Eli nodded, then motioned to the shed.

They stopped at the door. Eli looked around, then removed bolt cutters from his pack. The lock snapped easily and within seconds they were inside. "Don't turn on the overhead light," he said. He pulled out a little flashlight and shone it around.

Chelsea hadn't thought about what she'd expected to see inside, probably the usual things bought off TV then tossed into storage, kids' toys, and boxes of old clothes. But instead there was a single row of stacked file boxes, all of them shoved up against the back wall. From the look of the cobwebs and the dust on the floor, they hadn't been touched in years.

"What now?" Chelsea asked.

"You start at that end and I'll take this one."

"Do you have any idea what we're looking for?"

"None," Eli said as he opened the first box. It was full of receipts from Longacre Furniture and different suppliers. They had been tossed into the box, with no file folders, no organization. Eli looked at the dates and saw that they were years apart. "I think someone emptied folders into here."

Chelsea had also opened a box. Some of the documents in it had been wadded into balls, as though they'd been discarded. The second box she opened had been shredded. She held it up so Eli could see the contents, which were long strips of confetti.

"I think someone cleaned out trash bins and threw the contents into these boxes," she said.

"My assessment exactly. I think it's useless for us to try to find something in here. We have to turn these over to someone else."

"FBI? CIA? FedEx them to your friend the president?"

Eli took out his phone. "No. Someone more important. I think we should give these to Dad and let his accountants put it all back together."

"Ha! They'll turn the boxes over to some underpaid women to sort through, then they'll —"

"Sorry to interrupt your female-persecution complex, but most of Dad's accountants are women, and I gave him some German software that can piece together the shredded strips."

"Why don't you turn this over to the FBI?"

"They'd want to know how and where I got it. Dad will never ask. What was that?"

"I didn't hear anything."

Eli motioned for her to turn off the light on her cell phone. It was completely dark in the little building. She didn't hear him move but only felt him when he threw his body over hers. She made a sound when she was pressed up against the cold, dusty concrete floor, but then stayed still as they waited in silence. If anyone came in the door, they'd see Eli long before they realized there was a body under his.

They lay together for minutes, neither of them moving, but nothing happened.

Eli rolled off her. She couldn't see him but could hear what sounded like the click of his pistol. "I'm going outside," he whispered. "Stay here."

Chelsea sat up and listened. When Eli opened the door, a bit of light came through from outside, and he slipped out, closing the door behind him. It was so quiet in the little building that she could hear her heart beating.

Crawling, she searched for Eli's pack, found it, and rummaged inside. There were several objects that she couldn't identify, but when her hand hit the bolt cutters he'd used to cut the lock, she took the tool out.

She felt her way along the wall until she reached the door. If it opened, she'd be behind it.

When she heard the door opening, she raised the cutters high.

Eli's hand caught them midair and took them from her. "It was no one," he said, and turned on his flashlight to look at her. "You okay?"

"Fine." She took a breath. "Actually, I feel good. Is your dad coming?"

"Yes. Men are on their way. Some of my cousins —" He waved his hand. "It would be better if you don't know. But, yeah, people are coming to get these boxes. I need to get them out of this shed. Could you give me a hand? We'll toss them over the fence, then hide them. We have to do this in silence and darkness. Think you can do it?"

"Of course," she said. "When do we start?"

Eli gave her a grin of such happiness that she felt her knees go weak. She hadn't seen that smile since they were kids.

"Robin and Marian, all grown up," she said and had the satisfaction of seeing him take a tiny step toward her. But he caught himself.

"If we didn't have this task to do, right now I'd remove your clothing."

"No, you wouldn't," she said.

Eli frowned.

"Because I'd have every stitch off before you could get to me."

For a second his eyes blazed at her, then he turned away. "Too bad we have to take care of this now."

Outside, the wind had picked up and it felt like it might rain. Pilar was waiting for them.

"I knew I heard something," Eli muttered. "Get on the other side of the fence and I'll toss boxes to you. Or will they be too heavy for you?"

"Puh-lease," Pilar said.

"Don't be a jerk, Eli," Chelsea said.

Pilar and Chelsea looked at each other and smiled.

"*Two* of you?" Eli said under his breath, then went inside to get the first load of boxes.

Chelsea was glad to see Pilar go over the fence in exactly the way she had. "Ballet?"

"Seven years of it," Pilar said. "I grew too tall to pursue it."

"Me too," Chelsea said and again they exchanged smiles. The first four boxes came sailing over the fence and they caught them before they landed. "So how's Lanny?" Chelsea whispered. With the wind in the trees, their soft voices were covered.

"Great. I think maybe he's The One."

Chelsea almost laughed, as that's what she'd labeled Eli — but with a different meaning. "Planning to quit Eli and settle down? Kids? The works?"

"I haven't got that far, but I am done with Eli." She grunted as she caught a box so heavy she nearly fell. Chelsea helped her. "See what I mean? He's always doing things like this."

"Is he? You mean things outside the government?"

"Oh, yeah. He got shot in one of them, but he did bring down three men who were selling government secrets. But the way he did it was illegal. If the US didn't need him so much, he might have been put in prison. What was he like as a kid?"

"The same," Chelsea said. "I don't think he's changed at all. Except physically."

Pilar gave a little laugh. "Half the women in the office have made a play for him, but he doesn't even notice them. Jeff started spreading it around that Eli had been in love with a girl who died and couldn't get over her. I think that was supposed to make them back off."

"They tried harder?"

"Definitely! They started dressing to

entice him. I'm sure the huge increase in sales of push-up bras created a surge in the stock market."

"What about you? You interested?"

"Not in the least. He's too nerdy for me. I have a blue-collar background. Lanny can repair a transmission. He has grease under his nails. He —"

"Pilar," Eli said through the fence, "where is Dad?"

"Right here," came the deep male voice of Frank Taggert. "Chelsea, you look beautiful, as always."

"Mr. Taggert," Chelsea said and kissed the man's cheeks. He stood straight and tall, and even in the darkness she saw that the years hadn't put a pound on him. "You flew here just to help Eli?"

"Of course. He's my son."

Around them, in absolute silence, three men in black picked up the boxes and carried them away.

"How is Miranda?"

"Well," Frank said. "Come on, let's go."

"But Eli —" Chelsea began.

"He'll be here in a minute. Everything is taken care of. It'll be daylight soon and people will be getting up."

When Chelsea saw that Pilar was with them, she followed Frank down the road to where his car was parked.

Eli stayed behind to make sure a new lock was put on the empty shed, then vaulted over the fence and left.

One of the men reconnected the motion-sensing lights on the shed. They came on for a few seconds, then went off again. On the ground, the sleeping dog began to stir.

At last, everything was quiet and looked just as it had before the invasion of so many people.

Inside the house, Abby Ridgeway was sorry the show was over. Earlier, she'd awoken hungry and had pulled a bottle of water and a bag of corn chips out of the pantry. She'd meant to go back to her room and look at some adult websites her mother had forbidden with her blasted parental controls. It hadn't taken much work to figure out what her mom's password was.

It wasn't that Abby actually wanted to see the sites, but right now she was furious with her mother. She had given away the money for Abby's prom dress to that sleazy, slimy creep Orin Peterson.

In the last few years since her father . . . died — Abby refused to believe what she'd been told of her dad's death — she'd often told her mother what she thought of Orin.

But her mother always said that he had been through a lot that Abby knew nothing about. She'd told Abby about some of it: a dying wife, a bankrupted business, living on food stamps. Poor, poor Orin.

But Abby hadn't believed any of it. She and her friend Scully had done some research and found that Orin was still connected to Longacre Furniture. Abby told her mother what they'd found out.

Grace had asked Orin about that, and he'd said that yes, his name was still officially on the board but he received no money. In other words, he'd sweet-talked and cried and pleaded so much that Grace had believed him.

After that her mother refused to listen to anything Abby had to say about what had happened. Grace said that her husband had given his *life* to keep the shame of it all quiet and she was going to honor that. Abby was forbidden to ever again speak of anything that had to do with her father or Orin or even about Longacre Furniture.

Even after all the warnings, Abby had made some halfhearted attempts to find out more, but her mom's unhappiness was more than she could bear. Abby quit looking and she even forbade Scully to search or to speak of what had happened.

It had worked well because Abby saw her mother begin to get happier. She liked her job and for a while their lives had been pleasant. But then Orin called and Grace went running to him — and she came back poorer than when she'd left. The money for Abby's new dress was gone.

She knew her mother hadn't meant for Abby to find out. But on Sunday Abby wanted to go to the mall in Williamsburg to look for a dress, but her mom said she couldn't. She said she needed to talk to her boss, Mr. Frazier, on Monday. Abby knew what that meant: Orin had taken the money and her mom was going to ask for a loan. Abby hadn't said anything, just walked out of the room in silence.

It wasn't easy to hold that much anger. Her mother had reassured her that they'd buy a beautiful dress, but to Abby, it was the principle of the thing.

Tonight it was her anger that woke her. Her teeth were clenched, her hands made into fists, and she was in pain.

She got up and went into the kitchen to get something to eat. She didn't want her mother to know she was up, so she didn't open the fridge with its bright light and a noise that her mother always seemed to hear. As she was on her way back to her bedroom, she walked past the window and a movement caught her eye. At first she didn't pay any attention to it. Rex was a great watchdog that barked at the slightest movement. But then Abby backed up. To her disbelief she saw the shadow of what looked like a woman sailing over the top of their fence. She was so graceful, it looked like she was performing on some dance show.

As Abby stared out the dark window, she saw a man close behind the woman. The two of them went to the shed in the back — what Scully called the Forbidden Building because Abby's mom never allowed anyone to enter it — and slipped inside.

Abby grabbed her phone to call the sheriff. But she didn't. Maybe it was her anger at her mother, or maybe it was her extreme curiosity. Of course, years ago, she and Scully had found the lock combination and had investigated. Inside the shed were just boxes full of old receipts. Why would these two rather elegantly dressed people want to break into an old shed?

She pulled up a stool to the side of the window and ate while she watched the show. At one point she cranked a window open and it creaked. She barely had time to close it before the shed door opened and the man came out and looked around. He even came close to the window and looked in.

Yet again, Abby stayed behind the curtain, her finger hovering over the keypad of her phone. But she still didn't touch it. The man — who she saw quite clearly — turned and went back into the shed.

The second he was inside, Abby again opened the window a bit. Another woman arrived, then the two women went back over the fence. Minutes later, she saw the man begin to toss boxes over the fence. She thought maybe she heard voices, but in the gathering wind, she wasn't sure.

She saw the shadow of a man — heavier than the first one — close up the shed and put a lock on it. She was willing to bet it wasn't the lock that her mother knew the combination to. The outdoor light flashed for a moment, then went off.

Finally, there was silence. Abby sat still for a while, but her instincts told her that all the people were gone.

Long ago she'd found the little red book where her mother kept all her passcodes. Tiptoeing, Abby went to her mother's desk in the spare bedroom and looked. In the next minute she was running across the yard in her bare feet. She tried the combination six times but it didn't work.

Yawning, she started back to the house and nearly tripped over Rex. At first she was sickened as she thought they'd killed him, but he was just sleeping. How interesting, she thought, and went back inside and got into bed. She couldn't wait to tell Scully everything.

10

Frank dropped Pilar and Chelsea off at Eli's house, saying that someone would return Chelsea's car the next day. The men didn't explain to the women where they were going. They just drove away, leaving the women standing on the sidewalk.

"My car is over there," Pilar said. "I've got a long drive ahead so I better go."

"Take the other guest room," Chelsea said as she went to the front door.

"Thanks," Pilar said.

Ten minutes later, Chelsea was in the shower. She was exhilarated from the evening, but also exhausted. She felt like she wanted to sleep for a week, but at the same time she thought she might never sleep again.

She shampooed her hair, then held her head back under the showerhead. As the hot water cascaded down over her long hair, she closed her eyes. She wondered what Eli and his dad were doing now. Sitting in a coffee shop somewhere and discussing everything? Talking together about things that Eli seemed to think Chelsea wasn't smart enough, involved enough, whatever, to help him figure out? Were they — ?

She opened her eyes to see Eli, naked, standing in the shower with her.

All the questions in her mind disappeared. She put her arms around his neck and kissed him. It was a kiss that in seconds went deeper.

Eli picked her up, his hands on her round, curvy bottom. Her legs went around his torso, pulling him to her, and he set her down on his hard maleness.

It filled her. Her head went back as his lips were on her neck. He moved her so her back was against the tile wall. The water beat down on them as his strokes increased in depth. Chelsea clutched at his back, pulling him closer.

When she came, he kept on stroking, slowly and gently until she returned to life. "My turn," he whispered, and she held on for his last strokes.

He held her against the wall, his lips against hers. "You still have shampoo in your hair."

"And you're sweaty," she said.

Smiling, he set her down, backed her under the shower water, and began to massage her scalp as the shampoo came out. As he touched her, his chest was against hers.

"You could open a chain of salons with this technique," she said.

"I'm only interested in here and now and one client." He looked her in the eyes.

"Good answer." She picked up the bar of soap. "I think you have body parts that need washing. Mind if I do it?"

"Please," he said, then closed his eyes as Chelsea moved her hands downward.

The smell of pancakes woke Chelsea. When her stomach gave a growl, Eli reached out for her. She kissed the back of his neck.

Last night, there'd been twice in the shower, interspersed with lots of soapy fondling and exploring of each other's bodies. Then they'd moved into the bedroom. When they'd knocked a chair over and Chelsea said, "Shhh. Pilar is next door," they went downstairs to his bedroom.

Hours later, when they collapsed on the bed, the sun was up, peeping under the shades. They flopped back on the bed, their hunger for each other sated for the moment, and fell asleep, their bodies intertwined.

"I'm going to get something to eat. Keep

sleeping," Chelsea said.

He didn't reply and he didn't move.

As soon as she was out of the bed, she realized that she had no clothes downstairs. Eli and she had both been nude when they came down the stairs, and she had a few bruises from the stair treads. She couldn't help thinking that she was glad Pilar hadn't left her room during that short, energetic trip on the stairs.

In the walk-in closet she put on a pair of Eli's boxer shorts and one of his white dress shirts. It wasn't much, but it was a great deal more than she wore on most photo shoots. She thought about trying to untangle her hair but didn't.

She padded barefoot across the living room and as soon as she entered the kitchen, she saw Lanny Frazier. He was leaning against the counter, coffee mug in hand, and looking her up and down. He was a large, handsome man, his eyes half-closed, inviting.

Chelsea gave the look back at him. "I guess I should have brushed my hair."

"Not on my account, Tequila Lady," he said, his voice slow and seductive as he let her know he remembered her from the bar.

Pilar, a plate in each hand, stepped between them, her eyes on Lanny's. "She's all used up. Last night she and Eli sounded like a herd of cattle."

"Yeah?" Lanny said.

Chelsea wasn't fooled by his glances. She knew when a man was interested in her and this one wasn't. Not really. She took a piece of bacon off one of the plates Pilar was holding. "Yes, I'm taken, but I'll put you on my list." She paused. "At about a hundred and twenty."

There was a little guffaw of laughter from her left and she saw a big kid — no, a huge, enormous boy — sitting at the breakfast table, his head down, a sketchpad in his hands. He looked like a bigger, younger version of Lanny.

Chelsea went to sit by him at the table. "Drawing anything interesting?"

He turned the pad around to show a sketch of Chelsea, her long legs exposed, yet looking demurely innocent. Lanny was looking at her in a lecherous way.

She laughed. "Perfect. Have you met Eli?"

"At the gym," the boy said.

"Oh? Did you bench-press Jeff?"

He looked at her, his eyes full of laughter.

Lanny sat down across from Chelsea. "This is my baby brother, Shamus. He leaves for college in just a few weeks. We're going to miss his constant chattering. Can't get the kid to shut up."

"I think his drawing says everything about you."

Pilar put the plates in front of the two males and gave Chelsea a look to stop flirting. She was wearing a pair of shorts and a little T-shirt, and looked quite as good as Chelsea did. "You want some pancakes?"

"Sure," Chelsea said. "Just one. No, make that three. Eli wants me to get fat."

"You could use a few pounds," Lanny said. "So where is he hiding?"

"He's sleeping," Chelsea said.

"Ha!" Pilar said. "He never sleeps. I gave him a list of people he has to call and he'd better do it! They want him back at work. And he often calls his mom." As she handed Chelsea a plate of pancakes, she stared at her.

"Don't look at me," Chelsea said. "I'm not keeping him here. I'm just visiting. Eli can go back to saving the world anytime he wants to."

Pilar gave a curt nod, but she said nothing as she went back to the kitchen.

In the ensuing silence, Chelsea began to feel a bit awkward. She knew Pilar and Eli were friends and that meant they looked out for each other. But that didn't include dumping guilt on Chelsea because she wasn't giving up her life to chain herself to a kitchen. She wasn't going to spend her days waiting for hubby to come home. He got all the fun; she got the drudgery.

She looked at Lanny sitting across from her. "Doesn't Grace Ridgeway work for your family's company?"

"She does. But if you're hoping to become BFFs with her, it won't happen."

"Why not?" Chelsea asked as she bit into the pancakes.

"She stays to herself. My mom keeps trying to fix her up on dates but Grace won't go. But then, after what happened with her husband, it's understandable."

"Suicide, wasn't it?"

"That's what Colin was told. He's —"

"The sheriff. I met him. Gorgeous man."

"Better not let his wife, Gemma, hear you say that. She's . . ." Lanny made a few punches like a boxer. "Shamus and she work out together."

Chelsea looked at the boy, at the sheer size of him. "Olympic shot-putter, is she?"

Shamus, bent over his drawing pad, smiled.

Pilar, full plate in hand, sat down between Chelsea and Lanny. "Gemma is built so well I'm thinking of joining Mike's Gym and putting on the gloves."

Lanny looked at her. "But if you're living in DC . . ." He trailed off as the realization of what she might be saying hit him. He looked down at his pancakes, smiling.

Chelsea turned to Shamus. "Do you know Abby?"

He nodded, then handed her his big sketchpad.

The drawing was of two young people, a boy and a girl. She was very pretty, with long dark hair, while he was cute in a nerdy sort of way. His ears stuck out rather prominently.

At first Chelsea thought it was a picture of her and Eli as they'd been as kids, but there were too many differences for it to be them. She looked at Shamus. "Is this Grace's daughter, Abby?"

He nodded.

"Who's the boy?"

"Scully," Shamus said.

"And he is . . . ?"

Lanny spoke up. "The only person my little brother actually talks to is Gemma, my sister-in-law, so I'll have to translate. Scully is Grace's kid's best friend. I've seen them together at the shop several times." He took the pad, looked at the drawing, then handed it to Pilar. "Nobody gets why she hangs out with him. That girl is a beauty."

"She's fifteen!" Pilar said.

"Yeah, I know," Lanny said. "But give her three more years and she'll be ready to walk down a runway." He looked at Chelsea.

"Easier said than done. How tall is she?"

"About five-eight, I guess."

"Too short," Chelsea said. "What about the kid with her?"

"He's inches shorter than she is, if that's what you mean," Lanny said. "Poor kid doesn't have a chance."

Chelsea picked up the pad.

"They remind you of Eli and you?" Pilar asked.

"They do." Chelsea looked at Shamus. "You wouldn't happen to know who she's going to the prom with, would you?"

"Baze," Shamus said and took his pad back. He quickly drew something, then turned the pad around. A very good-looking young man in a football jersey was smiling.

"Ah, right, I got it. Scully with the ears is the best friend, but she dates the football player." She was looking at Shamus and waiting for his nod, but the boy just frowned. "I take it that you don't approve."

"Scully is my friend," Shamus said.

As Chelsea looked at the picture, she remembered how she'd felt at that age. All those hormones, all that curiosity. Like young Abby, Chelsea had been very pretty — and the boys let her know it. They teased and flirted with her, laughed, and appeared out of nowhere. She'd close her locker door and there would be two beautiful young men there, smiling at her.

In her family, she'd been one of several daughters and not even considered the prettiest one. Her older sisters were achievers, whereas Chelsea let things happen rather than pushed for them. For most of her childhood she'd been content to follow Eli around as he came up with ways to help people.

But then puberty hit and there were all those boys saying wonderful things to her about how pretty she was, what a nice voice she had, how smart she was. One boy said her hair was like "silk on a starlit night."

All of it had taken her by surprise, had shocked her, as she'd never seen herself as a beauty. One time she'd asked Eli if he thought she was pretty.

"As compared to what?" he'd asked. The best she could get out of him was when he told her that beauty in a human didn't matter. It was what was inside that counted.

Now, as an adult, she knew he was right, but when she was fifteen and being offered rides in red convertibles and being asked out by boys who were big, strong, and beautiful, a person's inner beliefs weren't what she cared about. When the senior captain of the football team asked her out, she didn't hesitate in saying yes.

It was hard to believe now but when she'd told Eli about her coming date, she'd expected him to be happy for her. To her, she'd achieved something rather wonderful. But his coldness, his refusal to talk about it, had made her angry at him.

Had she really expected him to congratulate her? she wondered as she looked at Shamus's drawing. Maybe she'd hoped that Eli would . . . what? Challenge the football player to a duel? With what? Keyboards?

"Are you okay?" Lanny asked.

Chelsea handed the pad back to Shamus. "I'm fine. I was just remembering some things, that's all." She turned to Shamus. "How's Scully taking the fact that his friend is going to the prom with another guy?"

"Scully is staying home that night."

"Right," Chelsea said. "That's what Eli did when I went out with someone else. What about you? You have a date for the prom?"

Lanny snorted. "My little brother doesn't single out girls. He goes out with a group of them at a time. At halftime in football games the cheerleaders climb on him. How many of them do you hold up at one time?"

In answer, Shamus turned the drawing pad around. It was a picture of him standing up with four cute little cheerleaders hanging on to him. Two had a foot at his waist, holding his hands as they leaned far out to the side. A pyramid of two girls stood on his shoulders.

Chelsea laughed. "I'd like to see that."

"See what?" Eli asked from the doorway. He had showered and was freshly shaved and dressed.

"How's your mom?" Chelsea asked, letting him know she knew he hadn't been sleeping.

"Great. She sends her love to you."

Chelsea was annoyed that he was his usual cool, remote self after the night they'd spent together. But when the others looked away, his eyes changed to so hot the hair on the back of her neck stood up. She started to leave the table but Eli turned away to fill a plate with Pilar's pancakes. He sat down between the two women.

"Anything going on that I should know about?"

Lanny spoke first. "Your girlfriend has been quizzing us about Grace Ridgeway and her daughter. I think Scully is going to be collateral damage. So what's up about them? If Grace is in any kind of trouble, our family will help."

"There will be no problems," Eli said between bites. "I turned everything over to my dad, and he's going to look into the papers we found and . . ." Eli shrugged. "That's it. I thought maybe we could all go out on a boat today. I have some relatives who are really good on the water so I've spent quite a bit of time with boats and we — What?!"

Everyone was staring at him. Pilar, Lanny, Chelsea, and even Shamus were all looking at him as though they couldn't believe what he was saying.

"Let me guess," Chelsea said. "You get us all on a boat, then you suddenly remember that you forgot your sunscreen and you . . . What? You swim away? How good a swimmer have you become since I last saw you?"

Eli filled his mouth and didn't answer.

"None of the agents can beat him in a pool in the training sessions," Pilar said.

Eli gave her a look of disgust. "Traitor!" he mumbled.

Lanny was frowning as he looked from Eli to Pilar. "Is there anything between you two besides work?"

"No!" Eli and Pilar said in unison.

Shamus gave a little laugh at their tone.

Chelsea stood up. "I think I'm going to stay here today and do nothing. Maybe I'll take a nap. Pilar, I bet there's a lot of work Eli needs to do, so maybe you two could drive up to DC for the day." She gave an exaggerated yawn. "Yeah, a nap would be lovely." She started to leave the room.

Eli caught her hand and motioned for her to sit back down. "Okay, no boat, no nap."

"What about saving the world?" Chelsea asked.

"That's been put on hold too." Eli couldn't help a small smile.

"So what *are* we going to do today, Great Leader?" Chelsea asked.

"Anyone wanta tell me what's going on?" Lanny asked.

"Pilar will," Eli said. He was looking at Chelsea. "What's in your mind?"

Chelsea looked at her nails. "I need a manicure and I thought I'd do a little shopping. Not much, just some."

Eli looked at her. "You're planning to buy Abby a prom dress, aren't you?"

"Possibly," Chelsea said and looked at Lanny. "Where can I go shopping?"

"There's a big outlet mall in Williamsburg."

"Sounds good," Chelsea said and again

365

started to get up, but again Eli caught her hand.

"You can't get involved in this. I'm concerned about . . . about some things."

Chelsea sat back down. "What have you found out?"

Eli gave a glance at Lanny, then Shamus. His eyes told Chelsea that he couldn't speak in front of them.

But she wasn't buying it. She had no doubt that if at all possible Eli would exclude her from everything. She looked him in the eyes. "Remember when we were kids and every time you thought there was danger you tried to exclude me? It didn't work then and it's not going to work now."

Eli glared back at her. "You want to buy her a dress so she can go out with Axel, don't you?"

"Did I miss something?" Lanny asked Pilar. "Who is Axel?"

"My guess is that he's Chelsea's high school football player." She didn't take her eyes off Chelsea and Eli, who were glaring at each other like dogs ready to attack.

"You're not going to stop me," Chelsea said, her teeth clenched. "Whoever Abby goes with, she deserves to look good."

"And where has your beauty taken you? Heard from your polo player yet?"

"No, but when I do, I'll let him know how glad I am to see him."

"I think . . ." Lanny began as he stood up.

"Yeah, we should go," Pilar said, and they both looked pointedly at Shamus, who hadn't moved.

The boy was tapping on his cell phone. Within seconds, he handed the phone to Chelsea.

She was still glaring at Eli, her eyes angry, and she had to read the phone twice before she saw it. She looked at Shamus. "Is this real?"

Shamus gave a nod, then stood up and closed his sketchpad.

"Thanks a lot," Chelsea said and returned his phone to him. "I'll get dressed and . . ." When she looked at Eli, the anger returned to her face.

"Where do you think you're going?" he growled at her. "Because if it has to do with this case, I'm not going to allow you to —"

"Allow me? *Allow* me?!"

Lanny got Pilar and Shamus out of the house quickly.

Inside, Chelsea, still glaring at Eli, said, "Are they gone?"

"Yeah." His shoulders relaxed. "Are there any more pancakes? And what was on the kid's phone?"

"A couple of them are on the stove, and it was the Twitter Road on the phone. Shamus — that darling child — asked somebody where Abby was going to be today and was told that her mom is dropping her and Scully off at the outlet mall at eleven. Poor kid is to pick out her dress with the help of a computer geek."

Eli was looking out the window at the car parked in front. Shamus was in the backseat, while Lanny and Pilar were quietly talking by the front.

Smiling, Shamus raised his hand in farewell. "The kid knows our fight was an act to get rid of them."

"I think Pilar does too, but she wants time alone with Lanny. She's talking about moving here."

"So you said. The truth is that I think you should stay here today. I bet you can get your nails done here in Edilean."

"I'm sure I could. Then *you* could help nerdy Scully with Abby's prom dress. Actually, it might be worth it to see what you two would come up with. My guess would be a lacy collar and little ruffles on the cuffs of the long sleeves. And of course a floor-length skirt."

"I think that sounds great."

"If you're a Sister Wife. Come on, let's get

dressed and go to the mall."

Eli was on the couch with his laptop, pretending to read what the general had sent him, while he waited for Chelsea to get dressed. This morning it hadn't been easy to act unconcerned when he'd found out Pilar had told Chelsea that he wasn't sleeping. But the second Chelsea was out of the room, Eli had started making calls. He wanted to know how serious all this with Orin Peterson was.

First he called Frank. So far, there was no word about the papers. The shredded documents were still being put together on the computers.

Next he talked to his mother. She'd met her first husband — Eli refused to call Leslie Harcourt his father — in Edilean and she might know something.

Miranda was a wealth of information. She'd not kept in touch with anyone in Edilean, but she had read every story in the news about the small town.

"A few years ago there was a major scandal in town. A man ended up getting killed and there were arrests. It had to do with some old paintings." Miranda took a breath. "The important part of all this is that a man named Mike Newcomb is a law enforcement agent and he handled it all. He lives in Edilean. You think he knows what you do for a living?"

On his end of the phone, Eli smiled. Mike ran the gym where he worked out, and he'd always felt that there was more to him than just owning a gym. But Mike had never even hinted about himself — another thing Eli liked. "Mike is good friends with the local sheriff so, yeah, I'm sure he knows all about what I do."

"Good!" Miranda said. "I don't want you to be alone." She paused. "How are you and Chelsea?"

"Great," Eli said, but then let out his breath. There was no use lying to his mother. She'd know. "She's not going to stay with me, if that's what you want to know."

"Have you asked her to?"

"She'd laugh in my face. She checks her email every few minutes and is always disappointed that her polo-player boyfriend hasn't contacted her."

"In that case, I'm glad you didn't outright ask her. I know how much you love Chelsea, but —"

"Mom, talking about this is embarrassing."

"I know it is, but remember that I'm the

one who held you while you cried after she left. And I'm the one who has seen the way you've tracked her over the years. And I coined the phrase NC, meaning Not Chelsea, for all those poor girls who never stood a chance with you. And I —"

"All right!" Eli said. "I get it. What's your point?"

"As much as I love her, Chelsea isn't as clear in her purpose in life as you are. If you tell her you want her to settle down with you —"

"She'll run. Or jump on the back of her Venezuelan polo player's horse and ride away."

"If I remember correctly, you're rather good on a horse. Like your dad."

"Mom, please. This is a different time. Women today don't go for men on black stallions."

"You think not?" Miranda didn't give her son time to reply. "My advice is that you shouldn't make things too easy for Chelsea. Think of it as one of your software games. If the warrior could walk straight to the princess, neither would want the other."

"I don't think computer games and black horses have anything to do with real life."

"Are you sure about that? Absolutely and totally *sure*?"

"When it comes to Chelsea, I'm not sure of anything. I have to go. Pilar's got some guy here who Chelsea says is a three. I, unfortunately, am a one."

Miranda laughed. "I don't know exactly what that means, but I can guess. I think I'll call Chelsea's mother and have a chat."

"I'd rather you didn't do that," Eli said. "Chelsea can make up her own mind about what she wants."

"I'm sure she can, but I'd lose my mother-hood badge if I didn't interfere."

Eli laughed. "That won't happen. I really do have to go. I —"

"I know. You have forty-some calls to make for your job. What happened to your taking some time off?"

"After Chelsea leaves, I think I'll double my schedule. Tell the kids I love them and to try to behave."

"I will," Miranda said. "Eli, dearest, remember that Chelsea likes a challenge."

"I never forget it," he said and clicked off.

By the time he left the bedroom, Chelsea had found out some about Grace and her daughter. Eli was glad of that. Maybe if Chelsea focused on the kids she wouldn't ask so much about Orin and the contents of the papers.

After Chelsea went upstairs to get dressed,

Eli called Mike Newcomb. All Eli had to say was that he needed some help and Mike agreed immediately. Eli couldn't help thinking what an odd place Edilean was that big secrets were being kept. Eli told Mike that he needed to find out about the suicide of Gilbert Ridgeway.

Mike didn't ask questions, just said he'd get on it right away.

By the time Chelsea came downstairs, Eli had everything in place. She had on jeans and a big white shirt, her hair hanging down around her shoulders, and she looked great.

"Are you sure you want to go shopping with some giggly teenagers?" he asked, suggestion in his voice.

When she sat down on the couch beside him, he closed his laptop. "What have you heard?" she asked.

"Nothing. The papers we stole haven't shown anything yet. It's entirely possible that Orin is innocent."

"Except for being a lying, cheating piece of scum."

"Which is not punishable by law," Eli said.

"Too bad. You ready to go? I'd like to see this kid Abby. Don't you find it interesting that her best friend is a nerdy little geek?"

Eli couldn't help wincing at the descrip-

373

tion. "She probably wants to improve her mind."

"Ouch!" Chelsea said as they went to the front door.

Turning, Eli stopped and kissed her. But when it became deeper, he pulled away. "Another minute of that and we'll never leave."

"Mmmmm. Shopping or sex? You always impose such difficult questions." He half pushed her out the door.

Eli drove into Williamsburg, down Richmond Road, to the huge collection of outlet stores.

"Nice," Chelsea said as he drove through the three parking areas. "I could do some damage here."

Eli backed into a slot in the middle area, near the Ann Taylor and Michael Kors stores. As soon as he turned off the engine, he went to Ben & Jerry's to get them milk shakes.

"I couldn't possibly," Chelsea said even as she took the strawberry one he'd bought for her. She took a deep drink. "I don't think I've had one of these since I was a kid. What are you going to do after I leave?"

Eli drank of his vanilla shake. "Get a life," he said. "I think I've been waiting to start one, but Jeff with his new girlfriend, and

Pilar and Lanny, have made me want . . . I guess it's companionship. For years, Jeff and Pilar and I were a team, but it looks like that is going to change."

"Because of me?" Chelsea asked.

"No. Because I held them back. I wasn't aware of it, but I was making sure Jeff didn't leave. I came up with things for him to do so he had to cancel dates."

"You were jealous?"

"I don't think so — but maybe I was. I was certainly jealous of his freedom to move on."

"But now you can go forward?" Chelsea was trying to understand what he was saying. He'd held back from any permanent relationship all these years because he was . . . what? Waiting for her? "I thought that maybe last night changed things between us," she said stiffly.

Eli, watching out the windshield for Abby, smiled. "Last night was great." He glanced at Chelsea, then back. "It was really, truly the best sex I've ever had, but let's face it, in the scope of a life, sex doesn't mean much."

"I think a good sex relationship is *very* important," she said softly.

"Sure. At first it is. Look at my parents. The first few years they were together, they went to bed about six p.m. I was too young to understand about that passion where you can't keep your hands off a person. Fingertips touching sends electricity through your body. The sound and smell of a person's breath can make you weak with desire. Your mind is taken over with thoughts and images of the other person. Her hair, her eyes, her skin all penetrate your very being. Your shake is melting."

Chelsea was staring at him, eyes wide.

"Your shake? You'd better drink it or it'll melt."

"Oh, yeah. Sure." She took a sip. "I've never heard you talk like that. I didn't even know you felt like this." She bent forward to kiss him, but he didn't turn toward her.

"Of course I do. But only about you." He kept his eyes straight ahead. "My point is that sex doesn't last. It's fun, like it is now for you and me, but what happens tomorrow?" He looked at her as though waiting for an answer.

Chelsea was still thinking about what he'd said about his desire for her.

"Do you agree that the sex between us is extraordinary?" he asked. "At least it was for me. But you'd know better than I would."

"You mean because of my extensive experience?"

Eli gave a shrug.

"Just because I've not dedicated my life to the US government doesn't mean I've jumped into bed with a hundred men."

He looked at her. "What does the government have to do with this? I just said that last night was the best time I've ever had in my life. On the stairs! That was like nothing I've ever experienced before. You were great."

"Why do I feel like I'm being put down?"

"I have no idea," Eli said, his face innocent. "My point wasn't about you and me specifically, but in a general way. Sex doesn't last over the long term. Now even my parents would rather spend Saturday at home watching a movie on TV."

"How the hell do you know?!" Chelsea said in anger. "Are you there on Saturday nights? Have you set up spy cameras in their house? For your information, a good sex life is one of the strongest bases for a good marriage."

"That's nice to hear. I'll keep that in mind for the future." He looked back out the windshield.

Chelsea was frowning as she watched customers wander along the sidewalks and in and out of the many stores. "Are you saying that you'll settle for a less interesting sex life if you get the other things you want?"

"I'm going to have to, aren't I?" Eli said. "I'm certainly not going to find sex like you and I have with someone else. I'll just have to make do."

Chelsea leaned back in her seat, staring straight ahead. "I never want to settle for anything," she said softly. "I want it *all.*"

"I hope you get it. Look! Is that Abby?"

Walking along the deep sidewalk in front of them were two teenagers. She was tall, with a very pretty face, and lots of chestnut hair. Beside her was a skinny boy who was about four inches shorter than she was. They were an odd-looking couple.

"Do you think we looked like that?" Eli asked.

"I think they're our mirror image." She looked at him. "I wonder whose idea it was to make girls gain their full height before boys do?"

"My guess would be older men. Less competition for them."

Chelsea laughed. "Probably so. Old men used to hit on me when I was in high school. And by old I mean about twenty-five. What about you? I never knew about the bullies, so were there any girls you never told me about?"

"Amber Wilson."

"You're kidding! She was . . ."

"One of the pretty ones," Eli said, his eyes on Abby and Scully. They were looking in the window of a shoe store.

"When did she — ?" Chelsea began but stopped because coming from the opposite side was a small crowd of teenagers. They were loud and laughing, punching each other. Two of the girls were tapping away on their cell phones.

"He sees them," Eli said, nodding toward young Scully. "And he's not going to say a word."

"Is that his pride or stupidity?" Chelsea asked as she stepped out of the car. Bending, she looked back at him. "I'm going to go listen."

Eli was out of the car instantly and he took her hand in his. They looked like every other young couple, with no hidden agenda.

They eased around the crowd of teenagers to stand in front of the shoe store window. They could see everything in the reflection of the glass. As always with teenagers, they were oblivious of the older couple.

"Mine's a sort of greeny blue," a girl was saying. "What about you, Addy?"

"It's *Abby,* short for Abigail," Scully said. He was behind her, glaring at all of them.

"Oh, right," the girl said. "It's hard for me to remember since we just met two days ago."

"You've been in classes together for three years." Scully's voice was rising.

Abby put her hand on his arm. "It's okay," she said softly. Through all of this, she hadn't taken her eyes off a tall, big, handsome boy who was looking around at the stores as though he was unaware of the turmoil around him.

"Hi, Baze," Abby said softly.

Turning, the boy looked down at her and gave a little smile. "You okay?"

"Sure." She just looked up at him, seeming to be incapable of further speech.

"What color is your dress?" he asked. "I need to know for the flowers."

"Oh. Uh . . ." She took a step back from him — which wasn't easy considering that Scully was right behind her.

"It's white!" Scully said. "And she doesn't need any flowers."

Smiling, the big guy put out his hand to touch Scully's shoulder, but the smaller boy pulled back.

Baze gave a sigh, then looked over their heads at the group. With a curt nod, he indicated that they should leave. There was no doubt that he was the leader. "See you later," he said to Abby, then the group moved away, herd fashion.

Chelsea and Eli were still holding hands, still staring at the window.

"You were rude!" Abby said as she turned on Scully.

"And you acted dumb. Are you going to start doing his homework for him?"

"Baze has a 3.8 average. He doesn't need me to help him with anything. I don't know why you're so angry. You said high school dances are for the masses, for people who can't think for themselves, and that you had no intention of going."

Chelsea glanced at Eli and he gave a nod of agreement — which Scully saw.

"And you agreed with me," Scully said.

"Yeah, well, that was before Baze asked me to go with him. Do you realize what this date could mean? Next year I could be one of the popular girls. I — we — could be invited to parties and —"

"I'm sure they're going to ask you to bring your skinny sidekick with you. Don't you realize that that guy only wants you because you're pretty?"

Abby's face was showing her growing rage. "Do you think I want him for his *brain*?"

When Chelsea let out a little laugh, then

381

tried to cover it with a cough, Eli practically pushed her inside the store.

"I wanted to hear more," she said. "And by the way, I'm on her side. He didn't ask her to go to the dance, but he's jealous that she's going with someone else. That's not fair. She can't win whatever she does."

"Like she would have gone with Scully. Ha!" Eli picked up a man's boot and looked at it.

"Who knows what she would have done if he'd just *asked*," Chelsea said between clenched teeth.

"He knew the answer without asking. She's cursed with being pretty, and he knows that will cause her a lifetime of problems."

"Only you think physical beauty is bad. But have you looked in a mirror lately? You grew into a guy off the cover of a magazine. Why couldn't you have done that in high school?"

"Because I was half a head shorter than you and we made fun of people who went to a gym. You were born beautiful; I wasn't."

Their voices had risen so much that two customers were staring at them. Chelsea took a step toward the front door, but when she saw Abby and Scully outside, she looked back at Eli. "We should . . ."

"Yeah," he said. "We should focus on now." He started walking down the aisle, Chelsea beside him. "If you're going to tart up the girl for her date with the football player, how does that help Scully? But then, I guess he doesn't matter, does he? The point is to replace the dress money Peterson stole, so the 'nerdy little geek,' as you call him, is of no consequence."

Chelsea put her hands into fists at her sides. "Are you trying to make me feel guilty?"

"Yes. Is it working?"

Her anger left her and she smiled. "Yes, it is. So what's your plan?"

"I don't have one. I just don't want the kid to have to see the love of his life in some dress that makes her look like she stepped out of heaven. I don't want him to have to watch her get into a limo with some meat-headed jock. That's all."

Chelsea knew he was referring to her first prom. The gorgeous dress she wore, the beautiful young man, the limo. She'd gone to Eli's house — to her friend — to show off. He'd been wearing sweats and he'd barely looked at her. She'd been so hurt by his inattention that tears had made her mascara run. With the selfishness of a teenager, she'd not even thought that Eli had been hurt on that night.

"So change it," she said. "Turn Scully into something other than a nerd."

"That would take six years of growth and a whole lot of iron," Eli muttered.

"If you can't do it, that's not my problem." She moved past him. "I'm going to see if they have any heels tall enough for my taste, and I'm going to figure out how to get Abby to let me buy her a magnificent dress. She's going to look so good those other girls are going to develop hernias from jealousy suppression." With that, she left Eli to go to women's shoes.

Chelsea was looking at a pair of heels so tall she knew they'd make her reach six feet. But Eli would still be taller, she thought with a smile. Rodrigo not so much, but he had other attributes. That at the moment she couldn't remember any of them didn't matter.

When she put the shoes back in place, she was startled to see Abby staring at her intensely.

"Who are you?" Abby asked. "I've seen you before."

Chelsea smiled to cover her discomfort. "I've been on the cover of a few magazines. Maybe you saw them."

"Maybe," Abby said, but she looked skeptical.

Chelsea fiddled with a pair of red sandals. "I didn't mean to eavesdrop when you were outside, but what are you wearing to your prom?"

At the very personal question, Abby stepped back. "I don't think that's any of your business." She nearly ran out of the store.

"What did you do to her?" Eli asked as he stopped behind Chelsea.

"I'm not sure, but I may get questioned by the police. You have any luck with the boy?"

"Didn't try. I think we need an introduction to these kids. We should find Jeff and ask his girlfriend to introduce us."

"Sounds good," Chelsea said, "but I don't know how I'm going to get that girl to agree to let me buy her a dress — or send her one. Come on, let's go back to the car. I'm going to email Mom to overnight me a dress she has in an upstairs closet."

"Think Abby will like it?"

"At that age, all a girl wants to do is show skin and sparkle."

"Girls change as they get older?"

"Not funny," she said, but she laughed.

They left the store and walked back to the

car, then sat there while Chelsea tapped a long email to her mother. She'd just pressed SEND when the two back doors of the car abruptly opened. Chelsea didn't move, but Eli was halfway across the seat, as though he meant to attack whoever had flung the doors open.

It was a moment before he sat back down, and Chelsea saw that Abby and Scully were sitting in the backseat.

Abby spoke first. "It was the ballet slippers. When I saw some really cute pink ones in the store, they made me remember where I saw you. You went over my fence, and both of you cleaned out the shed."

Eli and Chelsea were so stunned that they just looked between the seats at the two kids in silence.

"Who are you?" Scully asked. "You don't look like thieves."

Eli nodded toward the glove box and Chelsea opened it. She knew that his firearm was hidden at the top, but she didn't think that's what he wanted. Instead, she reached in and pulled out a leather case and handed it to Eli.

He held up an FBI badge.

Scully took it, examined it, then looked at Abby. "Told you so." He looked back at Eli. "Is this about Orin Peterson?"

"I can't talk about a case. It's —" Eli began.

"It has to be!" Abby said vehemently. "You have to get rid of him, get him out of our house!"

"What's that slimeball doing in your *house*?" Chelsea asked.

"Chelsea!" Eli said in warning. "You can't —"

"Yes, I can!" she said and looked at Abby. "Tell us what's going on."

"He was in my room. He —"

"He made a pass at you?" Chelsea asked in horror.

"No," Scully said. "He's searching for something but we don't know what. We covered for you on the shed, but he's not interested in it. His wife died and —"

"No, she didn't," Chelsea said with a glance at Eli. "I think you two should tell us from the beginning everything that's happened."

Abby started to speak but Scully put his hand on her arm. "We want to know why you two stole everything that was in the shed."

"If you saw us there," Eli said, "why didn't you call the police?"

Scully looked at Abby for a moment, then back at Eli. "We didn't want to upset Abby's mom. She's afraid of what's inside that shed. But we know there's nothing of importance in those boxes."

"You two went through them?" Eli asked.

"Every page," Scully said with pride.

"What does that man want from us?" Abby said, and there were tears in her eyes.

"What does he *say* he wants?" Eli asked.

"I think we need to go somewhere private so we can consolidate information," Scully said, sounding like an adult.

"There's a restaurant —" Eli began.

But Scully cut him off. "Take us back to Edilean."

"We're strangers to you," Chelsea said primly. "You can't just ride off with us."

"I took photos of you two and sent them to Shamus. He says you're okay, so let's go."

Eli looked at Chelsea, his eyebrows raised.

"Robin and Marian Les Jeunes the Next Generation seem to be alive and well," she mumbled as Eli started the car.

"We'll go to my house, a place where Shamus has been," Eli said.

Scully nodded as he took Abby's hand in his.

Thirty minutes later they were all seated at the breakfast table at the house in Edilean, with lemonade and cookies before them. Abby, with Scully's help, began telling her story.

Two nights before, Orin Peterson had shown up at their house with a cheap suitcase — and he was crying. He said his beloved wife had just died and he had nowhere else to go. The next morning, after Grace left for work, Orin had asked Abby about the combination to the lock on the shed. He said he just wanted to make sure it was in a safe place.

"That's when I put everything together," Abby said. She looked at Chelsea. "First horrible ol' Orin showed up and asked about what's in the shed. Then you did a ballet step over the fence, and you guys took everything."

"What did you tell him?" Eli asked.

"Nothing at first. I said I had to go, then I called Scully."

"And he had a plan," Chelsea said. "Eli was like that. Still is. He always has a plan."

"You?" Scully said in contempt. "I bet in high school you were on the football team. Or did you go in for basketball?" There was venom in his voice. "Do you even know how to turn on a computer?"

"Scully!" Abby said.

"I manage," Eli said with a bit of a smile. "What did you do about Peterson?"

"It was Scully's idea to tell him that we'd

taken everything out of the shed and put it in a neighbor's big dumpster," Abby said proudly.

"How did he react?" Chelsea asked.

Abby shrugged. "He was glad, I think, but I'm not sure. He'd spent the day searching. Everything in my room had been moved. Not a lot, but enough that I knew it was different. What does he want from us?"

"And what do you two want?" Scully asked, his eyes narrowed at the adults.

"Honestly," Eli said, "we don't know what the man is after. We don't know anything about him for sure."

"Except that he steals money from Abby's mom," Scully said. "Have you ever seen a man do that?"

"Yes," Eli said. "When I was a kid, I had to watch my biological father come up with lie after lie to get my mother to give him money. He didn't need it; he just wanted to win the game."

"Orin needs it," Abby said. "He's poor." She looked at her hands.

Scully spoke up. "Abby's mom said they have to be nice because of what Abby's dad did to him."

"He did *not* do that!" Abby said. "I'll *never* believe it!"

"I know," Scully said softly, "but —"

"I don't think your dad did anything bad, either," Chelsea said, "and I have some photos you should see." She got her camera and quickly flipped through to the ones she'd taken of Orin and his healthy wife at their big house beside a lake.

"This is his house?" Abby asked, sounding confused. "Who is that woman?"

Now it was Chelsea and Eli's turn to tell how everything had come about. Chelsea did most of the talking, starting with the overnight camping that she'd hated so much. "It was all dirt and mosquitoes," she said, "but Eli wanted to do it, so of course I followed him. Here, I'll show you."

Getting up, she got the box where she knew Eli kept photos of the two of them as kids. There was astonishment from the teenagers as they saw how pretty Chelsea was, and how thin and geeky Eli was.

Throughout the story, Scully kept his eyes on Eli, watching him and seeming to be puzzled.

When Chelsea finished her story, she showed Abby a photo she'd just received from her mother. "It's a dress I wore when I was younger. My mother keeps everything. I thought it might fit you."

The dress in the picture was pale pink, floor length, strapless, and covered with thousands of tiny crystals. They were most dense at the waist, then gradually lessened top and bottom.

"Wow," Abby said. "That's beautiful."

"My mom can send it if you'd like, and you can wear it to the dance."

"Could I?" Abby said in wonder. "But I don't have shoes."

"I have some Manolos that might fit you."

"Oh." Abby seemed to be incapable of speech.

"Let's go upstairs and see what we can find," Chelsea said.

Eli stood up. "Want to see my new game?" he asked Scully. They went into the living room and turned on the TV. In seconds, the game box was on. They sat side by side, their hands filled with the controllers.

"How did you get the new *Trafalgar Warriors* game?" Scully asked. "No! Don't go that way. There's always a trap there."

"I know," Eli said. "It was too predictable so I changed it. Go left, but avoid that rock. I put snakes under it."

"You . . ." Scully looked at Eli. "You wrote this game?"

"I had to do something. The government pays me nothing, and how was I going to win Chelsea back if I was broke? Leap over that open pit."

392

Scully agilely moved the controls to miss the demon that jumped out of the hole. "Win her back from what?"

"From all the catastrophes that that damned beauty of hers causes. You ever wish Abby was born ugly?"

"All the time," Scully said. "But you look like her."

Eli shrugged. "I grew taller and put on some muscle. How tall is your dad?"

"Six-two and my mom was five-ten."

"Then the odds are that in a couple of years you'll shoot up."

"But what do I do *now*?" There was such vehemence in his voice that he missed a pitfall and his warrior fell dead. He put down the controller. "Abby likes some dumb jock named Baze. He's only asking her out because she's so pretty and he wants to make his ex-girlfriend, Ashley, jealous. As soon as they get back together, he'll dump Abby."

"I'm sure you're right," Eli said. "Then you'll have to listen to her heartbreak. Wait until you see pictures online where she's laughing with some guy who's not as smart as his horse."

Scully's eyes were wide. He'd never before met someone who truly understood his problems. "If all this about Peterson comes out, I'm afraid Abby's mom will move. I heard her say she's always wanted to see California. Why are you looking at me like that?"

"Because I'm seeing my past in your future. You ever wonder how you could do things differently?"

"Abby says I never asked her to the dance, but —"

"She would have laughed at you and not believed you were serious," Eli said. "I know that too well. I have an idea. What if you went to the prom on your own? With someone other than Abby?"

"I don't want to go with anyone else," Scully said.

Eli picked up his phone and flipped through the photos to stop at a picture of his two cousins Lainey and Paige. They were very pretty young women, wearing thin summer dresses, their long hair blown by the breeze.

"They're . . ." Scully said.

"Right. They are. Tall, beautiful, smart, talented. How about if I get them to fly down here and go as your date?"

"*Both* of them?"

"Sure. Why not? Actually, I think they should come sooner and spend some time teaching you a few dances."

"I can't dance."

"Of course you can't. At your age, I couldn't either, but I learned. How does all this sound to you?"

"Great, but I need to help Abby. That man —"

"Chelsea and I will figure out Abby's problems. Besides, it might do her some good to be told that you're doing something she doesn't know about. As for her moving, what's your dad like? He's a widower, right?"

"Yeah. My mom died when I was four and it's been just Dad and me. He likes Abby's mother a lot, but she won't go out with him. Abby says she feels guilty over what she thinks her husband did."

"Embezzled funds? Bankrupted a big company? Put Peterson and his sick wife on the poverty line?"

"Yeah," Scully said. "All of that. Abby's tried to get her mother to go to Richmond to see that the furniture store is still thriving, but she won't do it."

"Both stores are doing well," Eli said. "And no matter what Peterson says, he still owns them." The sound of the laughter of the two females as they came downstairs made them stop talking.

"What are you two up to?" Chelsea asked.

"We were looking at the polo scores," Eli answered.

"Did Rodrigo win as usual?" Chelsea was smiling. "I think we should take these guys home. You and I have some things to do."

"Can you take me to my dad's store?" Scully asked Eli. "I'd like for him to meet you."

"In that case, Abby and I need to do some shopping," Chelsea said. "Just let me get some things and . . ." She gave Eli a look, then turned back to the teenagers. "Make yourselves at home. Kitchen is there, bathroom is to the left."

Seconds later, Chelsea and Eli were in the bedroom. "What did you find out?" Chelsea asked as she went to the bathroom to repair her makeup.

"The kid is heartbroken about Abby going out with another guy. I know how he feels. You in that pink dress with Axel. I saw him a few years ago. He has a beer belly and he's behind on his child support."

Chelsea glared at him in the mirror. "Could you stop with the guilt? I'm here now and if we ever get any time alone, I'm going to rip your clothes off. Isn't that enough for you?"

Eli gave a one-sided smile. "How about a quickie up against a wall?"

Chelsea halted with the lipstick tube in her hand as she considered, but then applied it. "Tempting, but we can't. Kids have no sense of time or privacy. Besides, I'm beginning to think all this is serious. Abby is afraid of Peterson. What have you heard from your dad?"

"Just that nothing has been found out. But I don't think Peterson would go to Grace if she didn't have something he wanted. We just need to figure out what it is."

Chelsea stepped back into the bedroom. "You don't think there's more than money involved in this, do you?"

Eli knew what she meant. He lowered his voice. "That maybe Abby's father didn't commit suicide? That maybe Peterson had a hand in his death? Yeah, I do. And I worry about Abby and Grace. I have Mike Newcomb looking into it."

"Who is he?"

Quickly, Eli told her of his conversation with his mother.

"Why didn't you tell me this before?"

"I would have, but you were in the kitchen wearing my underwear and flirting with Lanny."

"And I got a lot of information about Grace from him and his brother. You'd be amazed at what long, naked legs can accomplish."

"The same with shirtless men and women," Eli shot back at her.

For a moment they looked at each other, their eyes angry, but they soon turned to hot. Eli grabbed Chelsea's arm and spun her around so her back was to the wall. His mouth was on hers before she hit.

His tongue searched her mouth, his hands slid down to her round bottom, and he lifted her up. Her leg came up around his hip. As his kiss went deeper, he lifted her so both her long, slim legs were around his waist.

Her hands slipped under his shirt, running over the muscles, feeling the strength of him, the very maleness of him.

There was a knock on the bedroom door but they ignored it.

Eli's hand went to Chelsea's breast.

The knock came again, followed by a turning of the doorknob. If Eli hadn't locked the door, it would have opened.

"Hey!" Abby said from the other side of the door. "My mom just texted me that she's on her way home. I don't want her there alone with that man, so could we go?"

Reluctantly, Eli removed his mouth from Chelsea's skin. "Be there in a minute." He set her to the floor and looked at her. His eyes were still fiery, but also full of regret. He stepped away from her. "You go. I'll be out there when I'm presentable."

She glanced downward. He wasn't in any condition to be seen. "I'll take Abby home, then I'll come back here. No. Actually, I have to talk to Pilar, but you and I will have dinner together and —"

"I can't. Jeff wants us to go out with him and Melissa. I think he wants to tell me that he's going to quit working for me. He —"

Again, Abby knocked on the door.

With a sigh, Chelsea opened it.

"What happened to your lipstick?" Abby asked.

"It was kissed away." Chelsea stepped into the hall, closing the door behind her. "You ready to go?"

"Yeah, sure," Abby said. When she passed Scully, she gave a lift to her eyebrows and followed Chelsea to the front door. The two women left the house.

A few minutes later, Eli entered the living room.

Scully was holding a copy of the second *Trafalgar* game, the one that wasn't on the stands yet. "Can I . . . ?"

"Sure, take it," Eli said and they went to the car.

Once they were inside, Scully said, "So

how did you get her? What did you do?"

"If you mean Chelsea, she isn't mine. She keeps telling me she's going to leave."

"To do what?"

"I don't know. Travel around the world, I guess. Again."

"I like to *do* things and Abby does too, but right now she's so dazzled by her football player that she can't remember that."

"I know Chelsea is enjoying the adventure of trying to find out the truth about Peterson. But when that's done, what will she do while I'm at work?"

"Help *other* people?" Scully suggested.

Eli glanced at the boy. "You have a brain, don't you?"

"Right now I'd trade it for your pecs and abs," Scully said.

Eli laughed. "I should introduce you to my cousin Raine. When we were kids he called me Toothpick."

"I hate bullies."

"Raine isn't one. I called him Stump, as in tree stump. Actually, he was the best trainer in the gym. Listen, I don't write these games alone. There's an entire team that handles them. Maybe you'd like to have some input on the third game. Any interest?"

Scully was staring at Eli in openmouthed astonishment.

"I take it that means yes?"

"My dad owns —"

"I know," Eli said. "He runs the local computer store and he's a good programmer. You spend a lot of time in the back of the store with him. You're better with software, while he takes on the hardware problems."

"If you know so much about us, why did you ask me?"

"All the info on paper can't tell the deeper facts about a person. I especially wanted to hear how you felt about your dad."

"What did you find out?"

"That maybe you love the guy as much as I do my dad."

"Yeah, I do," Scully said softly.

"Think there's any chance of him getting together with Abby's mom?"

Scully smiled. "That would be great, wouldn't it? Then Abby and I would be together and . . ." He shrugged. "Don't tell her about that idea, would you?"

"Only if you don't tell Chelsea my secrets."

They looked at each other and grinned in agreement.

11

When Chelsea got back to the house it was nearly four and all she could think about was how to distract Eli. Above all, she couldn't give him time to look in her eyes and see that she was hiding something from him.

In these last days she'd come to remember the good and bad of being with someone who knew her so well. With her past boyfriends, all she'd had to do was look good and that was enough. If she was upset about something, they never even noticed.

But Eli wasn't like that. He knew that under her woman's body was the girl he'd known since they were kids.

After she'd dropped Abby off at her house — and Chelsea had taken care not to be seen — her mother called her. Since Chelsea was going to be late to her meeting with Pilar, she didn't want to pick up, but she knew her mother wouldn't send the dress if she didn't explain.

"Hi, Mom," Chelsea said in her most cheerful, nothing-is-wrong voice. "I'm sure you want to know about the dress. Well, you see, this kid I met through friends doesn't have anything to wear to her school prom, so I thought —"

"Screw the dress," her mom said. "I want to know about you and Eli."

Chelsea rolled her eyes. Trust her mother to go for the throat. "We're fine. Great. Couldn't be better. We're getting married next month because I'm three months pregnant with Eli's child. It's going fast because he did it all through some genetic hocus-pocus he's experimenting on for the government. I'd explain it but it's Top Secret. He —"

"Chelsea!" her mother said sternly.

"Sorry," she said. "Eli is fine and so am I. I have to go."

"Why? What's so urgent?"

Chelsea grit her teeth as she looked at the dashboard clock. She didn't have time to concoct some polite lie. "We think there may have been a murder connected to something Eli and I are looking into it." Instantly, she knew she shouldn't have said that! Her mother would probably call the police and —

"That's wonderful," her mom said. "Really great. Fabulous."

"Mom," Chelsea said in disbelief, "Eli and I are sticking our noses into what could be a *murder*!"

"I heard you, dearest. It's just like when you and Eli were children. You're helping some deserving girl go to a party, and there's someone else who I'm sure is a victim of a great injustice. Oh, yes! It all sounds very good. It's so much better than hearing you talk about what Clive and Nigel said to make you cry. I have to tell your father about this. I think we'll break open a bottle of champagne. Give my love to Eli, and I do mean that. Love. Bye, my darling child." She hung up.

As Chelsea tossed her phone onto the passenger seat, she shook her head in bewilderment. Were her parents normal? Shouldn't her mother have been *worried* at the mention of murder? And what was all that about her past miseries? Didn't they *care* about what those men had put their daughter through? Infidelities. Emotional cruelties. Such profound insensitivities to her needs that they were like knife wounds. Didn't her parents —

Chelsea looked at the clock. She didn't have time to ponder her past problems. Pilar had asked to talk to her and to keep it secret from Eli, and that's what Chelsea was doing.

As Chelsea drove back to the house, she was thinking about her meeting with Pilar and all they'd talked about. Chelsea had been given a great deal to think about. Maybe there could be a future that didn't involve how she *looked.* They'd met at a little restaurant, sitting across from each other and keeping their voices down so they wouldn't be overheard.

"I was wondering about something," Pilar said. "We all knew that Eli's heart was already taken — and broken. Are you going to put it back together?"

"I might," Chelsea said, smiling. "So tell me your ideas for our future."

"When Eli finds out what you and I are thinking about doing . . ." Pilar shook her head.

"Let me handle him," Chelsea said. "Now tell me how you think I can change my life."

When Chelsea entered the house and heard the shower running, she straightened her body and her face. The last thing she wanted was for Eli to ask her questions about what she'd been doing for the last few hours. But then, she knew exactly how to distract him.

As she went through the bedroom she flung her clothes off so that by the time she reached the bath she was nude. She opened the steamy shower door and stepped inside.

Eli picked her up, her long legs going around his waist, and instantly entered her. "I thought about you all afternoon. I wanted to finish what we started."

"Me too," she said, his lips on her neck.

The hot water beat down on them as Eli's long, slow strokes began. Chelsea leaned back against the wall, her body slanted to give him better access. His lips touched her body, his hands running over her.

Their lovemaking was intensified by a yearning from having been started and then interrupted.

Afterward, they held on to each other, the water still coming down, the shower even more steamy.

"I missed you," Eli whispered, his bare chest against hers.

She was too busy kissing him to answer.

He set her down, then soaped his hands and began washing her. "What did you find out?" he asked.

"About what?" There was a tiny bit of a high pitch to her voice and she knew she needed to cover it. "I told my mom you and

I were involved in something dangerous, and she was happy about it. It really annoyed me." She was glad she was facing the shower wall so Eli couldn't see her face.

"She knows I'll protect you."

"From guns?"

He turned her around to lather the front of her. "What makes you think guns will be involved?"

"I don't. It's just a possibility. Did you meet Scully's dad?"

"Yeah, and I found out that the two kids met through their parents. Scully's father, Nolan, went to Frazier Motors to put in a new computer system. It's not what I would have installed but —"

"They met then?" Chelsea took the soap from him and began to lather his body.

"They did. Scully said his dad hadn't been interested in any woman since his wife died, but that he liked Abby's mom very much."

"Let me guess," Chelsea said as she ran her hands over Eli's bare, muscular chest. Then did it again. And again. "Grace broke it off. She said she had too much in her past to go forward."

"That's exactly right." He put one of Chelsea's legs on his hip and stroked it with soapy hands. "I remember how annoyed I was when you outgrew your bike. I thought the length of your legs was totally unnecessary."

"What do you think now?"

"I need every inch of them."

"I need lots of inches too," she said, her mouth by his ear, her hand between his legs.

Smiling, Eli turned her back around. "Do you know that —"

"Grace blames herself for her husband's death? Beats herself up for not knowing he was so miserable that he wanted out of life?"

"That's what Nolan said." Eli was looking at her in awe.

"How'd you get him to talk to you so intimately?"

"My persuasive personality," Eli said. When Chelsea looked over her shoulder at him, her face skeptical, he laughed. "I asked him."

"Just flat out *asked* him?"

He ignored her meaning, turned her back around, then with as much full body touching as he could manage, he stepped out and grabbed a towel. "I asked if he'd be interested if I got him and Grace back together, and his story came out."

"Since when are you a matchmaker?"

"I am whenever you are in my life. I've come to realize that people shouldn't live their lives alone. Both Pilar and Jeff are going in different directions, and you're going back to some dull-brained jock, and —"

Chelsea pulled the shower door closed and put her head under the water. She'd heard it — or a version of it — too many times before. The truth was that right now she wasn't sure what she was going to do, but her meeting with Pilar was making her see possibilities for the future.

In the bedroom, Eli was smiling. He'd already told Jeff and Melissa that he couldn't make dinner but would they please take Chelsea out. Eli wanted to make sure she was occupied for the evening while he was, well, busy. He'd traded favors with an FBI friend to get Peterson, Abby, and Grace out of the house for the evening so Eli could look around.

Now all he had to do was come up with an excuse to go out for the evening. He thought it would be better if he told Chelsea he was doing something Top Secret for the government. Maybe he'd name-drop. She'd seemed impressed by the president, so maybe he'd use him. If he was going to lie, he might as well make it a big one.

Chelsea was silently walking around inside Grace's house. It was nearly dark outside but she didn't dare turn on the lights for fear someone would see her. Earlier, when she'd told Pilar what she planned to do as soon as she got Eli out of the house, Pilar had lent her a tiny flashlight that had a pinpoint beam.

"People are less likely to see it than a regular flashlight."

Chelsea was glad to find out that Pilar knew so many tricks.

"I listen," Pilar said with a shrug. "It wasn't as though anyone ever gave me any real responsibility."

"Not even Eli?"

"Especially not him," Pilar said.

That had been hours ago, and now Chelsea was looking around Abby's bedroom and trying to imagine what Orin Peterson was looking for. A photo? A document? But wouldn't Abby know that she had either of those?

Unless someone else had hidden it, Chelsea thought. Maybe it was Abby's dad who'd secreted whatever it was away.

Furniture! she thought. Since both Orin and Abby's father sold furniture, maybe they knew of some secret compartment.

She turned the light toward Abby's bed. It was plain wood, painted white, and looked old enough that her father would have seen it. There were round knobs on the four corners, but when she twisted them, they didn't move. She felt down the square posts, feeling for anything that could conceal a hidden compartment. There was nothing.

Next she'd have to get down and look up under the bed. She had just bent down when a hand went over her mouth.

For a few seconds she struggled and tried to bite the hand.

"It's me," Eli said, and removed his hand.

"So all that about going to dinner with Melissa and Jeff was a lie? No government work?"

"I don't have time to argue with you now. Peterson just parked his car down the road." He put his hand tightly on her arm and began pulling her toward the back door.

"Damn!" Chelsea said. "He must have sneaked out of the restaurant." In spite of Eli's pulling, she didn't move.

When Eli looked at her in the dim light, he gave a sigh of exasperation. He knew her look of stubbornness so well. She wasn't leaving. "Oh, hell!" he muttered, then flung the closet door open and practically shoved her inside. He got in beside her and pulled the door closed. "Did you set this up?" he growled through clenched teeth.

"Of course," she said, unconcerned about his anger. "While you were playing video games with Scully, I arranged with Abby for her to take her mother and ol' Orin out to dinner on money Abby said she'd saved from her allowance. But then, I thought that tonight you were busy doing something for the president. Something that was so secret that you couldn't tell me about it." Her expression told him what she thought of that lie.

As she looked back toward the room, she was glad the closet doors had fixed louvers. They'd be able to see what Peterson did when he got here. She wasn't worried about his finding her and Eli because she had Abby's permission to be here. "How did you know I was here?"

"I didn't at first. But when Jeff texted me that my FBI friend found an empty house, and that you said you couldn't go to dinner, then Peterson, Abby, and Grace showed up at an expensive restaurant, it didn't take much to see what you were up to." They were in the back of the closet, close together in the narrow space. "What do you have on?"

"A black silk shirt," she said. "Silk against skin is one of the great wonders of the earth."

"Bet I could get it off," he said. "And my hands might feel even better than silk."

They started to kiss but the soft sound of a door opening took them back to why they were here.

When Orin turned on a bedside lamp, they could see him clearly. Just as Chelsea had done, he ran his hands along the bedposts.

The light inside the closet was dim but they could see each other well enough for Chelsea to shake her head no. She'd already looked there.

Orin left the bed and went to the far wall to Abby's desk. It too was old. He pulled out a drawer, didn't so much as glance at the contents, but held it up to look at the bottom, the sides, and the back. He examined the front of the drawer, seeming to search for a hidden compartment.

Chelsea made a face at Eli to say that the man was certainly thorough.

Just as Orin slid the drawer back into its slot, the doorbell rang. Instantly, Orin reached under his jacket and pulled out a gun.

Chelsea had to bite her lips to suppress a gasp. It was one thing to be hiding from a man who was trespassing, but another to be caught by a man wielding a gun.

With a look of I-told-you-so, Eli pulled Abby's heavy winter coat over his head —

and Chelsea went under with him.

Eli had his phone in his hand, the wool coat covering the light, and he tapped out a message to Jeff. DIVERSION NEEDED. ABBY'S HOUSE. NH4.

As soon as he sent the message, he lifted the coat from them and looked back at the room. Orin was looking out the window at whoever had rung the doorbell. It rang again, but he made no move to answer it.

After a few minutes they could hear voices and footsteps outside. Whoever had been there was leaving. Orin stepped away from the window, put the gun back in his pants, and started on the second drawer.

In the pretty little restaurant, Jeff and Melissa were having dinner. Since their first meeting they'd rarely been apart. Jeff was staying in the dreary apartment above the sheriff's office, and Melissa had come up with every excuse possible to be there with him.

For the last couple of years Jeff had felt restless, as though he wanted more in life. For a while it had been a dream come true to get to follow Eli around the world, even to get calls in the middle of the night. It had even been exciting to visit Eli in a hospital.

But somewhere in there the extreme excitement had become boring. When he visited his kid sister, he found that he envied her her two kids. He wished he could know where he was going to be next month. Hell, he'd like to be sure where he'd be spending the night. At any minute, Eli might call, and Jeff would have to leave.

Right now, for all that Jeff seemed to be on the outs with Eli, he knew their friendship was strong enough to withstand whatever Jeff decided his future would be. But now was not the time for that discussion, for Eli was totally absorbed with Chelsea. After years of seeing his boss ignore women, it was startling to see him so fascinated with one.

Melissa had seen it too. "What will Eli do if Chelsea leaves him?" she asked as the waiter poured the wine.

"Bury himself in work," Jeff said. "And I do mean that literally. My worry is that when he goes into the field again, he won't be . . . careful. He takes too many risks as it is."

"I don't mean to be negative," Melissa said, "but I can't imagine someone like Chelsea settling down and making cupcakes for the school fund-raiser."

"What about you?" Jeff asked. "You like

cupcakes?"

"I'm rather good at baking," she said, smiling.

"I'm beginning to think that you're good at everything."

"I'm —" She broke off because Jeff's phone buzzed. She knew he had two cell phones, one that he often turned off, but the one with the black cover was always on, always with him. Right now it was on the table beside him.

Jeff didn't hesitate in picking up the phone and looking at the message. "I have to go," he said as he stood up, dropped a fifty-dollar bill on the table, and hurried out of the restaurant.

Melissa caught up with him when he reached the valet stand.

Jeff turned to her. "Where does Grace Ridgeway live?"

"I'll drive you there."

"No!" he said. "It's Eli and it's NH4."

Melissa glared at him.

"It's our own code. It means Need Help, Level Four. That's the top. There might be firearms involved."

"Oh?" She opened her handbag to pull out a .45. "Like this one?"

Jeff looked at the weapon, then at her. "I think maybe this tells too much about me, but I'm so hot for you right now that if I didn't have to go save Eli, I'd pull you into the bushes."

The valet arrived with Melissa's car. "I have lots of shrubs around my house, and when we finish this, I'll show them to you. Get in. I'm driving."

"Yes, ma'am," Jeff said, grinning as he got into the passenger seat.

When Eli and Chelsea heard the siren coming toward the house, they smiled at each other.

Orin looked up at the sound, but he didn't seem to think it had anything to do with him. He was examining the fourth drawer. But when the dark sedan with its blazing lights stopped in front of the house, he dropped the drawer and ran for the back door.

"Stay here!" Eli said to Chelsea, then leaped out of the closet.

Chelsea didn't think about what she did, but as she'd always done, she just followed Eli. But when she burst out of the closet, she saw that Orin had a gun pointed at the middle of Eli.

Chelsea's mind seemed to work with lightning speed. It looked like Eli was going to leap and Orin was going to fire. There was no room for Eli to get away from a bullet.

Remembering the lecherous way Orin had looked at her, she grabbed the top of her shirt with both hands and pulled hard. Buttons went flying — and exposed her breasts in a bra so tiny it was barely a whisper of black lace.

For the flash of a second, Orin's eyes left Eli and went to Chelsea's nearly bare chest. And in that second, Eli was able to knock the gun from Orin's hand. It hit the far wall and went clattering down.

But Chelsea's trick of exposing herself almost backfired when Eli saw what she'd done. "Bloody hell!" he said just before he made a leap for Orin.

But when Orin saw Eli's momentary distraction, he ran toward the door. Chelsea tried to step in front of him, but he pushed her so hard that she fell against Eli. She knew Eli was furious at her as he worked to get out of the spiderweb of her long hair and even longer legs.

He tossed her onto the bed, then ran to the door. Chelsea was close behind him.

When he stopped in the doorway, blocking her exit or even from seeing outside, she yelled, "He's going to get away!"

Eli stepped aside to let her stand beside

him. In the backyard near the shed, Orin was clinging to the concrete block wall, frantically and futilely trying to get his out-of-shape body over it. Below him was Rex, the Ridgeway family dog, barking loudly as it jumped up, trying to bite Orin's heels.

"Get it off of me!" Orin shouted as his thick legs fought to get up the wall. "Get it —" He screamed as the dog clamped its teeth into his calf.

Eli stepped forward, but then Melissa came through the side gate, gun drawn.

"Down!" she ordered the dog, and it obeyed.

"I'm going to sue!" Orin yelled as he fell to the ground.

"You're under arrest," Melissa said as she put handcuffs on him and began to read him his rights.

"What for?"

"Trespassing. Attempted child molestation. We'll come up with something to keep you locked up until we get to the truth."

Orin glared at Eli and Chelsea. "It's those two who've been stalking me." As Melissa pulled him toward the gate, he sneered at Eli. "I'll have you in jail for this! I have connections! I have —"

"Shut up!" Melissa said and pushed him through the gate.

Jeff, who had stayed to one side as he watched it all, went to Eli and Chelsea. "You guys okay?"

"Fine," Eli said as Rex came up to him and he stroked the dog's head. "You have any safety pins? For Chelsea's shirt?"

"Give me a break," Chelsea said. "I saved your life, so what do a few missing buttons mean?"

"You could have —"

Watching them, Jeff grinned and put his hands in his pockets. "I'm going with Melissa. Chelsea, would you help me pick out a ring to give her?"

That so startled her that she quit arguing with Eli. "So soon?"

"When you know, you know. I gotta go. See you later."

When they were alone, Eli turned to Chelsea and smiled. "We got rid of them all."

"That we did. You want to go home and . . ." She shrugged.

"I'd love to." He put his arm around her shoulders. "Home. I like the sound of that."

"Mmmm," Chelsea said as she rubbed her bare legs against Eli's. "So what's on the agenda for today?"

"I figure you'll spend every minute on getting dressed. You are planning to go to the dance tonight, aren't you?"

"You know me so well," she said as she began kissing his neck. "Dealing with my clothes is just what I'm going to spend the entire day doing."

He pulled away to look at her. "I don't like the sound of that. What are you actually planning to do?"

Chelsea rolled to her back. Last night Melissa said she'd turned Peterson over to Dr. Tris, the local physician, with instructions to hold him as long as possible. He'd still be in the hospital during the prom tonight, so there was no danger that he'd show up. As long as whatever he wanted hadn't been found, he would be a menace. Last night Eli had spent hours on the phone calling people in the government, pulling in favors, to find out about Orin Peterson and the truth behind Gilbert Ridgeway's death.

Even though no one had found whatever it was that Orin was after, Grace now had a reason to throw him out of her house.

Chelsea knew that Eli was going to try to get her to swear that from now on, the case would be in the hands of the authorities. No more sneaking about in the middle of the night.

"Actually, you're right. Abby and I are going to do a girl day," Chelsea said, her eyes wide in innocence. "Hair, nails, feet, all of it. My mom sent the dress for Abby and one for me. And your tux needs to be pressed. It's a busy day ahead. By the way, Abby sent me a text asking if we knew where Scully was. What have you done with him?"

"What makes you think it was me?"

Chelsea narrowed her eyes at him.

Eli chuckled. "My cousins flew in, and while you were wherever you were all yesterday afternoon, they were giving Scully dance lessons."

"That was really nice of you." She flung the covers back to get out of bed, but Eli caught her hand.

"In case you missed it, that was a hint for you to tell me where you were."

"The First Lady called me to ask —" She broke off at his look. "You're not the only one who can lie. Where were *you*?"

"Since we both ended up in the same place, I guess we were doing the same thing. How long will it take to do your hair today?"

"Hours," she said, smiling. She got up, pulled on one of his T-shirts, and went into the bathroom.

When she came out, Eli was leaning back on the pillows, his hands behind his head.

"You either tell me what you're planning or I'll have you kidnapped and held in custody until after the dance."

"Oooooh. By Men in Black? Men so physically fit they can hardly wear a suit? Will they have those little microphone thingies in their ears? Can they —"

"Chelsea!" Eli said in warning.

She sat down on the edge of the bed and began to rub moisturizer on her legs. "Okay, I'll tell you — but only because we *need* you. And it's nothing bad."

"*We* is you and who else?"

"Pilar. I really like her! I've never had a lot of women friends in my life."

He looked at her long leg that she was stroking. "Can't imagine why."

"You're sweet. But anyway, do you think you could make Grace's computer at Frazier Motors stop working for a day?"

"Enough that the local repairman, who happens to be Scully's dad, has to be called in to fix it?"

She kissed him on the forehead. "Now who says men don't have brains?"

When she started to get up, Eli pulled her down onto the bed and began kissing her. "Are you the one doing matchmaking now?"

"I am." She kissed him back. "Pilar's already told Lanny about it, and he's ready for a system breakdown. We're all just waiting on you to go to the dealership and do it. It's early, but Lanny will let us in before the place opens."

"Puh-lease," Eli said as he kissed her more.

"You can break a computer from a distance?"

Her tone of innocence made him laugh. "You know I could have done that when I was eight. You're up to something and I want to know what it is."

Smiling, Chelsea rubbed her leg between his. "Speaking of 'up' . . ."

With a groan of exasperation, Eli pulled her on top of him.

12

They made an entrance. Chelsea insisted that they wait until thirty minutes after the dance started before they entered, then she and Abby went in front, Eli and Baze behind them.

Chelsea's gown was a deep, rich blue halter top, with the sides open to the waist. There was a slit up the side of the skirt almost to her hip. The fabric had tiny brilliants woven into it so that it shimmered in the shadowy lights, glowing like candlelight under silk. In her ultrahigh heels she was six feet tall and very impressive.

Beside her was Abby in her strapless dress with thousands of crystals catching the light.

They paused at the doorway and looked around them. The high school gym had been decorated in blues and greens, with sparkling ribbons hanging from the ceiling. Suspended in the center was an old-fashioned mirrored ball that cast tiny, flattering lights over everyone.

Abby started to step forward, but Chelsea gave her a look to stay still. The four of them just stood there in silence, waiting.

After a few moments the nearest dancing couples stopped to look at the latest arrivals. They were properly awed. The gowns Chelsea and Abby wore looked like the runways they had come off of.

A couple stepped aside, then the next tier did, then the next, until it was clear from the band on the stage to them.

The lead singer, a kid who'd graduated from the school three years before, looked down the aisle that had been opened and saw the two beauties in the glimmering gowns. He signaled his band to stop playing. Turning, he said something to them, and they began playing a song called "Let the Party Begin."

Chelsea smiled at the young man. "Now we can go," she said to Abby, and the two couples slowly went forward.

The music changed to a slow tune, and Baze took Abby in his arms while Eli led Chelsea into a dance. The entire audience watched for a few moments, then joined in.

"So this is what it's like to be a popular kid," Eli said as he held Chelsea close.

"In high school, being popular is like being Queen of the World. But alas, then you leave the closed environment and go out into a world where there are lots of queens."

Smiling, he kissed her cheek. "It was a nice thing you did for Abby."

"Speaking of which, where is Scully?"

"Around." Eli dipped Chelsea.

"He will be here, won't he?"

"Oh, yes. With bells on. I won't let history repeat itself with yet another nerd being left out."

"I'm sorry I did that. I was so young that I really did believe you when you said you didn't want to go to the prom."

"But I didn't," Eli said as he extended his arm for her to turn around in a circle, then come back to him. "I wanted you to stay with me. Just me. To know no one else, to like no one but me. If I'd had my way, I would have locked you in a house and never let you out. I was a selfish little bastard."

Chelsea frowned. "I don't think that's true.

"I think it's time that I learn to give as well as take. You asked where I was yesterday afternoon. I was arranging my retirement."

"What?" She pulled back to look at him, but he pushed her head back down on his shoulder.

"Since you've been here, I've realized that

work isn't enough in my life. If you will stay with me, I will retire and we'll do whatever you want. Travel, live on a boat, anything you need to make you happy. We'll —"

"No," Chelsea said.

He looked at her, his face stricken. "No?"

"I mean no, you don't have to do that. Pilar and I are going to open a detective agency here in Edilean."

Eli stopped moving to stare at her. "You aren't talking about an agency that uses guns, are you?"

"Yes. In fact, Pilar has arranged for me to take shooting lessons."

"Shoo . . . shooting lessons?" He could barely say the words.

"My time with you has made me remember how much I liked what we did when we were kids. I got distracted for a few years, what with modeling and, well, other things, so —"

"Polo players and race-car drivers."

"Whatever. Pilar thinks my connections in those worlds will help us solve cases. And of course she knows some very high-end people. Did you know that she had an affair with — Oops. I can't tell you that. But anyway, we're trying to come up with a name for our new agency. You have any suggestions?"

"I forbid it," Eli said, his eyes steely with anger.

"I'd laugh, but with the open sides of this dress I'd pop out. Who are you to 'forbid' me anything? And what happened to your new realization of your selfishness?"

"I'm your husband-to-be, that's who I am. And a detective agency is too dangerous."

"How does a computer geek manage to live in the nineteenth century? Married or not, you can't forbid me anything. You —" She broke off at the sound of a familiar tune that came from Eli's inside pocket. Since she had no place to put a phone, she'd slipped hers into his jacket.

Before Eli could speak, Chelsea took the phone out. "It's Rodrigo and I have to take this." She made her way across the gym floor to go into the school. Eli was right behind her.

Inside, the lights were dim, but they could see about a dozen young couples wrapped around each other, slammed against the rows of lockers, and kissing.

"Rodrigo," Chelsea said into the phone, then listened. "You're ready to take me back, are you? Let me guess. You need someone with a brain to take care of your schedules. And of course I'm to make sure your horses are looked after so you have lots of time to party. What happened to cute little Tiffany?"

She listened. "I see. A twenty-two-year-old can't handle everything?"

Eli felt like snatching the phone away from her, but he controlled himself.

"Do you? Well, Roddy, dear, I'm afraid you're just going to have to find another 'love of your life' to put up with you. I'm staying where I am and I'm going to marry the guy who is the love of *my* life. And by the way, he is much better in bed than *you* are."

She clicked off, then looked at Eli. "Now where were we?"

"I don't remember," he said as he took her into his arms and began to kiss her.

Minutes later, he said, "Ah, yes, about this agency. We need to talk about that."

"I agree," Chelsea said. "Right after we discuss what kind of ring you're going to buy me. We need to —" She broke off because Baze threw open the big doors that led out of the gym.

"Where the hell have you two been?" he half yelled. Behind him was Abby and her face was white. With a shaking hand, she held out her cell phone.

Chelsea and Eli, heads together, read the text message. CME HOME NOW. BRNG RABIT.

"What does it mean?" Chelsea asked.

Baze gave Abby a moment to reply, but when she couldn't speak, he answered, "Abby's dad gave her a rabbit on a key chain. It's in her locker."

"Let's go get it," Eli said, and he and Baze took off running down the hall. The kissing couples didn't so much as look up at the commotion.

Abby stayed where she was, seemingly rooted in place. Chelsea looked at her.

"There are too many errors. My mom didn't write that, but it's her phone."

"I think we should go," Chelsea said and held out her hand. "Eli will take care of it, but we need to help him."

Abby drew a breath, then took Chelsea's hand and they began running. This time, with the women in their glorious dresses and high heels, the males of the kissing couples stopped to look — which caused the females to put a great deal more enthusiasm into what they were doing.

When Abby and Chelsea reached the locker, Eli and Baze were waiting, both of them tapping away on their cell phones.

"I hope that's the sheriff you're contacting," Chelsea said.

Eli nodded. "It is, and Jeff and my cousin Paige."

Chelsea wanted to ask about that, but Abby was trying to work the combination to her locker. Her hands were shaking so badly that she couldn't turn the dial, so Eli helped her. Baze didn't look up from his phone.

Abby removed the key ring from a hook stuck onto the back of the door and handed it to Eli.

"Flash drive," Eli and Chelsea said in unison. Because the lid had been glued in place, no one had realized it was more than just an ornament.

"Stay with them," Eli said to Chelsea, but her look made him know that she wasn't going to do that. With a sigh, he held out his hand to her and they began running in the direction of the parking lot.

"Nolan," Grace said, "I can't thank you enough for all you did today." It was just after 6:00 p.m. and they were at her house. A pizza had been delivered and he was opening a bottle of red wine. "It was really strange how you'd get my computer working, then it would shut itself down again."

"Yeah, it was," Nolan said, but his eyes didn't meet hers. All day he and Eli had exchanged texts. As soon as Nolan had fixed one thing, he'd text Eli and immediately something else would go wrong. By afternoon it became a game between the men. THAT ALL YOU GOT? Nolan had texted, and the next problem had occupied him for an hour before he fixed it. Afterward, he texted Eli, HOW ABOUT SOMETHING CREATIVE? It took him thirty minutes to find the little green dragon that Eli sent to the computer.

Nolan showed none of this to Grace. Instead, he just worked and listened. It hadn't been easy to get her to start talking. He accomplished it by asking her advice on how to deal with Scully. Did she know what the kids were up to?

After that, they'd sat in her office, and while Nolan worked on her computer, Grace talked. There were several times when he was shocked at what she told him about Orin Peterson and the times she'd given him money.

"I don't know the truth," Grace said, "but I think maybe the real story isn't what Orin's told me all these years."

Nolan wasn't sure what she meant, but he was beginning to think that there was more to her late husband's suicide than just despondency.

"Maybe I didn't . . ." Grace whispered.

"Maybe Gil wasn't . . ." She didn't finish her sentences, but Nolan had an idea that maybe the burden of guilt that she carried was being lifted.

Toward the end of the day, Nolan sent Eli one last text — FINISHED — and the computer continued to work. Nolan was packing up when Grace invited him to her house for pizza.

"Yes," he said. "I'd love to." He was afraid to say any more for fear that she'd see what was in his heart. When she'd first moved to Edilean they'd dated for four glorious months. It had been wonderful!

At first their two children had nothing to say to each other. Grace's pretty daughter was concerned with clothes and makeup and boys, while his son was as nerdy as they come. But through repeated visits, Abby's brain came to the fore and Scully learned some desperately needed social skills. By the end of that summer, Nolan thought they had become a family.

But one day, Grace called it off. She said some things about guilt and her late husband's suicide, but none of it made sense. All Nolan knew for sure was that one Saturday she went to meet with her husband's former business partner, and when she returned, she told Nolan she couldn't

434

see him anymore.

Nothing he said dissuaded her. For a few months he pursued her but she wouldn't budge. In anger, he went out with a couple of other women, but he didn't like them much.

After the breakup, Abby and Scully stayed friends — and there were times when Nolan was downright jealous. When she came to pick up Abby, he'd see Grace in her car, but they never talked.

Until today. Today she'd been different. It was as though something inside her had been released. She'd talked and even, a couple of times, laughed.

When she'd invited him for pizza, he didn't hesitate in saying yes.

"I'm sorry about Abby going to the prom with a football player," Grace said as she filled the wineglasses.

He agreed, but he wasn't going to betray his son by telling of Scully's hurt. "It's all right. Scully's happiest when he's in front of a computer."

"I know how much he cares about Abby. But the kid, Baze, is nice too."

"And he can dance," Nolan said. "And he knows how to talk to people and all those things I should have taught my son. If I knew how to do them, that is."

Grace laughed. "I think you're quite adept in social matters. Scully could be too if he had some training. It's just that Abby needs to learn that there is value in a male besides a muscular body."

Nolan smiled. "I've been thinking of joining Mike's Gym. Think that if I had some biceps I could win a girl's heart?"

Grace looked at him over her glass of wine. "I think you can win the heart of any woman just the way you are."

Nolan put his hand out to hers and she took it. In the next moment they were standing, their arms around each other, and kissing.

"I've missed you so much," Nolan whispered against her lips. "The time we spent together was some of the happiest of my life."

"And I've missed you. I'm so sorry I hurt you."

"Isn't this nice?" came a voice from a few feet away.

Turning, they saw Orin Peterson standing there holding a gun pointed at them. His shirt was misbuttoned; his trousers had no belt. There was a bloody scrape on his forehead. He looked as though he'd escaped from somewhere.

"Where's the rabbit?" he asked.

436

Grace stepped out of Nolan's arms. "Orin," she said as calmly as she could manage, "you look like you could use some food. The pizza is hot. How about if I make you some coffee?"

"Shut up! I've had enough of your whining. Where's the rabbit?"

"I think —" Nolan began.

Orin fired the gun at him, and if Nolan hadn't turned his head, he would have been hit. "The next one strikes," Orin said. He looked back at Grace. "Where the hell is it?"

"I have no idea what you're talking about. Nolan needs to go home, then you and I can sit down and talk this through. We'll find whatever it is that you want, but I can assure you that I've never owned a rabbit."

"Don't patronize me."

Grace's body was shaking but she didn't want him to see that. "I know your wife died recently but —"

Orin laughed. "You really are the stupidest woman I've ever met. All I had to do was dump a load of guilt on you, take some money, and you'd crawl back into your shell. But now I'm sick of waiting. I've had four years in hell because of you. I was always worrying, always afraid you were going to find out."

Grace took a step farther away from Nolan. Maybe if she could get Orin to concentrate on her, Nolan could slip away and get help.

"I didn't mean to do anything bad to you, Orin," Grace said. "I didn't want you to be in misery. Your poverty —"

"Oh, hell! Just shut the crap. Where is the little metal rabbit? And since you're too dumb to figure it out, I'll tell you that my wife is quite well. In fact, she was the one who planned everything. Paula has always been the smart one. That that husband of yours snooped into things wasn't something we thought would happen. I offered him twenty percent of everything if he'd keep quiet but he said no. Twenty percent! He was even dumber than you."

Grace was beginning to understand what Orin was saying. "You . . . you and Paula killed my husband because he knew too much?"

With a snort, Orin shook his head. "So now you finally stop crying and use your brain. Too bad it's all for nothing. I want —"

"It's a flash drive, isn't it?" Nolan said. "Shaped like a toy rabbit."

Grace drew in her breath. She knew what Orin wanted — and where it was.

At her sound, Orin looked at her for a moment and saw the fear there. Terror. A smile came across his face. "I *knew* it! That smart-aleck kid of yours has it, doesn't she?" On the kitchen island was Grace's cell phone. Grabbing it, and hardly removing his eyes from them, he texted Abby to come home immediately and bring . . . He looked at Grace. "Is it on a key ring?" He could see by her eyes that he was right. He finished the text and sent it. "Won't be long now and she'll be here."

Orin tossed the phone down and turned to Nolan. "So you're the town computer nerd. Years ago, I had to listen to Grace rave about you. Took me nearly two hours to get her to believe she wasn't worth a second husband. After all, she was such a bad wife that the first one killed himself just to get away from her." Orin was smirking. "Grace is such a coward! That kid of hers has more courage in her little finger than she has in her entire body."

"So what's on the drive?" Nolan asked. He was inching toward the sideboard, his right hand held behind him.

"None of your business. You know, all this is happening because of that nerd kid you have. I've always been afraid that he'd see that little rabbit and know what it was.

Paula told me it would never happen, but I knew it was only a matter of time. Was that a car?" Orin listened. "No. I'll be glad to get out of here. I'm going to cry so hard at your funeral, Grace. Murder-suicide. Such a romantic story about a woman the whole town knows is deeply depressed."

Grace looked at Nolan, her eyes telling him that she was going to *do* something. He gave a quick shake of his head, pleading with her not to risk it.

On the kitchen counter was Abby's cute little red Jambox. It was the size of half a brick and nearly as solid as one. Abby used it to play her music louder than the computer speakers allowed. Grace had often been amazed at how much sound could come out of something so small.

When Orin turned his sneering glance at Nolan, she grabbed the solid little box and threw it as hard as she could toward Orin's head, then immediately dropped down to her knees behind the island.

The Jambox hit the side of Orin's head, not enough to knock him down, but it cut him.

"What the —" Orin managed to say before Nolan leaped on him.

The two men hit the floor hard and the gun went sliding. Grace, still squatting behind the counter, flung herself forward and grabbed the gun.

She was shaking, but she stood up and held it at arm's length, just as she saw them do on TV.

But Nolan, younger, taller, and stronger than Orin, had him under control. Orin was flat on the floor, arms and legs splayed, with Nolan's knee in his back. "You have any plastic ties?"

"Yes," Grace said and rummaged in a drawer until she found some — long ones, left over from tying up the Christmas tree. She grabbed several and handed them to Nolan.

As he took the ties, he gently pushed the gun she was still holding away from his head.

"Oh, sorry," she said and started to put it on the island, but didn't.

Nolan secured Orin's hands behind his back.

"I'll give you two twenty-five percent," Orin said. "It's a lot of money. Hey! I'll give you my lake house. It's a lot better than this dump. You can —"

Yesterday Abby had dropped mustard on Grace's favorite red silk scarf, spot-washed it, then hung it on the coat-closet door to dry. Grace pulled the scarf off and handed it to Nolan.

"Thanks," he said, smiling at her. He tied it around Orin's mouth. "That's better." He used another tie to fasten Orin's ankles together, then stood up. "That should keep him from running away while I'm distracted."

"We need to call the sheriff. What could distract you from that?"

"This," Nolan said as he pulled her into his arms and kissed her.

"Mmmm" was all Grace could say.

When Sheriff Colin Frazier and his deputy, Melissa, burst into the house, with Eli and Chelsea close behind them, three of them holding guns, what they saw astonished them.

On the floor, tied up as if he were being prepared for roasting, was Orin Peterson. Standing inches away were Nolan and Grace, their bodies intertwined and kissing, oblivious to all the commotion around them. However, still clutched in Grace's hand was Orin's gun.

Colin nodded to Melissa, but she was already on her way to remove the gun from Grace's hand.

"You two," Colin said, but the kissing couple didn't move. Louder: "Nolan!"

Reluctantly, Nolan pulled away from Grace, then was startled to see the people there, especially Eli and Chelsea. They were dressed for the prom, with Eli in a tux and Chelsea in a revealing blue dress that was just plain dazzling.

"Let's get him out of here," Melissa said. She cut the tie on Peterson's ankles, then Colin, a huge man, hauled Orin up with one arm.

"I can't wait to see what's on that little rabbit," Colin said and started for the door. He paused by Eli and Chelsea. "Thanks for not trying to handle this by yourselves."

"I don't think they needed either one of us," Eli said, nodding toward Nolan and Grace.

When the sheriff and his deputy were gone, Eli and Chelsea went to the dining table. Nolan and Grace were sitting there, holding hands, and quietly talking.

"How did you know?" Nolan asked Eli.

"Abby knew Orin's misspelled text wasn't from you," Eli said.

Grace took a deep drink of her wine. "Orin was going to . . . to . . ."

"I know," Chelsea said. "He wanted Abby to bring the flash drive here to him. He meant to kill . . ." She didn't finish the sentence.

"I didn't get to see Abby in her dress," Grace said, and suddenly the tears began. "She said I didn't need to bother, that her new friend Chelsea was helping her." She looked Chelsea up and down. "I understand because you look like you're off the cover of *Vogue.*"

"It's okay." Nolan patted her hand. "You're just upset over what happened, but you'll be all right. You just need —"

"Men!" Chelsea said under her breath, then held out her hand to Grace. "Come on, let's get you dressed so you can see your daughter in her prom dress. You!" She turned to Nolan. "Go shave and put on your best suit." She looked at Eli. "Use all your spy techniques to get the owner of that little dress shop on the corner downtown to open up and let you buy that red dress in the window."

"Chelsea," Eli said in a voice of great patience, "I can't do something like that. My credentials don't —"

She moved so she was nose to nose with him. In her heels she was nearly as tall as he was. "If you ever plan to get me in bed again, if you have any hope of getting me to stay in this one-horse town, you will *do* this. Do you understand me?"

Eli started to speak, but Nolan grabbed

his arm and pulled. "One red dress coming up. Need any shoes?"

Chelsea looked at Grace. "This one is a keeper."

"I think so," Grace said.

Chelsea looked back at the men, who were still standing there. "Go!"

The two men hurried out of the house and Chelsea looked back at Grace. "Where's your drawer?"

Grace looked blank.

"Where's that drawer full of giveaway makeup, moisturizers, whatever you've accumulated over the years?"

"Oh," Grace said. "*That* drawer. This way."

It was late when the two couples got to the prom, but it was still in full swing. The band was on a break, but the teenagers were milling around, laughing and talking loudly.

Abby was standing by the entrance door, still shaking, still scared of what was coming. Would the sheriff come to her with horrific news?

When the door opened and her mother came in, Abby nearly collapsed in relief. She flung herself on her mother, the tears at last coming.

"It's okay," Grace said, holding her daughter's head to her shoulder. "Everything is fine. This is your prom and you should dance. Where is Baze?"

Abby didn't lose her grip on her mother but she sniffed. "He said I was no fun and he went back to Ashley. I want to go home and stay there forever, but you look beautiful."

Grace pulled her daughter's face away to look at her. "He wasn't worth you, and thank you. Now, I want you to get back on that floor and —"

She broke off because the music began, only this time it was a much better band. It was loud and professional.

Chelsea, standing nearby, said, "Who are they?"

"I would imagine it's the band I hired for Scully," Eli answered.

"You did what?" Around them, the teenagers were looking at the band in awe. The kissing couples started coming back into the gym.

Eli gave a small smile. "You're not the only one who can make plans in secret. Shall we go see the show?" He held out his arm for her.

While they'd been away, dealing with Orin, new speakers had been set up and instead of local kids playing, some men in their forties, maybe fifties, were on the stage. Their faces had lines and wrinkles that only decades of substance abuse could produce. Their leather outfits looked as though they'd been through a lot of partying. One guy with a guitar nodded at Eli, then looked at Chelsea and gave a thumbs-up.

She looked at Eli. "Friend of yours?"

"He's needed help a couple of times, so he owes me." Eli pulled her into his arms, her back to his front. "I think you'll like their music."

Abruptly, the band stopped playing. There was a drumroll, and everyone turned to look toward the back. The gym doors opened with a crash. Standing in a spotlight was Scully, wearing a tuxedo. He was flanked by two beautiful young women wearing short, revealing dance costumes.

As the band began again, this time very loud and throbbing, exciting, Scully and the girls danced into the room. Everyone stepped back to watch.

The dance show the three people put on was nothing short of spectacular. It was a story of the two beautiful young women fighting over the guy in the tux. The girls pranced and mock-fought, and Scully — who had mastered the art of looking disdainful — tried to make up his mind over which woman he wanted.

The dancing and the music had everyone clapping and cheering. Which woman should Scully choose?

When the girls seemed about ready to get into a brawl, Scully stepped away from them and walked toward the surrounding crowd. They parted to let him pass.

Scully walked to Abby, who was standing by her mother. Her eye makeup had run a bit, but that just made her look more like a beautiful damsel who desperately needed rescuing.

As the music pounded, Scully held his hand out to her.

With a smile that dazzled, Abby accepted his hand and walked with him to the center of the floor. When the music slowed, Scully began to dance with Abby in an old-fashioned ballroom style. He dipped her, flung her out to the end of his arm, then pulled her back. It didn't take Abby long to begin to add moves of her own. Everyone around them was clapping, smiling, cheering.

When the music stopped, Scully pulled Abby to him and kissed her full on the mouth.

The entire school erupted into cheers. As Eli's two pretty cousins slipped sparkling crowns onto the heads of Scully and Abby, confetti rained down from the ceiling, covering everyone.

Again, the crowd parted as, holding hands and wearing their crowns, Abby and Scully left the gym.

"Limo outside?" Chelsea asked Eli.

"Oh, yeah. And midnight pizza."

Turning, Chelsea put her arms around Eli's neck. "I think that was the nicest thing I've ever seen anyone do. Do you know that I love you?"

"No," he said softly. "I don't. Before I believe it, you'll have to tell me every day for the rest of my life."

"I will," she said and kissed him. "I promise."

Eli smiled at her, took her hand in his, and led her out the door, through the parking area, and to the football field.

"I think we should see to Nolan and Grace," Chelsea said. "They've had a traumatic evening and they came with us. How are they going to get home?"

"I gave Nolan my car keys," Eli said.

"Then how — ?" She didn't finish because Eli gave a whistle. "I didn't know you could whistle. When did you — ?" Her eyes widened.

From the dark of the goalpost came a

horse, a magnificent creature as black as a moonless midnight. It wore a black saddle emblazoned with silver that caught the light and threw it back.

The horse stopped by Eli, bowing its head to him. In one quick leap, he vaulted into the saddle, then with a smile, he bent and offered his hand to Chelsea. "Together," he said.

"Yes. Together," she answered, then took his hand and let him pull her up behind him. The slit in her gown parted, exposing her bare leg almost to her hip. Her face was pressed against his back, her arms tightly around his waist.

Eli gave one long, lingering caress to her skin, then he nudged the horse forward, and they rode away into the still darkness of the night. Together. Forever.

ABOUT THE AUTHOR

Jude Deveraux is the author of more than forty *New York Times* bestsellers, including *Moonlight in the Morning*, *The Scent of Jasmine*, *Scarlet Nights*, *Days of Gold*, *Lavender Morning*, *Return to Summerhouse*, and *Secrets*. To date, there are more than sixty million copies of her books in print worldwide. To learn more, visit JudeDeveraux.com.

The employees of Thorndike Press hope you have enjoyed this Large Print book. All our Thorndike, Wheeler, and Kennebec Large Print titles are designed for easy reading, and all our books are made to last. Other Thorndike Press Large Print books are available at your library, through selected bookstores, or directly from us.

For information about titles, please call:
  (800) 223-1244

or visit our Web site at:
  http://gale.cengage.com/thorndike

To share your comments, please write:
  Publisher
  Thorndike Press
  10 Water St., Suite 310
  Waterville, ME 04901